BIRTHRIGHT

PATRICIA DIXON

Copyright © 2022 Patricia Dixon

The right of Patricia Dixon to be identified as the Author of the Work has been asserted by her in accordance with the Copyright, Designs and Patents Act 1988.
First published in 2022 by Bloodhound Books.
Apart from any use permitted under UK copyright law, this publication may only be reproduced, stored, or transmitted, in any form, or by any means, with prior permission in writing of the publisher or, in the case of reprographic production, in accordance with the terms of licences issued by the Copyright Licensing Agency.
All characters in this publication are fictitious and any resemblance to real persons, living or dead, is purely coincidental.

www.bloodhoundbooks.com

Print ISBN 978-1-914614-73-6

ALSO BY PATRICIA DIXON

PSYCHOLOGICAL THRILLERS / SUSPENSE / DRAMAS

Over My Shoulder

The Secrets of Tenley House

#MeToo

Liars (co-authored with Anita Waller)

Blame

The Other Woman

Coming Home

WOMEN'S FICTION / FAMILY SAGAS

They Don't Know

Resistance

The Destiny Series:

Rosie and Ruby

Anna

Tilly

Grace

Destiny

*For my wonderful friend Tina Jackson
With love always,
Trish x*

Objets inanimés
Objets inanimés, avez-vous donc une âme qui s'attache
a notre âme et la force d'aimer?
Alphonse de Lamartine

Inanimate objects, do you have a soul which sticks to our soul and forces it to love?

PROLOGUE

Chateau de Chevalier, Loire
1931

Ophélie, la Duchesse de Bombelle, watched as the maid retreated, waiting patiently until she left the room before unwrapping the parcel that rested on her lap. Ophélie hid her eagerness to see what was inside, recognising the writing immediately, the spidery scrawl of previous missives etched in her mind, words that laid his heart at her feet and himself bare.

There was no doubt that he had left his mark in more ways than one because she had thought of nothing else since leaving Paris. So much so that if she closed her eyes he was there by her side, pipe tobacco, red wine, too close yet not close enough. The agony of resistance, the mere memory of him caused a reflex, delicate fingers rested in the small of her neck where his lips had skimmed her skin and tested her resolve to its limits.

She was being foolish, Ophélie accepted this. She knew the man well enough to understand that she was one of many, his ardour and roving eye as renowned as his art – yet now she had fallen under his spell it was hard to escape the magic. Hence, she had fled Paris and returned to her country home where she was safe, not from him but herself and an overwhelming, suffocating desire. Propriety and the fear of scandal had been her saving grace.

It had irked immensely that le Duc was aware of his good friend's intentions, that he was pursuing his wife, and thought it a great joke. Her husband had batted away her early concerns, so sure of himself and his role in their marriage, confident in his arrogance and ignorant to his wife's most inner desires, he'd assured Ophélie that the man was harmless. And of course, le Duc was flattered and yes, as much as she feigned offence, deep down, so was she.

They were used to his ways. He was part of their circle, not on the periphery either, but the star attraction so hard to avoid; the magnet at the centre of their avant-garde world. And then came the moment when they were alone, mere minutes yet the thrill of what passed between them was so intense that Ophélie knew it would last a lifetime, see her through the dull days, and the nights she shared a bed with her husband, more so.

The maid was gone, and she was alone. Pulling the string from the brown paper, she cast it aside to reveal a box, cardboard, nothing fancy and even this made her smile. Her fingers trembled slightly, and her heart fluttered. She was a girl again, flushed, giddy, lost in the blissful abandon of youth. Lifting the lid, Ophélie saw her gift was shrouded in muslin, a painting, of course. She unfolded it carefully, pulling back four corners of fabric one by one to reveal the canvas mounted in a carved frame, delicately engraved with filigree. She recognised the painting immediately; one she had admired during a visit to his studio. That he had remembered was in itself a message – their brief conversation, her voice heard above the others who were gathered, her admiration of this piece of work – that he had taken note and sent it to her.

Ophélie allowed her fingers to gently trace the image, his style recognisable in an instant, a dreamy depiction of a figure with a disorganised face and twisted body. A woman reclining on a red chair, her head tilted to one side, eyes closed in her heart-shaped visage, serene in sleep, golden hair cascading, bare shoulders embellished with beads, her left breast exposed, hands at rest. The colours were a joy on the eye; mauve, yellow, crimson, blue and green. But the painting brought Ophélie no peace, only envy because she wanted to be that woman, the one who inspired, captured in oil for all time, forever eternal.

There was a note, and for a second, she did not want to read it for fear it may incite feelings she could not resist. She forbade herself to weaken, no matter what it said or how strong the temptation yet immediately she unfolded the paper and her eyes fell on the scrawl, her heart returned to Paris. His words, his understanding was as precious as her gift, not measurable in francs, immaterial. This was the currency of intimacy, and she would treasure it always.

Paris, September 14th, 1931
My darling Ophélie,
Please accept this token of my admiration and unrequited love. You have captured my soul and taken me prisoner and whilst I accept you can never set me free, I cannot accept a life without you in it. If your friendship is all I may have, please, make that your gift to me.
Do not be a stranger, return to Paris soon,
Always yours,
Picasso

1

ANTOINETTE

**Chateau de Chevalier, Loire
Present day**

This is my favourite time of day. As I leave my bedroom, nestled in the eaves of the attic, I move through the chateau undisturbed and apart from the ticking of clocks, everywhere is silent. As always, my beautiful home waits patiently, to wake and begin a new day, beaten to the crack only by the birds that are busy heralding the dawn with their joyous song and I too begin my chores. Actually, that is a misuse of a word because for me, my work is a labour of love, caring for the chateau and its treasures, and watching over the family that reside here even if some of them do try my patience.

I stop on the third-floor landing and take a moment to embrace the estate because from here I can see across the treetops, mighty oaks and elms that have surrounded the chateau for centuries, and beyond, swathes of valley that meet the banks of the Loire. It is a beautiful sight, a palette of green hues, smudges of nature, the unknown artist at his best.

The birds are busy this morning, catching their breakfast. They always seem so happy to be alive and free, to gather food for their young, basking in the virgin rays of dawn, warming their feathers in the summer sun, soaring above the turrets in blissful ignorance. I envy them so. Yet I am thankful for their music that never fails to lift my heart, one that dips the moment I allow myself to ponder the fate of this beautiful place, my home. No matter how much I try to avoid it – and I have – I must face the truth. Something bad is coming.

Melancholy strikes and I imagine the many windows crisscrossed with lead are saddened eyes, cast downwards, perhaps holding back a tear. The ramparts are the shoulders of the chateau, sagged and despondent. I can feel the weight of its worry as though it was my own burden. Yet like me, the chateau refuses to give in. It clings on, to hope. It trusts. That is all it has left. I have left.

It is this faith, not in God or a king, but in those who inhabit its ancient walls that shrouds me in more sadness because as always, the future of Chateau de Chevalier depends on those that guard its history, who, like the musketeers of old are prepared to fight to preserve its memories.

Every room is steeped in them, from the attics where the servants slept, where babies were born on the wrong side of the bed sheets and young girls new to service wept for their mama. Thirty-six rooms, all with their own tales to tell. The king stayed here, and so did his mistress. Every single Chevalier heir was born under this roof, and most of them took their last breath surrounded by weeping women and the odd scurrilous son desperate to take his rightful place.

When I first came to the chateau, like many of those young women before me I had marvelled at the fairy-tale castle from afar and once inside I was smitten. So different from my childhood home on the edge of the village, a farm where, along with my family, I enjoyed simple pleasures, food, life. Here, inside these walls it is another world. Most think that I am fanciful and don't believe that when I touch the things in the chateau, I feel their souls. But it's true. Each object, a book, a paperweight, a ladle, a kettle, has been held by someone who lived a life, their handprint underneath mine. They left their mark. They were here and that essence remains.

And it is for this reason that I understand why Mademoiselle Fabienne wishes to hold onto her heritage. She, more than many of the de Bombelle family who reside here, should have the chance to retain her birthright. This is her home, where she has the fondest memories of her dear mama and brother, now departed. She talks of them often, swimming in the lake, swinging from trees, her mama seated on a blanket below, eating honey straight from the hives. Shivery winters huddled around log fires, the gardens blanketed by russet leaves, rabbits digging up the lawns, all the stuff her legend is made of. Chateau de Chevalier is in her blood; she adores it. And I adore her.

But we are on the brink of losing it all. Yes, I know it is wrong to listen at doors and sometimes watch, unseen, be privy to conversations that are private. In this case I salve my conscience by telling myself it is for the greater good and it does make me smile, knowing that my dear mama is correct. I am so very nosey.

Monsieur de Bombelle has made a grave error, again. He is a terrible businessman and ever since he took over the estate he has made one bad judgement after another and is now scraping the bottom of the barrel. His dreadful new wife proves my point in both circumstances. I do not like her. Nobody does. She pulls his strings in more ways than one and has grand plans of her own that include the chateau, but not in a good way. She is dangerous, a scowling woman whose face is shrouded in shadows that hide who she really is, masking the darkness in her eyes. She makes me shudder.

The atmosphere is terrible since Mademoiselle Fabienne returned from London when she heard about the plans and now, war has been declared. Battle lines have been drawn and the new Madame de Bombelle is proving a worthy adversary.

Where are the old-guard chevaliers when we need them? A loyal musketeer would solve all our problems of this, I am sure. A swift slice with the sword, off with her head and then maybe we could rest in peace.

I begin to pace. It is a habit I cannot rid myself of. I need to think. I must not panic. I must gather my energy for the day ahead and the summit with the lawyers and accountants where I am sure sparks will fly like the fireworks on Bastille Day. That it should have come to this. Father against daughter.

I head down another four flights of stairs to the long gallery, my favourite place where I will find comfort. I often begin my day here. Rebirthed by the sun as it rises in the east and shines through the enormous windows at the gable end of the chateau, I gather its energy. The moon also has the same effect and, in the evenings, if I stand at the other end of the corridor, I can gaze at it and the stars while shadows fall along the gallery.

The moment I reach the landing I am immediately invigorated by rays of silver-white that illuminate the dust motes and bathe the long corridor in an ethereal light. It reflects off the polished chequered tiles, then upwards to the carved, garlanded cornices, a ladder, two brush lengths and a tied-on duster, high. I know this: I have cleaned them many times.

The gallery, as is most of the house, is lined with oak panels and runs the width of the first floor. It is split in the middle by the walnut staircase that winds through the centre of the house.

Here, on either side, the walls are adorned by the chateau's treasures, those that mademoiselle had refused to sell, much to her papa's annoyance.

It is a place to browse and ponder history, lovingly displayed, collated and chronicled by the one person who could save us. Mademoiselle Fabienne de Bombelle, at present the last in the line of Les Grand Ducs de la Maison de Bombelle. She is a young lady with the heart and pride of a lion, unlike her father who has disappointed me immensely, a weak individual on the brink of breaking his daughter's heart. Such a simpering mouse. I wish that the kitchen cat would swallow him whole.

I tut because I am cross. How could it be that this grand chateau, graced through history by proud fighting men, defenders of the faith, their queen and many kings, protectors of brethren and family could have fallen so low at the hands of a fickle descendant. An incompetent man whose head has been turned by a woman not fit to enter the grounds, let alone the doors of this precious place. I know. I know her type and her family. I despise them.

The rumours about the Sabers have rumbled on through time; no smoke without fire; long memories; hardened hearts; whispers that can still be heard amongst the old guard, lest we forget. But that is another story that cannot be proved. Not by me, anyway.

I wish there was something that would help, written in the journals. They rest on bureaus that line the flocked walls. Sadly, the gaps in history tell their own tale, of nobody left to write it down and pass on what they saw during a terrible time. Perhaps that's why I like to spend so much time here, looking for a clue, anything to save us.

Mademoiselle looks too, everywhere. We have stood here together many times, reading the journals, smiling at the photographs, piecing together the past so it may be passed on, admired by fresh eyes. Making the sign of the cross I pray to God this comes to pass.

Looking downwards, my hand skims above the page of a precious journal as I read the entry. The elaborate script is barely legible yet stubbornly resists the conspiracy of chemicals in the air. The words cling to the delicate paper, holding onto a time gone by: 2 *Mai 1898, la fete de le Duc de Chevalier*. The birthday party of Monsieur de Bombelle, the great-great-grandfather of Mademoiselle Fabienne. The entry is accompanied by a photograph, sepia, yet even in its simplicity the beauty of the chateau shines through, telling of an era long before my time. The white stone of the chateau is the backdrop, the turrets at either end point high into the sky, about to pierce the cloudless blanket of what I imagine is cobalt blue. The twelve steps that lead to the glass-fronted door are lined by all the servants, protected from the heat of the day by the stone porch above.

It is a Bombelle tradition that at special celebrations everyone gathers on the steps in their best uniforms, family at the front. Each generation must take part, scowling children in the grip of their nanny's hand, le Duc and Duchesse right at the centre flanked by grandparents clinging onto life, wheeled outside and captured on film, just in time, for posterity.

I am in one of these such photographs. A wedding. I remember the day very clearly because I stood next to Gregoire, the chauffeur. A strand of my red hair had come loose, and he whispered a warning to me, but it was too late, the camera clicked, and we all went back inside. My dear Gregoire is gone now, the new wife sacked him and sold the car, a beautiful vintage Facel Vega. That woman is lethal; something Monsieur Bombelle would do well to remember.

My attention is drawn back to 1898 and the sepia photograph of the *fete* and my mood dips further, knowing that for those in the photograph, their *joie de vivre,* joy of life, would soon be decimated by the first, terrible war. I shudder at this single word and again make the sign of the cross.

When I dust the artefacts, even though it is part of my job and I take my work seriously, I avoid making eye contact with any photographs that depict the brave men, young soldiers from the village and two of the Duc's sons, who marched towards the front lines of the Great War. Some of them – including a son of the Duc – would never see their homes and families again. How it hurts my heart.

I do, however, allow my eyes to rest for a moment on the face of our Duchesse who turned over her precious home and tended the injured. She is on the lawn, surrounded by the stoical nurses in starched uniforms who worked tirelessly alongside her. What sights they must have seen, and thankfully before my time. And in the case below, her medal. *La Légion d'Honneur,* preserved and polished for all to see.

I move along the row and my heart picks up the pace because I know that when I reach a certain photograph, the images captured there are a portent of doom and I want to cry out, tell them what is coming. I read the date.

Juillet, 1939. The pre-war days, the last year of freedom when they thought or maybe prayed it would never happen again. A second war was coming. The house was filled with servants who scurried like ants, eager to please and were happy to bask in the afterglow of the Paris set who regularly arrived for the weekend and filled the chateau with love and laughter. Actors, musicians, writers and artists, not particularly the elite of French society, more the free-spirited, of mind and body. The beautiful and gregarious avant-garde who refused to conform, pushing boundaries and themselves to the edge. They had no idea they would soon be termed 'deviants' by the invading scum.

The montage of photographs, letters and invitations tells its own tale and despite their irony manage to make me smile. The photo depicts the most glamorous of events where carefree – or perhaps careless – young things have brought a chaise longue onto the lawn, just for a lark. Their lithe bodies are draped at angles, others standing behind, lifting glasses, posing for the camera, laughing into the lens of adversity.

In another, couples are gliding down the marbled stairway for cocktails, swishing their gowns, draped in finery, or more humble attire. The men in their dinner jackets, androgynous interlopers, famous faces hiding their fears behind a fog of ignorance and cigar smoke. Popping champagne corks like bullets with no idea that soon, cannons would line their horizons, darkening their days, blocking out the sun.

Instead, they drowned their thoughts, erudite, radical, deluded or whatever in absinthe and wine. They danced until dawn, throwing caution and decency to the wind as they swam naked in the lake, relishing in a wanton abandon that was about to be ripped from their grasp, smothered by a grey fog of Nazi uniforms, jackboots and oppression. It's all there, in black and white, what happened, what was about to happen.

This is why I do not allow my eyes to look further so I leave them in a happy time, before our Belle France was invaded and the scourge rampaged southwards and infested this beautiful chateau. That is when the rot set in, what they did, what they took. It marked the beginning of the end and the route to where we are now.

A garrison of troops reaping wanton destruction, tarnishing every room of the chateau, disrespecting the home of another. Trucks churning up the lawn where the beautiful people once lounged, soldiers' muddy boots trampling where Louis XVII once walked, the *cave* looted and our treasures, stolen, spirited away in the night and lost forever. They took many things, the grey devils, not just souls and lives. They took away the future.

In those images I see my own fate. The fate of Chateau de Chevalier.

To cheer myself I turn my back on the scourge and admire the rich tableaus of family portraits. I love to look at the enormous paintings most of all. History daubed in oil. I always hide my mirth out of respect, especially to the Grand Duc, done no favours by the artist who faithfully depicted his portly frame squashed into a chair while the buttons of his waistcoat strain across a rotund belly. They were not handsome, the forebears of the chateau, that is for certain, yet in the spirit of Renaissance and Revolution, even now they manage to inflict their will.

Knowing eyes peer out, black dots of coal set into pale skin, boring holes through their failing descendants. The women especially cannot hide their ire, rouged cheeks flushed with anger, lips set in a grimace, or perhaps their corsets are pulled a little too tight. I understand their displeasure at both circumstances but what has been, cannot be altered. And for that I am sorry.

Those who have remained are now forced to watch from their uncomfortable chairs on the walls of the chateau, weeping at what they see, unable to turn away. These are the old guard, the survivors, proud to be back in their rightful place.

Everyone knows the story. When the invasion began, the Duc called from Paris and ordered the immediate removal of the antique furniture, his collection of priceless masterpieces and *objets d'art*. But le Duc was betrayed. The first truck got away, but the second truck was intercepted right there outside the chateau, the precious cargo of paintings taken by the Nazis and lost forever. No doubt they are now stored in private galleries of collectors without scruples, old masters that will never see the light of day. The Bombelle treasures that could save the chateau if only they could be found, even one.

I sigh. The history of the chateau is written, and I accept

that I cannot alter what has passed but maybe, I could change the course of the future, if only I knew how. Mademoiselle Fabienne is doing her best, fighting the good fight and as always, I will remain by her side, helping in any way I can, guiding her.

I hear a footstep. It is she. An early riser like myself. I must go because today is a big one for all of us. I give the old guard a courteous nod of the head, hoping as I go that all of my prayers will be answered. Not that one of them will be turned into a mouse and eaten by a greedy cat, or that the other will lose their head. I simply pray that mademoiselle keeps on looking because it's out there, the solution.

She just has to find it.

2

FABIENNE

Fabienne stood at the bottom of the stairs, checking her watch before calling out. 'Antoinette, Antoiiinetttte.'

Seconds later she heard footsteps above and *voilà,* the woman herself appeared, scurrying down the stairs.

'Ah, there you are. Could you help me? Remember that old desk in the cellar? I want to bring it up and see if it can be restored. It's already getting warm outside so maybe we should get organised now, otherwise we will die of heatstroke.'

'Yes, of course, mademoiselle. I was just in the gallery, counting the artefacts. I know everything by eye, but I like to keep check just in case something small is taken. I have a terrible fear that she will pilfer something, and I will not notice. I can just imagine her selling a vase and buying herself a Dior handbag.'

'You're a diamond, Antoinette. And less of the mademoiselle, we're not in 1622! I swear you live in a dreamworld. In fact, maybe I should make you wear a maid's uniform, a nice black dress and white pinafore, ooh, and some thick woolly tights and sensible shoes. You'd look so smart.' Fabienne raised her eyebrows, enjoying teasing her best friend.

'Come on, let's move the desk and then we can make a start on our business plan. We need something to show them later this afternoon.' Fabienne winked at her loyal assistant and friend who was just as determined to prevent any of the *objets d'art* being sold off as she.

'I still don't think your papa has lost his mind so badly that he would let the witch take something. She would have to sell it without him knowing. She won't get much down at the *brocante,* that's for sure.'

'I gave up trying to fathom my father the day he got married because, let's face it, that was when he really lost his mind!' Fabienne gave a flick of the head and was followed by Antoinette, both tickled by the comment, neither of them fans of her stepmother, Veronique.

The desk was stored in one of the eight cellars and as they made their way, Fabienne's mind continually ticked over, the upcoming meeting foremost. She was determined to show her father that she meant business and was not prepared to sell anything, even the smallest trinket to restore the chateau. He had got them into this mess so he should be helping to get them out. All she wanted him to do was listen to her plan, but he refused, flapping his hands and shooing her away like she was a child again – but the worst insult, the one that made her eyes sting, was that he had sided with Veronique.

Fabienne's panicked business plan, a last-ditch attempt at knocking some sense into her father, had been conceived late the previous night while she and Antoinette lay on the lawn, drinking beer and gazing at the stars.

'Do you really think we could do it, save the chateau? It's a grand plan but in my head it seems so viable. Others have done it.'

Antoinette had nodded. 'You are right. It will be hard work but together I'm sure we can convince them. And I am not afraid of hard work. Have you seen me cleaning the cornices in the gallery with a big stick? I should be in the circus. Anyway, we have to try. I feel this is my home too, and I want to save it as much as you do – so let's go for it.'

They had clinked bottles, sealed the deal. The last defenders of the Chevalier faith.

Fabienne was so angry and disappointed by her father who, now his back was against the wall, wanted to take the easy way out and sell the chateau to an English couple who had grand plans to turn it into a hotel. Great idea, big round of applause for the entrepreneurs. So why could her father not see the potential and do the same? Because Veronique, her stepmother, had her beady eyes on a villa on the Côte d'Azur and needed the money from the sale to buy it and fund her glitzy retirement.

No wonder Fabienne's father was penniless, hitching up with a spend-aholic. Then to make matters worse, Veronique's shady brother had shown an interest, not in the chateau, but the land it stood on. Antoinette had overheard him saying to Veronique that Chevalier would be better flattened, and the estate used to build new homes. That man could get where water couldn't, conjuring planning permissions, and over the years he'd slowly bought up most of Cholet. But it wasn't happening, not to her home, not while Fabienne drew breath.

The whole sorry situation was at the forefront of her mind day and night, even while they were taking the stairs to the kitchens below. When they reached the cellar door Fabienne's hot temper was simmering nicely despite the rush of cold air that gave her goosebumps as they made their way downwards. *That woman and her family reckon they have it all stitched up! Well, I'll show them they're not as clever as they think.*

It had started with a plot of land. Unbeknown to Fabienne, her father had sold off a huge plot on the edge of the estate to a development company who had acquired planning permission from Veronique's brother, the *Maire* of the town. On paper everything seemed to be above board and many towns were doing the same, building new homes in rural areas earmarked for urbanisation. However, Fabienne suspected that the *Maire* had far more to do with it than he let on. He would have got a sweetener, a payoff, that was for sure. She had let that go: the land belonged to her father and not the estate. But when he blew it all on a holiday to Mauritius, spending not a penny on the chateau, alarm bells started to ring.

Antoinette felt the same, but her assumptions were based more on rumour and the suspicious mind of her elderly great-grandmother, Eglantine, who whiled away the hours in *La Maison de Retraite*, recounting stories of old to her fellow retirees or anyone who had the patience to listen.

She had gone into decline almost thirty years before, after the death of her husband who, sadly, she still believed was alive. Antoinette remembered that as a child, her grandmère would always get in trouble over family dinners for saying inappropriate things, or as her mémère would say, talking rubbish. And as her memory and grasp on reality deteriorated none of them knew what was real or fantasy. Still, she was quite content in her starring role as the care home's most senior resident who had been entertaining them all for over twenty years with her antics and stories.

Being the only patient member of her family and someone deemed to have plenty of time on their hands, Antoinette was Eglantine's most frequent visitor, even if she didn't always realise who she was.

According to Antoinette, via her grandmère, the Saber family had a very unsavoury and dubious past and even though there had been periods where they weren't in positions of power, every now and then one of them would pop up and get their creepy little fingers on the key to the Maire's safe.

The darkest period of Saber history was at the end of the Second World War when one of them was hung by The Resistance for being a collaborator. By all accounts, wartime Maire Saber was an obnoxious man who couldn't wait to hand over the keys of the town to the invading *kommandant*, and more or less invited him and his marauding soldiers to the chateau where they were billeted for the duration. Rumours abounded of goings-on in there, and the death of a young woman was the most horrific. By all accounts, the murderers were protected by the traitor himself.

Ever since, against the odds and shrouded in a cape of shame and mystery, the Saber family had managed to thrive, owning the best properties for miles around and, due to making what everyone surmised were shrewd investments, lived a fine life. Now one of them had set their sights on the Chateau de Chevalier.

The gloom of the cellar and the thought of her precious home being invaded by Nazis and now Veronique, caused Fabienne to shiver as she moved empty crates and boxes. 'There it is. It's a lovely piece and I think it will clean up nicely. I have to do something while I'm here otherwise I'll go mad.'

Antoinette agreed. 'It's probably got woodworm so we will need to douse it in vinegar and leave it for a few days. So maybe we could make a start of emptying the library and cleaning the books and shelves. The dust in there is horrendous. I don't think it's been touched for years.'

'That's a plan. We'll move this and then bring up some of these boxes to store the books and you never know, we might even find a few first editions in there.' Fabienne picked up one end of the desk and waited while Antoinette brushed something off her shoulders, grimacing.

'Come on, let's go. I do not like to spend too much time down here. This part of the house gives me the creeps.' She lifted her end of the desk and began backing up the stairs, taking them carefully while Fabienne followed, ducking to avoid the huge cobwebs that hung in dust-covered loops from the beams and brickwork; even the cord of the light bulb was matted with the stuff.

'Okay, let's go before the tarantulas get us.' She and Antoinette had already braved every one of the cellars in the chateau, screaming when huge spiders had interrupted their scouring of each corner in search of anything that might have been squirrelled away.

They climbed upwards towards the open door and the light from the kitchen, their trainers hardly sounding on the smooth stone stairs worn with time and indented by hundreds of footsteps.

Antoinette puffed as she spoke: the stairs were steep and the desk was heavy. 'Next time you want something bringing up I'll ask Rudy. You know how eager he is to please you and more than willing to be your slave, sex slave especially.'

Fabienne laughed out loud. 'Your brother never gives up, does he. I thought he'd be over his schoolboy crush on me by now so do not encourage him. Anyway, he's engaged, and I haven't time for men. They are too much trouble.'

Her voice echoed in the shadows below and as she followed Antoinette, Fabienne imagined someone stood behind, hands against her back, protecting her in case she fell. Ever since she was a little girl, she'd believed that the ghosts of the chateau were her secret friends, for a short time had been convinced she could see them. Then as she grew older, they faded, visiting less often so instead she made them up, using the entries in the journals and stories in history books to make her ancestors real. She wasn't afraid of ghosts, not one bit, and it gave her comfort to imagine them by her side or wandering the rooms and halls. It was their home too.

'Hey, earth to planet Fabienne...' Antoinette was brushing dust off her hands and clothes, the desk safely deposited on the pale-grey marble of the foyer.

'Sorry, I was miles away. Let's get the vinegar and put this right out front and let it air in the sun, lower the tone a bit and remind a certain person that it's come down to this, flogging old furniture to pay the electric bill.'

'I wish I could help you with money, you know that, don't you.' Antoinette was pulling open the drawers but found nothing apart from dead flies.

Fabienne smiled. 'Of course I do. But you being here while I'm in London is worth more than money. Knowing you're keeping an eye on everything, including Papa and Veronique, is a godsend.'

'Hey, it's a two-way street. I get to live in a chateau and how many people can say that? I love giving my address and I'm always tempted to add a title. I do have a royal name after all.' Antoinette winked. 'The only downside to my dream job is having to be at the beck and call of Veronique the Viper. But for you, I take a breath and count to ten, sometimes a hundred, once it was thousand and she was so pissed off with me.'

Both women giggled and then headed back towards the kitchen, Fabienne's spirits lifting at the thought of scoring a point, coffee and breakfast. It had worked well, employing Antoinette as housekeeper at the chateau which continued a weird and coincidental tradition. Throughout history the name had cropped up in the journals many times and now, the modern-day equivalent was once again installed at the chateau. Maybe it was really meant to be in more ways than one because Antoinette had always adored Fabienne's home, ever since the first time she'd stepped inside.

When Fabienne was four, her mother and younger brother Baptiste had been killed in a freak car crash on one of the winding roads just outside the gates to the estate. Her father in his self-absorbed pity could not cope with life, let alone a little girl who cried for her mama no matter how hard the nanny tried to soothe her. In the end, after what he considered 'doing his best', the solution to his own problems came in the form of a boarding school in England. Fabienne hated it as much as she dreaded going home, knowing Mama and *petit*-Baptiste would not be there.

The chateau was a lonely place for a little girl with only the cook and staff for company and she would spend hours in her mother's bedroom, hiding in the wardrobe that still contained Mama's beautiful clothes and scent, sliding her feet into shoes, bare feet, skin against imaginary skin. Or sitting at the gilt dressing table, touching the brushes and wisps of hair that were trapped in the bristles, lifting the lids of perfume bottles and inhaling, never dabbing. The liquid inside too precious to waste because the genie spirit of Mama was captured within.

One fateful day, after being shooed outside by Lauriane, the housekeeper, who believed in the benefits of fresh air and sun, Fabienne had wandered alone until she came across a group of children from the village. They were playing in the river and Antoinette had been amongst them and waved when she spotted the shy ten-year-old half-hiding behind a tree. Encouraged by a smile, Fabienne had joined in, skimming stones and paddling, sharing Antoinette's picnic and hearing a strange sound. Laughter. Her own.

They met every day for a week until rain stopped play, a terrible thunderstorm sending Papa's dogs into a frenzy at the lightning that ripped open the sky, scaring the cook. When the urgent sound of the doorbell added to the tension it had Lauriane and a curious Fabienne rushing to the door. There in a puddle stood Antoinette. Her yellow mackintosh was sodden, and her rain-soaked fingers gripped the handlebars of her bicycle.

'I went to the lake to see if you were there. I thought you would be sad if I didn't come. And now my tyre has popped.' They all looked at the tyre as though they needed proof, and seconds later as a flash lit Antoinette in a halo of light, she was dragged inside the foyer by Lauriane, and the dripping mackintosh removed.

Fabienne could still see the expression on Antoinette's face as she took in her surroundings, looking upwards to the fresco of angels on the ceiling, her mouth agape, eyes agog. 'It is beautiful, like a castle for a princess. Are you a princess?'

Fabienne vehemently shook her head. 'No, I am just me. Would you like some soup?'

It was the beginning of a friendship that had survived for almost twenty years. They wrote to one another while Fabienne was away at school, and then university and even an internship at an auctioneers in New York hadn't thwarted them.

When Lauriane finally retired, Antoinette was first in line for the job that was quickly upgraded to personal assistant to le Duc de Bombelle. With a qualification in business studies and knowing the chateau as well as Fabienne, it was her dream job. She lived in, making room at home for her sister who was sick of sharing, and did her best to keep Monsieur Bombelle in order even though it was for the most part a losing battle.

Meeting Antoinette had changed everything for Fabienne who, after dreading it, loved coming home. Papa aside, she was always welcomed by Antoinette and her family who made a fuss and a special meal, a tradition continued in the present. More often than not the homecoming feast was burnt or not quite cooked through because Antoinette was not a born chef. But it was always accompanied by plenty of wine and cheese and a worrying explanation of how Monsieur Bombelle had messed up, spent too much, and would not listen to reason.

The chateau's finances had remained in the hands of Fabienne's father and over the years matters gradually worsened. Antoinette found herself to be the only remaining member of staff. The cook resigned when her wages didn't get paid, the same with the gardener, and dear Gregoire the chauffeur and the vintage car were surplus to requirements since Monsieur Bombelle kept buggering off to Paris with his fancy woman, Veronique the Viper.

Fabienne and Antoinette knew it was going to happen, the marriage. What they didn't foresee was that the new Madame Bombelle would not love the chateau as much as they. In fact she hated it, all of it. And sometimes it seemed that she hated Fabienne even more.

When Antoinette told her about the land being sold, the deal had already gone through but what shocked Fabienne the most was that her father had suddenly gone from being shit to shifty. The visit from the English couple with a film crew in tow had blindsided Antoinette, who knew exactly who was pulling Monsieur Bombelle's strings. Veronique had set up the meeting and her lily-livered husband was fully on board, ready to sell the chateau to the highest bidder or, anyone who could pay off his debts and get Veronique a villa by the sea.

Within hours, Fabienne had asked her boss at the London auction house for leave, compassionate, unpaid, whatever was needed so she could get back home as soon as possible. She had consulted a solicitor friend and as she'd suspected, French law was complicated but at least she knew her rights.

While Fabienne was throwing things into a suitcase and heading for the airport, Antoinette's employment had been swiftly terminated, and she was told to leave by Veronique. Instead, the guardian of the chateau stood firm and refused to be evicted. There was a stand-off and she had remained, resolute, waiting for her friend's return and now resided there indefinitely, as Fabienne's guest.

The battle lines were drawn. The solicitors and accountants were due at 3pm. And Fabienne was ready for a fight. Would it be another duel to the death on a misty morning? Not quite. But the chateau was her everything, the link to Mama and *petit-Baptiste* and if she lost it, they might as well tear out her heart. Fabienne needed her heart and the chateau to survive. She had to find a way. It was as simple as that.

3

MAC

The journey from the *notaire's* office to his grandfather's house – his house – took only minutes yet Mac wished that it was an hour, a day, anything that would delay how he would feel the moment it came into view. Which was why he had pulled over and was hiding in a lay-by literally metres from his new home. His only home, since he'd lost the one in England to stupidity.

Come on, pull yourself together, man. You've got to do this, for Mum, and for Mémère and Grandpère. You can't let them down, again.

And there, in his last thought, lay the truth. That was what he was really scared of. Facing up to his mistakes, his neglect, his own weakness, a list of failings as long as his arms and legs that, owing to his six foot two stature, went on and on.

A huge part of him wanted to go back to the place he'd spent twenty-two wonderful summers, then for the next four had popped back whenever he could and then in the last three, had hardly been near. Not until it was too late.

It was the pathetic part of him that would prefer to stay in the lay-by or even turn the car around and head home, or, rather, back to England. He had to remind himself constantly that this was it, a farmhouse bequeathed to him by his grandfather, via his mother. This was his last chance to make good.

Regrets, he fucking hated them because there was just no way to erase the stain that stuck to you like glue once you'd messed up. Maybe, hopefully, in years to come the tinge of failure would fade. After all, what happened wasn't exactly his fault but he would always wish he'd seen the signs, listened to his friends and, yes, his mum. He hadn't and he'd paid the price. The greatest regret of all, though, was leaving things too late and being a selfish, loved-up knobhead who thought he had forever, and it wasn't until he stood by his grandfather's graveside that Mac had truly realised that time had run out.

The arrival of a car, seen through his rear mirror, interrupted the moment of maudlin self-indulgence and brought on a smile, when the two occupants began unloading their lunchtime picnic table. It was something the French thought nothing of, setting up at the side of a road and whiling away an hour while cars whizzed by. Reminded of trips to the seaside and his grandma unpacking a feast, Mac decided to make a move.

Just get on with it. You'll have Mum on the phone soon, asking a hundred questions. Stop being mard. Grandpère wouldn't like that.

The turning to the farmhouse was up ahead and he could already see the sign which might as well have said – 'This way to guilt central. Enjoy your day!' Instead, forbidding the tears in his eyes to fall and swallowing down the ball of emotion that blocked his throat, just like he had every time they arrived for the summer, Mac read the name out loud: *'La Fleurie'*.

Pulling a set of keys from the envelope given to him by the *notaire*, Mac thought it odd, having to unlock a door that was always open. He'd loved that his grandparents never felt the need to barricade themselves in or keep people out and rather than it make him feel nervous, it always gave a city kid an immense sense of calm. The silent message assured him he had nothing to fear. *Here you are safe, with us.*

He left his car parked at the gate which creaked and wobbled on the hinge as he pushed it open and once inside the garden, he stood beside the flower beds that were overgrown by weeds. From there he took in his home and the very thing he was afraid of engulfed him. Awash with nostalgia that rooted his feet to the spot, holding him firmly in its grip, his ears homed in on a familiar sound.

Amidst the almost silence, the song of the countryside hummed a lullaby. The buzz of a bee feasting on wild flowers. A tractor somewhere across the fields chugging back and forth. Crickets on the lawn. From the next house along the faint whine of a chainsaw. A biplane cutting through the blue sky overhead. Yet bizarrely, the two missing voices of those he longed to hear the most, who once called his name as he ran up the path, were the loudest of all. *Mémère et Grandpère.*

While Mac steeled himself, he pictured the five-year-old he used to be, the boy with zero patience and no time for reflection so instead, pushed past and raced up the path and into the arms of his grandmother who was already smothering him in *bisous*, catching up on kisses she'd missed since last time.

When in France, little Mac had loved to use French terms, picking up words so that later in life he could speak well enough to converse freely, using the language that sealed him to those he loved. He had mastered the accent, nurtured during the holidays but one he'd quickly learnt to abandon when he got home for fear of being ridiculed by his friends. French Boy. That's what they'd called him. La Fleurie was his special place, his secret, his anchor and he guarded it fiercely from the nasty boys at school who could tarnish it with their peevish words.

But oh how he had waited, and waited for Easter and most of all the endless summer.

'We are here, Mémère, it took so long. Is lunch ready, can I go to my room? Grandpère, where's my *vélo*, have you pumped up the tyres, can we go fishing *ce soir,* when the moon is out, and will you show me *les chatons,* I love kittens?'

A year's worth of waiting and expectation was packed into one minute of hugs and happiness. Wanting to do everything all at once in that first day when he had six weeks to fill up. Each time they arrived was like the first, re-exploring familiar places, re-climbing trees he knew every knot and branch of, re-seeing rooms he dreamt about, re-tasting food that he imagined when he ate his boring school lunch, revisiting his family who he missed like a limb when he went home.

Mac had never even considered that the place where he'd had the happiest times, somewhere that had never let him down and always delivered on its promises would one day belong to him. This was his grandparents' home; it was their place, where they belonged. And he couldn't quite grasp that the little farm he saw in his childhood dreams, always a dot on the horizon basking under the rainbow and waiting at the end of a winding road, was now his.

The property was on the very outskirts of Cholet, a small farming community that once served the nearby chateau. The farm was more than two centuries old and stood on the edge of its own private wood, cocooned by a semicircle of lush green trees to the right. To the left stretched acres of farmland and fields. Ten of which now belonged to Mac.

The house had long, low walls the colour of butter and cut into the thick sandstone was an arched doorway, encased by slabs of local white stone as were the four windows, just big enough for a head and shoulders to peep out. The kitchen was behind the first window on the left and the rest were dotted along the right. The blue shutters were all open, which he thought was odd because he was sure that before they left after the funeral he and his mother, fussing and jollying things along to hide her own tears and thoughts, had fastened them closed.

Expecting there to be a face at the window – more wishful thinking – Mac shook off the ridiculous notion and looked upwards to the three *dormers,* converted loft rooms once used to keep the chickens and pigs in winter.

It was a story that Mac had loved. One where his great-great-grandfather carried a grunting porker up rickety wooden steps and he'd always wondered if it was noisy below, listening to hoof steps and beak pecks overhead, and then there would be a dreadful smell of poo. Who took out the poo?

Such tales had confounded yet enthralled little Mac and he would lie in bed going over them in his head. Like the fact that below the house were tunnels and two *caves* where they'd hid their food from the Nazis in the war. Mac had been down there with Grandpère many times to bring up a bottle for dinner or some of the potatoes stored in the darkest corner, or best of all to check one more time that there were no Nazis lurking in the shadows. It was these things, the quirks, the history, that had made the farmhouse so special and a place of mystery in a land that time seemed to have forgotten, so far away from the noisy city he came from.

Back in the present, Mac scanned the roof and could see that some of the brown slates were missing and had slid into the gutter, causing him to expect a leak once he got inside. *Inside.* It was time.

Ignoring the thought, and fact that this time neither of his grandparents would be there to greet him, Mac strode up the path and placed the key in the lock. He pushed gently, prepared for stagnant air knowing that the house had been unoccupied since February but there was a distinct whiff of disinfectant and furniture polish. There was a familiar noise too, the hum of the old *frigo* that had been there for as long as he could remember – a huge fridge that reminded him of an ancient bank safe.

Closing the door, Mac needed a moment to take it all in. So he pulled a chair from the scuffed table, where he'd eaten so many meals, legs dangling from the seat next to Grandpère – and then before he knew it, his trainers had touched the floor. Where had the time gone?

He took in the timbered, low-ceilinged room and the burgundy leather sofa and armchairs arranged around the fireplace. Mémère's crocheted shawl was draped across the back of one and Grandpère's pouffe stood in front of the other where he would rest his aching legs and warm his toes on the fire. While Mac imagined them both sitting there listening to the radio, a giddy six-year-old took the spiral stairs two at a time, his footsteps running along the corridor overhead, passing two bedrooms and the bathroom until he reached his own at the gable end of the house.

Mac had thrown his backpack on the bed and unzipped the top, the iron frame creaking as he moved, pulling out the carefully packed contents before arranging them just how he liked. The teddy that Grandpère would tease him about was laid on his pillow not hidden under the covers out of sight. Mémère had told Grandpère off last time and said Mac was to ignore him.

Next, Mac couldn't resist taking a sniff of the cotton pillowcase that was embroidered with flowers, inhaling Savon de Marseille and a hint of lavender. Yes, that was good, exactly as he remembered, how it should be. He then placed his Spider-Man pyjamas underneath and his slippers at the side of the bed. His mum had the rest of his clothes in the car, but he had wanted to pack these himself and had written them on the list he'd been compiling for weeks. With his spends, fastidiously saved in a jar at home and counted at least once a month, he'd bought loads of comics from the shop at the port and these he slid in the top drawer along with his torch. Right at the bottom of the backpack his hand found the crinkly wrapping paper that hid his grandpère's birthday present.

August 14th was always a fun day because they had a big party where all the neighbours came, and the meal went on and on forever. The men got very drunk while the ladies complained about it and washed millions of plates. Once, they had a sheep on a stick and Grandpère allowed him to turn the handle so it rotated above the fire. He was so close to the flames it was brilliant, but nobody would have believed him at school, so he kept quiet.

Mac placed the woolly work socks in the second drawer down, along with the card he'd written out extra carefully before they left Manchester. They had been his idea. Grandpère always needed new socks and they would save Mémère having to darn his old ones.

On his bedside table was the little tin tray that said Ricard on the base. It was bashed and faded but Mac liked the smiley man who looked so happy to be drinking a glass of pastis, the same as Grandpère had before his lunch and dinner. Mac was allowed to dip his finger in and always grimaced when he tasted it, which made Grandpère laugh, even more when he dipped again. When he got big, Mac was determined to drink pastis too even if he still hated it because he so wanted to be like Grandpère. On the tray stood a jug and an upside-down glass, waiting for the night when it would be so hot that all the windows would have to stay open, and he would read about Dennis the Menace from under his covers.

The year before, Mémère had said he was big enough to fill

the jug in the bathroom and carry it himself because she knew he wouldn't drop it. And he was allowed to stay awake if he wanted so he could listen to the owls and the foxes outside and even though the noise was a bit scary, he still didn't need the hall light on. See, that was another reason he loved it there because they treated him differently, not like he was a baby of six.

Jumping off the bed Mac went in search of his treasure, something he'd hidden away before and thought of all the time at home. His friends didn't believe him, but he didn't care. He knew it was true. That he had a penknife. His and Grandpère's secret.

It was the end of the Easter break. He had cried so much the day before they were leaving that he and Grandpère went for a walk in the woods and here, Mac was given the penknife, 'for grown-up boys who do not cry and want to learn how to carve and skin a rabbit'. Mac hadn't been sure about the rabbit part, but he definitely wanted to whittle sticks. 'It will be here when you return, waiting for you just like the house and us, so no more tears. Go hide it somewhere you mother and grandmother can't find it. *C'est entre nous.*'

Mac had nodded, agreeing it would be between them when Grandpère tapped his nose and winked like he did when he told one of his stories about treasure and the brave men who once lived in the woods.

Mémère said that Grandpère talked rubbish and not to believe his stories, but Mac didn't care if they were true or false, he just loved the look in his grandpère's eyes while he told a tale, the whisper in his voice, like he was passing on something very important that he could only share with Mac. Like the time Grandpère's eyes went all watery when they went to the church and put flowers on the grave. His grandpère said it was where his older sister was, who'd been murdered by the Germans when he was only small. He was sad and that had made Mac sad, so they'd held hands. Grandpère's hands were rough and bumpy. Man's hands, strong and warm, they made him feel safe.

They even went to see the tree that never dies, that thousands of rusty nails could not kill, and they too had hammered one in, walked around the trunk three times and made a wish. Mac's hadn't come true yet, but he was only little, and he didn't know if his grandpère's had either, because you weren't allowed to tell. He hoped it had, or it would.

The penknife was on the top shelf of his wardrobe wrapped inside one of the woolly jumpers that Mémère had knitted. She knitted everything. Blankets, socks, hats for everyone – even the teapot and the toilet rolls. Mac dragged the chair from the corner of his room and stood on top, pulling out the middle pullover and *voilà,* as Mémère always said, there it was, his penknife.

He hadn't whittled anything yet, but he would, and he'd even help Grandpère skin a rabbit if he had to. Laying the blade on the palm of his hand Mac traced the lines on the pudgy flesh below and for a tiny second a bad thought entered his head then left again which was good. He didn't want to have bad thoughts in France and be reminded of bad people like his dad, because this was his happy place, and his mum's too.

A gentle tap on the door and a voice calling his name broke into Mac's thoughts. Leaving memories of his young self and the penknife he still possessed behind, he winced when the chair legs scraped along the tiles as he pushed it back in haste. On the doorstep was Marie-France, a basket on her arm and a look on her face that said she was happy to see him yet sad about the circumstances which brought him there. Mac had known

Marie-France all his life, the closest neighbour and best friend of his mémère and a summertime surrogate aunt.

'*Bienvenue* Mac, welcome home. I have brought you some provisions. Something simple for your dinner although you can come and eat with us, whatever you prefer. Jacqueline would be happy to see you and Alphonse too.' She passed the basket and smiled.

Remembering his manners and the law of the land Mac took the basket and invited Marie- France inside while his brain was on red alert. No way would he go for dinner and be mentally eaten alive by Jacqueline, the most man-hungry woman he had ever met in his entire life. And sadly, Quasimodo's long-lost twin.

'Thank you for this, Marie-France, but if you don't mind, tonight I'd prefer to spend some time alone with my thoughts. I'm sure you understand. But I will pop by to return the basket and say hello later in the week, if that's okay.'

She nodded and hid her disappointment well as she scanned the lounge and then looked left, towards the kitchen. 'I have kept everything clean for you. I knew you would return, and your grandmother would never forgive me if the place became a *bordelle*. She made me promise to look after your grandfather and now I will look after you. I will be here each Monday and Thursday. Will that be okay? I can do three days, but I said you won't make a big mess. You are a good boy, I know this.'

Mac was thrown, because a) he couldn't afford to pay a cleaner and b) he was quite capable of looking after himself despite what his mum said and c) did Marie-France think he was going to stay there permanently? Ah, that was it. Nail on head. His mother had been on the phone, and they'd hatched a plan and asked Marie-France to keep her eye on him. That made sense.

But from Marie-France's expression, she wasn't going to take no for an answer where the cleaning was concerned, and Mac really didn't have the energy or inclination to offend his French 'aunty'. Instead, he would speak to his mum and let her undo her meddling. Her mess. She could sort it out.

'Thank you Marie-France, two days is fine. Now may I offer you a drink?' Along with the bread and cheese and goodness knows what treats she'd squashed in there, he'd spied a bottle of milk in the basket and was sure that somewhere in the cupboards he would find coffee.

Holding up her hands with a martyred expression, his guest politely declined. 'Thank you but no. I am off to the church. There is a wedding tomorrow and I need to prepare. And you never know, now that you have returned to us, one day, we may have an Anglo-French union. That would make me and your grandfather so happy.'

Stunned, confused and terrified at the inference, Mac could only stare; words failed him while dread filled his heart. Marie-France, hand resting on her heart, filled in one of the blanks.

'It was his wish always, that one day you would come back and live here, at La Fleurie. He missed you so much when you were gone, they both did. They believed this was where you were meant to be and *voilà*, it is so.' At this Marie-France made for the door and after pulling it open laid her hand on Mac's arm. 'You will be happy here. And your grandfather will also be happy to know that his wish came true. That old tree has worked its magic.' With a wink she took her leave and left Mac open-mouthed but at least one mystery had been solved. Another problem remained.

Taking the basket into the kitchen Mac unloaded his feast. Sliced ham, no doubt from one of their pigs, tomatoes, black, yellow and greeny-red. A box of Camembert that announced its own arrival, pâté of unknown origin and after a sniff he was still none the wiser, rabbit maybe. Butter, not home-made but his favourite and laced with *Sel de Bretagne*: the salted kind from Brittany was another of his weaknesses. Prunes and blackberries, a wedge of brioche and a roule of crusty bread. Gazing at the food on the table only one thought pinged into Mac's head – it was all fit for a king, not a pauper who didn't deserve even a morsel.

How could he have told her, his Tante Marie-France that his grandpère's wish would not be coming true? Because once he had sorted through the house and the belongings contained therein, made the necessary repairs and tidied up the front and back garden, no matter what she or his mother said, his mind was made up. There was no life for him here. What could he do? How would he make a living?

The house was a lifeline and would help him start again which was why he'd already asked the *notaire* to come and value it and then it would go on the market. Yet regardless of his resolve, now he was there, back in his childhood playground, it pained him more than he'd imagined. While his head screamed that he would have to let go of the past once and for all, his heart clung on.

Stop this, you've made up your mind, stick to the plan.

But I love it here. Maybe I can find a way, do it up and rent it out.

And stay in Mum's spare room forever, you saddo.

Taking the provisions over to the frigo he opened the door and was given a slap around the chops by a whoosh of cold air that forced him to talk sense into himself. If he wanted a place of his own in Manchester, to get his foot on the property ladder, then no matter how hard it would be, sooner rather than later, La Fleurie had to be sold.

4

VERONIQUE

She had taken her time getting ready and everyone was waiting downstairs just as she intended. As la Duchesse, she had every right to be late and make a grand entrance but rather than give her pleasure, the thought made Veronique so very damn angry. That was nothing new, though, because for so long she had been angry at everyone and everything. Hating the world had become second nature.

It was pathetic. Grasping onto a spurious outdated and defunct title that was no more special than that of Madame Talone who was married to the slob who ran the *tabac* in the town. Veronique was no more a Duchesse than her husband was a Duc because the stupid title in this day and age was meaningless as was her union to Hugo Bombelle. *Stupide, stupide, stupide.*

To her utter disbelief, despite such dedication, grinning and bearing being married to a man almost twenty years her senior, the union had brought nothing of value apart from titbits. Second-hand remnants of a charmed life that les Bombelles once lived. And she thought she'd been so clever and wily, turning the tables and showing her smart-arse brother that she wasn't what he said and had a mind of her own.

Was she being ungrateful? Possibly. Apparently, residing in a chateau was what dreams were made of and had it been any other, away from the town where she grew up, it might have been enjoyable. She may have been able to turn a blind eye to its faults.

Add to this the intolerable trial of living in the shadow of a dead woman who everyone had adored, and Veronique could only take so much of the reminders that were everywhere. The ghosts of Hugo's wife and son lingered; their photographs looked out from frames in the *salon*, portraits in the corridors, then the townsfolk who never tired of recounting tales of the good old days when the 'real Duchesse' was alive. Veronique told herself it was envy, and she liked that, someone begrudging her the life they thought she had.

Things were better when they resided in the Paris apartment. She felt more settled there, well away from the past and her memories of Cholet. It was located in the third arrondissement of Paris and Veronique adored the Parisian way of life, the anonymity of being swallowed by a city, the stand-offish arrogance of wealthy acquaintances who had better things to do than reminisce. They were people she would politely acknowledge as they passed in a restaurant but had no desire to befriend or answer nosey questions about her past or where she'd been before she married darling Hugo.

She preferred the solitude of the city and the apartment, happy to hear the buzz of cosmopolitan life going on around her while she enjoyed her own company, her books and the radio. The only blip was having to share her moments of contentment with Hugo – the roof over her head had come at a price, and that price was their odd relationship, hers and Hugo's.

Not quite companions because she was required to fulfil his

needs now and then, they merely got along, shared a home, chatted about this and that, circumnavigating anything in their pasts that caused discomfort and basically convincing themselves that everything was going to be all right. But it wasn't and they couldn't pretend any longer.

In limbo, that was where she was stuck. Suspended between the past and a happy ending that was slowly fading from sight. Shackled to an old man and an even more ancient chateau, both well and truly past it, they prevented her from achieving what she truly craved and constantly eluded her. Not great wealth or power as some people might suspect because yes, she was shallow, but life had made her so, people had made her so. As the clock ticked, Veronique heard each second, and realised it was now or never, time to break free before it was too late.

Before she could do this there was one big problem she needed to solve. Hugo's stubborn, selfish, sentimental daughter who continued to thwart her plans. Fabienne's existence on the earth was a permanent irritation. It was she who blocked the way and threatened to derail what Veronique had thought was a splendid scheme, when in fact it was flawed from the outset.

Yes, she should have done her homework properly, but appearances were, and remained, deceiving. As others did when they saw Chateau de Chevalier and heard all about the Paris apartment, she had stupidly hedged her bets on what she beheld and what she remembered.

A chateau where the glitterati came to stay for weekends and the walls were lined with paintings and each room was adorned with priceless *objets d'art*. On paper, the collection that had been collated since the end of the last war was reputed to be worth a fortune. In her head she had struck gold. Veronique now accepted that she was deluded, duped by her own avarice and summarily punished.

The truth of the matter stung like hell. For a start the value of the collection was irrelevant and secondly, French law was an ass because no matter how much Veronique and her impoverished husband wished it otherwise, Fabienne could not be disinherited.

Making matters even worse, pre-marriage, her husband omitted to tell her about the stupid family tradition and equally stupid will made by him and his long dead wife. Upholding the Bombelle custom, the late Duchesse had bequeathed all chattels such as jewellery, those dreary journals, tatty old rugs from India and even pots and bloody pans to her daughter. In short, Fabienne held all the cards. She was digging her heels in and Veronique's villa in Nice was fast becoming a distant dream.

In reality the chateau was the same. A mirage that from the outside looked like a fairy-tale castle when in fact it was a money-sucking monster that needed to be put out of its misery. Veronique was more than happy to slice off its head.

The rain was another enemy and she dreaded winter or any inclement weather. The roof leaked in hundreds of places, the windows rattled and creaked, the wood was rotten and the single glazing useless and allowed the wind to howl through the rooms in a storm. The plumbing clunked and groaned and backed up. The taps spurted foul brown water or didn't produce any at all. Bath time was always a gamble. And she couldn't even bear to think about the toilet situation and the drains that regularly blocked. The electrics were a health hazard and yes, she had wondered if a good old outage or frazzled wire might one day start a fire and burn the place to the ground. Sometimes frustration engulfed her and regardless of logic she was tempted to buy a can of petrol and set the place on fire herself, simply out of spite.

Tutting, Veronique picked up the bottle of scent and as she dabbed Chanel No.5 behind her ears and onto her wrists, recalled the conversation where Hugo had trampled over her future.

She'd been browsing the internet and after peering over her shoulder, he casually suggested she refrain from looking at beachside properties as the whole thing was a no go.

Naturally Veronique had asked why and when Hugo finally plucked up the courage to explain their predicament, she listened, horrified, barely able to believe what she was hearing, teetering on the verge of another meltdown.

'What do you mean, darling? How is it possible that Fabienne owns almost everything? Surely the art belongs to you too. And what if your son was still alive, is it not unfair that he would have been passed over?'

Hugo had winced at the mention of his son who had died tragically when he was two. Yet while a pulse throbbed in his cheek, he attempted to explain. 'One of my ancestors fell on hard times and the chateau was only saved when he married into money, but this came with a codicil.'

'Which was?' Veronique crossed her arms and tapped her foot impatiently, wanting to slap Hugo so hard for not mentioning all this before they married.

'That her wealth, in the form of chattels, would be passed on directly through the female line, via the daughters of the family. Apparently, she was a headstrong young woman with an eye for business and perhaps recognised that the Bombelle men didn't always make the wisest of choices. Either that or she was a raving feminist who was making a stand against primogeniture. Her wealth rescued the family name, one almost ruined by incompetent male heirs.' Hugo lit another cigarette, his default setting when nerves got the better of him. Perhaps he realised in this case he was describing himself.

'Well, that's ridiculous and stupidly complicated and archaic. And anyway primo... thingy, was abolished years ago and what if there were no girls born to the family? Who would inherit the chattels then?'

Hugo had merely shrugged. 'It's really quite simple, my darling: it reverts to the males but unfortunately, it's watertight so we cannot make Fabienne sell anything in the chateau or the apartment. It all belongs to her.'

Veronique was in shock. 'Well, she is welcome to your smelly socks too. And your dreary collection of car magazines. In the meantime, we are prisoners who cannot afford to put a new roof on this crumbling pile or live our dream of retiring by the sea. It is totally unacceptable, Hugo, and you have to find a way to make her see sense.'

Again, he shrugged and added a very condescending roll of the eyes. 'How? What do you suggest we do? I wish I had the answers, my darling, but instead, I have a bank balance permanently in the red, mounting bills and you on my back twenty-four seven!'

A gasp. 'How dare you. I am trying to help you solve the problem not add to it.' Veronique was incensed because she was the injured party, not him. She'd been duped into marrying a wrinkly, fake millionaire when she was in her prime, not yet fifty and full of life. 'But I thought the collection was valuable. Wasn't your grandfather some big art dealer? Surely he made wise investments.' Veronique knew the family had lost their most priceless possessions during the war but had presumed the stock had been replenished.

Hugo merely tutted. 'You forget that the post-war years were tough for everyone and the damage done to the chateau by those Nazi pigs took time and money to repair. Yes, he managed to bring it back to its former glory but only cosmetically. He could never afford to buy artworks on the scale he had before and times were changing too, for landowners all across Europe. We have been lucky to survive this long.'

Veronique was not going to take the news lying down. 'Are the portraits in the gallery worth anything? Perhaps you could persuade her to let some of them go, split the difference so we can move on, let her mend the leaky roof.' A viable and perfectly reasonable option.

'Not really. They were commissioned and painted by obscure artists of the time and of no great importance in the art world. The antiques around the chateau are valuable but even if she sold all of them, it wouldn't help in the long term. A new roof alone would cost over half a million pounds, then there's all the other repairs that are needed. We would need to sell everything and then be left with empty walls and rooms.'

'Dear God, I'm living in a death trap and a waking nightmare! And I am sick of being under the thumb of your daughter who thinks she knows everything about everything.'

Hugo flopped into his armchair and opened his newspaper, retreating behind the broadsheet as was his habit. 'Oh, don't be so dramatic and petty. You have to give Fabienne some credit where it's due because she has made art her life and this chateau *is*, no matter how much it pains you, her heritage. Don't get me wrong, I'd be rid of it in a heartbeat, however, my hands are tied.'

Still not defeated, Veronique resorted to sarcasm in order to punish her pathetic husband, backing him into a corner at the same time. 'So, is there anything you do own, dearest? You know, in your own name. Have you actually made any money yourself or have you simply fed off your ancestors until there was no meat left on the bones?'

Hugo flicked his newspaper downwards and she could see

the anger in his eyes as she waited for him to retaliate. 'Actually, I own some land on the edge of town that I acquired before I was married. I won it from a chap who I beat at cards, and then there's my car. Both have been excellent investments but still not enough to save the chateau.'

Veronique felt the smile begin before it appeared on her face, triumph bubbling from within while utter disdain for Hugo's gambling addiction trotted on behind. 'Oh, how marvellous, darling. Then you can sell them both and take me on holiday. If your daughter gets almost everything when you are dead, you can make me happy while you are alive. Let's start with the car and the chauffeur, think of the money we will save on Gregoire's wages. I will do the honours and tell him he has to go. I will also ring my brother and ask him if he knows of anyone who wants to buy some land. I'm sure he will. René knows everything and everyone, doesn't he, darling?'

With that she left Hugo open-mouthed and red-faced, wincing from the sting of words that she knew cut deep. Back in the day her husband and brother had been good friends, but now their bonhomie had faded, the past still weighing heavy. But Hugo had paid his pound of flesh and even if her sly brother wanted more, there was nothing left to give.

As she had marched from the room, Veronique had caught sight of Antoinette scurrying across the foyer, no doubt listening at doors once again. Well, that little exchange would certainly give her something to report back to Fabienne and taking a point where she could, Veronique had smiled.

Despite this small victory it still irritated Veronique that Fabienne would not see sense and agree to sell. She could see it all, flitting from Nice to Paris as the mood took her. But no.

Fabienne resolutely clung onto the past and her inheritance and her tatty old things, especially those passed down after the death of her precious maman.

Even the dead Madame de Bombelle's boudoir was like a shrine that nobody apart from Fabienne was allowed to enter and God help Hugo if Veronique ever found him in there, lamenting his late wife!

The nursery was the same and gave her the creeps, reminding her of a scene from a horror movie with dust sheets covering the black-eyed rocking horse and Baptiste's bedroom furniture. She'd only ever been in there once when curiosity and maybe devilment had got the better of her. As she'd entered the room, her skin had began to prickle and her hair really had stood on end when the atmosphere and temperature dipped. If she'd believed in spirits then she would have said that they were telling her to get out, screaming in her ears that she was unwelcome, and why.

Fastening her earrings, Veronique sucked in her temper. Wound up like a bobbin, she knew her mood would only get worse once the summit began. Hugo had thought by calling in unbiased third parties, namely his lawyer and accountant, that they could get through to Fabienne. He wanted them to lay out in black and white the direness of the chateau's financial situation, and once she really understood, propose they sell to the young British couple. It would be the perfect solution.

A tap on the door preceded the voice of Antoinette, another thorn in Veronique's side. The bloody spy.

'Madame, they are here and are waiting for you in the study. Monsieur Hugo wishes you to hurry.'

Sucking in her irritation at everyone and everything, Veronique replied. 'I am on my way. Tell him to be patient.'

'*Oui*, madame.'

There was a time when Veronique had been grateful for

Antoinette because she was adept at running the house and taking care of the mundane, ensuring the cleaners did a proper job and arranging for minor repairs to be made. Nowadays, Veronique regarded Antoinette as the enemy within because she had alerted Fabienne, telling tales about the English and the film crew.

Veronique saw it as a portent, a lifeline and a chance worth taking. Unfortunately, Fabienne had been highly offended, saying they'd gone behind her back and that stubborn streak may as well have been painted right down the centre of her spine.

Well fine, if that was how she wanted it, that's what she would get. Veronique loved a challenge and board games were her thing. If the meeting with the lawyers and accountants didn't go the way she and Hugo hoped, then she would revert to plan B. Her husband and his errant child would be out of the equation. Her patience had reached its limits and she had the future to think of. And this *did not* include rattling round in a cold, leaky mausoleum for the rest of her days.

No, one way or another Veronique would have her villa in the sun, even if she had to scale it down somewhat. An apartment would do, just as long as it was hers, no men, no husbands, no brothers. Fabienne may think she held the keys to the door and all the cards, but Veronique had one more up her sleeve, something better than an ace. Her brother, René.

It wasn't that she loved her brother, it was quite the opposite. He was his father's son and the narcissist gene ran through his veins. They had always danced around one another, once Veronique worked out how to play the game of give and take, nothing ever given for free.

The day she realised her brother wasn't protecting her because he loved her, but because it gave him power had caused Veronique such pain. Hunger, the last slice of bread, a favour owed. The last bastion of family life had crumbled, a big brother who didn't really care and once her tears had dried Veronique realised that she had two choices. Be a victim like her mother or side with the devil. Lucifer won.

As well as being a successful businessman, René had many useful connections on either side of the law, within the law too. Like his father, René was quick to anger, and she knew more than anyone his ability for making things that irritated him disappear. The same applied to problems, like awkward members of the committee who were shuffled off, their seat soon occupied by someone more compliant. René was good at moving things. Money, stolen goods, people.

But his speciality was secrets. Like the one he held over her, that he referred to with a sneer. And then her terrible mistake that would forever be her greatest regret. What she suspected of him but could never prove. Something they never spoke about. A part of her past that was etched into her memory and left a deep groove in her heart. All of these had messed with her head, made her reliant on him when she had longed to be free.

Veronique often told herself it wasn't their fault, how they were. It was merely the result of her dysfunctional upbringing, watching a cruel father torment a woman who had the misfortune to be his wife. Three generations of loveless childhoods perpetuated by the legacy of shame had taken their toll and no matter who was to blame, Veronique had had enough of it all. Of making the wrong choice again, choosing Hugo and allowing René back into her life for propriety's sake, so nobody would ask questions. Tired of her brother wielding power, always there on the periphery of her life, waiting for a chance to pounce for his own gain.

Veronique sighed then stood and before leaving the room she stared at her reflection, and instead of admiration she felt nothing but disdain, utterly despising the woman she saw and had become. The charade would go on because, once again, Veronique needed René and she couldn't have it both ways. So, as much as she loathed asking a favour it looked inevitable, and the only way to guarantee his help would be to make it worth his while, take the crust of bread and pay it back, just like always.

5

FABIENNE

It was hard to believe yet she could see it with her own eyes, there in black and white, and far too much red, the true state of their financial affairs. Her father's study was in complete silence as those gathered, the family lawyer, old Monsieur Roussel accompanied by their stern-faced accountant Monsieur Landry and his young assistant Joel, who was doing his utmost to hide his feelings for Antoinette.

He and Antoinette had struck up a flirtatious relationship after their first telephone conversation which had begun rather awkwardly due to an unpaid bill. Since, Fabienne had been amused to hear that Joel had succumbed quite easily to Antoinette's charms and gave them extra time to pay. And it seemed he had other useful talents, not necessarily confined to book-keeping.

Once Veronique had deigned to grace them with her presence, the accountant had nodded to his assistant who solemnly passed around copies of the report. The tome of doom was neatly bound in a very professional embossed cover and all Fabienne could think was how much the printing had cost and that it would be reflected in Monsieur Landry's fee.

Not daring to look up until the tears in her eyes had dissipated, Fabienne rested her forehead in her hands and addressed her father, hearing her own disappointment in every word.

'Oh Papa. What have you done? I didn't know it was as bad as this. You should have told me.' By her side Antoinette shuffled, most probably feeling uncomfortable that she was privy to a family meeting though Fabienne had insisted she attend. If Veronique was present then Antoinette should be included too, as Fabienne's business adviser. She had the qualifications after all.

'I didn't want to worry you and hoped that my investments might pay off, but you should take into account that we have lived through a pandemic. Things have been tricky.' If Hugo was embarrassed by the loud tut that emanated from his wife, he could rest assured that everyone in the room probably felt the same.

Fabienne was past caring what the lawyer and the accountants thought of her incompetent father or their awkward family dynamic. This was her home, and she was sick of his pathetic excuses. In fact, she was fed up with him in general because for as long as she could remember he had been weak and unreliable.

She had clung onto the hope that he did love her really, and for a time convinced herself it was only grief that prevented him from showing her any warmth. But eventually the light dawned on the inadequacies of their relationship and the deficient moral fibre of her one living relative, and it had hurt her badly. The figures had only proved what she already knew.

Her father had paid for her education as a means to his own ends, and she owed him nothing. However, the chateau was a different matter.

'Papa, there is no time to wait until your investments come

good and can we please be honest for once? Even if you did actually make some money would you spend it on this place or on your wife? The last time you acquired funds where did it go? Oh yes, first class to Mauritius.' Fabienne looked up and into the angry eyes of her puce-faced father and waited.

Being inside a pressure cooker would have been more comfortable than the fusty, wood-panelled study as everyone waited for an answer, or an excuse. Which way would he go? Did he have the balls to stand up to his wife? Did he have the merest inclination to appease his own flesh and blood? Fabienne was unsurprised by his response.

'How can you ask me such a hypothetical question? It's ridiculous. And you have no right to mention my private affairs when we are here to discuss the chateau.' Hugo blustered while by his side Veronique smirked.

'You know what, Papa, it does not matter. It is of no consequence to me what you do with your imaginary windfalls because I have better things to do with my time. Like saving my home, so we need to move forward and find a way to get ourselves out of this mess.'

'And I suppose *you* have the perfect solution to everyone's problems. How did I not guess?' The derisory tone of her stepmother had everyone's head swivelling in one direction.

'Yes, Veronique, perhaps I do. One that doesn't include losing my home to fund your exorbitant spending habits.' Perhaps sensing the mounting tension M. Landry interrupted for which Fabienne was grateful. She needed a moment to quell the desire to beat Veronique to a pulp.

'I think we should listen to Mademoiselle Fabienne's idea because as you can see from the report we are in a dire situation. I cannot hold off your creditors much longer. So, please, continue.' M. Landry gestured that Fabienne should begin.

After closing the folder, unable to bear its contents any

longer, Fabienne glanced at Antoinette, who gave her an encouraging smile before opening her brand-new notepad. For some reason, in the tensest of moments, seeing her best friend serious and poised, pen at the ready almost gave Fabienne the nervous giggles. *Okay, so if Antoinette can bluff it out, then so can I.*

'Even before we knew the full extent of our situation, Antoinette and I had realised that the time for procrastination is over. Our business plan will be with you in its fully prepared form by the end of the week but for now, I will share our ideas and give you time to ponder. Antoinette will make notes of any concerns that may arise from this meeting, and we will address them within our report.' Fabienne looked to her friend who simply nodded and pushed her huge, black-framed specs further up the bridge of her nose.

Next, Fabienne stole a glance at her father who looked nervous while Veronique smirked and picked at her nails. Ignoring the swish of her stomach, Fabienne took a breath and ploughed on with her pitch. It was an idea that had been conceived the night before, courtesy of a six-pack of very strong beer. Even though it started out as a bit of a dream, a tipsy fantasy, the more she thought about it into the early hours, the more it started to make sense.

'To begin, I would like to make it very clear that despite previous suggestions, none of the artwork or valuables contained in either the chateau or the apartment in Paris will be sold to raise money. I have spent considerable time valuing each piece using my own experience and with the help of my colleagues at the gallery. I will, of course, provide you with an up-to-date figure based on the current climate along with a detailed inventory but for now, you can always refer to the insured value.'

Three heads nodded from behind her father's walnut desk

while on the other side, Antoinette scribbled God only knew what, and the other two, well they were about to get a huge shock.

'As I see it, the only way the chateau can survive is by opening it to the public and it will be of no interest to anyone if it is stripped bare of what antiques remain and as we have already established, selling the collection in its entirety will not raise enough money to solve our problems in the long term. It will only provide an interim solution. And whilst the Bombelles have always fiercely guarded our privacy, me included, we have to move with the times.'

Fabienne paused, expecting opposition but she sensed they were waiting for her to say something stupid before jumping in, so she chose her words extremely carefully. 'What I propose could work for all of us and be the compromise we need. I would like to utilise the chateau for three different purposes all of which I am sure will bring revenue and stability.' Again silence, so she ploughed on.

'I suggest we split it into four areas. The attics can be converted into two apartments. My side and yours.' At this point her father leant forward and opened his mouth as if to object but like an obedient dog he shrunk back when Veronique raised her hand and silenced him.

Fabienne wasn't fooled or comforted by this action and suspected that her stepmother merely wanted to hear it all before passing judgement. All she could do was soldier on.

'The third floor will be converted into luxury apartments that we can let. After the pandemic there was a run on country homes of all sizes that were snapped up by city dwellers from Paris, Rennes and Nantes, desperate never to be trapped in a city on lockdown again. So, why not charge a premium rate for a lease on a beautiful, serviced apartment within a chateau, located in extensive private grounds, well away from the hustle and bustle of city life. They can live the dream without actually taking on a whole chateau and instead, enjoy a small piece of it.'

Antoinette had ceased scribbling and now had a dreamy look in her eye, no doubt imagining the luxury apartments they'd conjured up somewhere around the third bottle of beer.

In the absence of verbal resistance and ignoring stony looks from her father and Veronique, Fabienne continued. 'Now to the second and first floor which I propose we convert into a boutique hotel and restaurant, all the usual attractions like a function suite, gym, etcetera. And finally, the ground floor which will host the reception area for residents and guests and also, an art gallery.' At this Antoinette's head turned as she eyed Fabienne quizzically because this hadn't been part of their beer-goggle dream.

The idea had literally popped into Fabienne's head, right there and then, like someone was whispering in her ear and once the words were spoken and she had repeated them, the possibilities were running riot in her brain.

Then came the bluff. 'I have a contact list brimming with contemporary artists who would love to show their work in a setting such as this and along with my connections I will be able to secure loans of art from other galleries, maybe temporarily exchange ours for theirs. It's a work in progress but I am convinced it's doable. In fact, together, as a package, what I propose will secure the future of the chateau and also bring much needed employment to the area.'

Seeing that both the accountant and lawyer were nodding appreciatively, and Joel was making notes faster than Antoinette was pretending to, gave Fabienne a boost of confidence.

'It's a win–win. The money from the rental of the apartments will continually inject capital into the business and as we grow our brand, we can perhaps expand and renovate the outbuildings, for example the stables. They would be perfect for luxury *gîtes*. This is a viable business plan and I know I can make it work, if you give me the chance.'

A clearing of the throat drew her eyes towards M. Landry who had raised his finger and she knew the crucial question was about to be asked. 'Mademoiselle Fabienne, I applaud your ingenuity and enterprise, but I am afraid I may have to be the bearer of solemn news because had you hoped to raise capital for this venture from the bank, I can positively assure you that none would be forthcoming. They are more interested in your father clearing his debts, which is why he has suggested the chateau be sold. I thought you understood this.'

Feeling sympathy for the pink-cheeked accountant who had the grace to look abashed at foreclosing on her idea, Fabienne knew it was time to drop the bomb. 'Since seeing the report I am fully aware of this fact. However, all is not lost because there is a way to raise capital *and* pay off Papa's debts.'

A hush descended and Fabienne knew without even looking that Antoinette would be holding her breath for this bit. 'Something has to be sacrificed so therefore I propose we sell the apartment in Paris to raise the required funds. It is worth millions and will be snapped up in a heartbeat due to its location.'

'No! Hugo, you must stop this at once. How dare she suggest these things. We are NOT selling the apartment; it is the chateau that must go.' Veronique's screech had cut the air and as she grabbed her husband's arm, she appeared to be squeezing her venom through his jacket because he'd gone a funny colour, ashen with overtones of blood-pressure red.

Fabienne didn't miss a beat. 'Actually, Veronique, how dare *you* interfere with family business so please, be quiet and listen to what I have to say otherwise leave the room. Your input isn't required. This is between me, and my father and you will have no say in the matter.'

It was M. Landry who intervened and cooled the temperature with wise words. 'Ladies, please. We will get nowhere if we resort to raised voices and vitriol so, Fabienne, do continue and once you have finished, we will give your father a chance to respond. Please, remember we are all searching for a resolution so let's keep looking.' Again, he gestured with his hand that she should continue, his words obeyed by everyone in the room.

Speaking directly to her father who would not even look her in the eye, Fabienne attempted appeasement. 'Papa, you know how much I treasure our heritage, the Bombelle-Chevalier name and legacy and it will break my heart to see the apartment leave the family, but it really is the only solution. It is our most valuable asset and can secure the future of the chateau which, if my plans come to fruition, will one day support itself and remain with us forever. For the next generations. Surely you can see that.'

Nobody moved or spoke. Joel's pen was poised yet his eyes were firmly fixed on Fabienne's father, as were everyone's. Hugo cleared his throat and avoided eye contact with his wife and daughter, turning instead to his lawyer and spoke about his only child instead of to her.

'My daughter knows full well that my wife and I reside in Paris for most of the year and that is where I do business. Therefore, it is wholly unreasonable for her to expect us to sell our home to save this one, which is decaying around our ears. So, I suggest a compromise.'

Fabienne did not expect this, a counter move, and couldn't imagine what it would be. And she could not imagine why if her father had a solution he hadn't mentioned it until now. She kept her counsel and allowed M. Landry to conduct proceedings, at the same time refusing to allow her heart to be wounded by her father's snub and derisory tone.

'Please proceed, Hugo. I am sure we are all most curious.' Landry raised a furry eyebrow to accompany his thinly veiled sarcasm.

'I propose we remortgage the Paris apartment and split the sum, a figure to be agreed by Fabienne and myself, between us. She can use her half to renovate this place or whatever she likes and the same applies to me and my wife. That way we both get what we want. Fabienne keeps the chateau, and we keep the Paris apartment.'

'And she gets her villa in Antibes or whichever town is unlucky enough to have that parasite in residence–'

'How dare you?' This time Veronique stood but unlike previously, behind her anger was the hint of triumph. Fabienne could see it in the eyes of her adversary, but the game wasn't over yet. As usual, her father hadn't thought things through, and she was about to tell him so.

'I dare because I am right, and you know it! And I also know that Papa has once again demonstrated to us why we are in such a mess because he's forgotten one very important element. How the hell is he going to make the repayments on the loan? Let's face it, he earns nothing and hasn't done for years so his idea is totally preposterous.'

When Hugo answered it was a mocking tone. Was he enjoying hurting her? Even considering this caused Fabienne to grab the arm of the chair, her knuckles white and her palm clammy.

'Isn't it obvious, Fabienne? You will meet the repayments from the profits you expect to make on the hotel, that I will partly own. This is your dream; you can live it but do not expect me to finance it from my own pocket.

'In fact, it is you that is selfish, wanting everything your own way. All you have to do is sell some of your precious treasure to make your monthly repayments, until you actually have customers or tenants. Either way, I really don't care. It's up to you. Remortgage the Paris apartment to fund the renovations on the chateau or watch it crumble about your ears. You will inherit it one day as you well know, but in the meantime, I want nothing to do with it. In fact, I am so thoroughly sick of this place, hearing about it, living in it and watching it rot that Veronique and I will return to Paris today. Any further questions?' When he reached out and entwined his fingers in Veronique's, like allies, he may as well have slapped Fabienne across the face.

Feeling the warmth of Antoinette's skin as she laid her hand over Fabienne's brought some comfort as father stared out daughter. Until she saw it, the twitch of a smirk and the cold flat look in his eye. For Fabienne it was the final straw. In that instant she knew that the relationship with her father, already threadbare, like a tatty rug that was one step away from being thrown out with the rubbish, had been set alight.

The flames of resentment burned deeper than ever before, brighter, hotter, more devastating than the fire that she saw in her dreams, one in which her mother and brother died. And through the imaginary smoke that burned her eyes and made them leak, Fabienne could still see clearly enough to make her decision.

'Do you think I'm a fool, Papa? To finance the whims of that viper and happily stand by while you squander your money while I use mine to make you more? It will just go on and on because we will be in more debt than before, until the chateau can be renovated. And even if I did sell some of the antiques, what if we can't make the repayments? Then we lose the apartment. It's too risky, you are a liability and I'm not prepared to be backed into a corner.'

The roar of anger from her father as he stood took Fabienne

by surprise because never had she heard him raise his voice to her, or anyone for that matter.

'It is you who is backing people into corners, Fabienne, for your own selfish, sentimental wants and I won't have it. I am sick and tired of being told what to do and blamed for things out of my control, so this is my final offer, take it or leave it.' Without looking in her direction he then spoke to his wife.

'Veronique, go and pack our bags, we are leaving immediately.' Next, he bade farewell to the solicitor and lawyer. 'My apologies for the tawdry spectacle as it was not my intention but I'm sure you can see what I'm up against. Should you wish to speak with me you know where I'll be. Good day, gentlemen.' And with that he marched from the room, Veronique almost running behind him, such was his haste.

Fabienne was flabbergasted yet resolute as she stood and shouted at his back. 'Then I will leave it, Papa. No deal. No villa. No spending sprees. And don't get too comfy in the apartment because I might just turn up with my friends and throw a party. Remember I have a key. It's my home too.' When the door slammed Fabienne almost screamed her final words. 'GOODBYE AND GOOD RIDDANCE!'

Taking a deep breath and realising her whole body was trembling she turned to face the room and saw only bowed heads shuffling papers and closing files. Even Joel was occupied with his briefcase.

Antoinette was quickly by her side, protectively wrapping her arms around Fabienne's shoulders, her voice hushed. 'I cannot believe your father came up with that. I didn't know he had the brains to be so cunning but I'm proud of you for standing up to him, and her.' She was interrupted by the others as they made to leave, led by Monsieur Roussel, who took Fabienne's hand in his as he spoke.

'My dear, we should give your father time to cool off and

think things through and hopefully when he does, he will see the wisdom in your plan because you are correct, taking a loan against the apartment is risky. If all else fails perhaps you can find an investor. The English couple might be interested but in the meantime I'm sure my friend here will do his best to hold off the creditors.' He glanced at Monsieur Landry who nodded his agreement.

'And please know that I do admire your determination and loyalty to your home so be assured I will pray for you at mass on Sunday. I have fond memories of this place, you know, and your dear mother and grandfather who loved the chateau as much as you. Now, we will leave you in peace. You know where I am if you need me. *Au revoir,* Fabienne. Try not to worry.'

They all trooped out, Joel leaving last and giving Antoinette a chaste smile.

Once they were alone, Fabienne flopped into the chair and allowed the frustration and hurt of the past hour to escape, not in the form of tears but the worst swear words Antoinette said she had ever heard.

'Okay, so now you've had a tantrum and made my ears bleed, what are we going to do?' Antoinette folded the cover of her notepad and clicked the button on her pen.

Fabienne dragged her hands downwards, contorting the skin of her face and wondered if this is how Edvard Munch's screaming figure felt as they stood on the bridge. 'I have no idea, no idea at all.'

But then, in the next moment she did. Because even if her father thought he'd pushed her to the edge, of a bridge, a cliff, the brink, she was not going to jump off. Fabienne was standing firm.

6

EGLANTINE

I don't like parties. I don't like balloons. I don't like pineapple sorbet. I don't like that big fat nurse who needs to take a shower. I don't like it when it is too hot, and today it is too hot. I don't like sitting next to Hubert at mealtimes because he's a slurper. I don't like these ugly brown shoes and I know I did not choose them. I don't like watching the news because it makes me angry. I don't like Macron. I don't like being here.

I'm not being grumpy, by the way. I just like to list all the things I don't like because it reassures me that at least I still have some free will. And that my mind has not turned to mush after living in this insufferable place where order and routine are king. A battle. That's what it is. To stay sane and keep all my marbles in my pouch, in my pocket, just here, nice and safe. I dare not keep my marbles in my head because that lot put chemicals in my food and it alters my mind. I know their type.

I cling onto sanity, I really do, because it's the last bastion of self-respect and I prize that over everything. That and being able to wipe my own bottom. Sorry, sorry, I've embarrassed you now. I didn't mean to make you uncomfortable. But let's face it,

I've seen enough of them go gaga in this place to know how easy it is and how quickly it happens.

One minute they are fine, closing their book and saying goodnight and then wake up in the morning possessed by a raving lunatic. Okay, so perhaps that's unfair and something they can correct with a couple of bags of saline but then there are others who just give up. They flop like saggy puddings. Or hold up their hands and surrender. I've seen it with my own eyes. And I'm not talking about when the Nazi invaders came. I mean this lot in here, the shufflers, not the dirty collaborators or the lily-livered Vichy.

I'm sorry, you look perplexed, that's because I wander in and out of the past and I will try to stay on track but it's because I have a quick mind, nothing else. I am not dallying with senility as some seem to think.

Back to my point – because I do have one. I will not surrender. I didn't make it through that ugly war and bring up seven children to fade away like a scar. I'm not a blemish, an unsightly reminder, a statistical blight or tiresome drain on society. That's how I feel, being in here and that's why I make a bit of a fuss now and then. I like to hear my voice and know they are still listening. If I want warm milk in my coffee I will have it, and if I don't want to sit in the plastic leak-proof armchair then I bloody well won't. *'You like this green chair don't you, Eglantine?'* NO. I don't. Listen to me. I wish they would listen. Properly.

Even Antoinette – she's my favourite great-grandchild but don't tell the others – doesn't understand what I am trying to say. Even though the words I am speaking are very clear in my mind, for some reason she gets them all mixed up and says she doesn't understand.

Between you and me, she can be a bit stupid, but I won't say that out loud. She's loyal and kind, but clearly not as intelligent as me. That'll be bad genes from her father's side. I don't like her father either. I must remember this for my list.

When Antoinette visits which is often, more often than the rest of them, she tells me all about what's going on up at the chateau. I love a good bit of gossip and always have. That was how we thrived, me and my comrades always staying ahead of them, the invaders and the collaborators.

The things I know about that place. A den of iniquity was what my own grandmother called it. And she would have known because her brother was a gardener at the chateau and reported the goings-on when the Parisians came to stay. Back in the old days, the townsfolk frowned upon the weekend visitors but they have always been a two-faced lot and knew which side their bread was buttered. And in the case of the Duc and Duchesse, that was nice and thick.

It's a terrible place, Chevalier, and I've tried to warn my Antoinette because when I found out that the Saber woman had married stupid Hugo my blood ran cold. That family, the Sabers, are the scourge of the earth, evil to the core and she – her name escapes me right now – is descended from a collaborator and so is that obnoxious brother of hers.

I remember everything. About them, the traitor, what happened up at the chateau. It may have been over eighty years ago, but I know it all like yesterday which was Friday because we had fish for dinner. See, I've still got it.

They forget I was there just like they forget I exist, or I am still me, Eglantine, a member of *La Resistance* who fought for Free France. I'm not just another 'guest'. That's what they call us, you know, when 'prisoner' would be more apt. Most of the guests are insipid, like the wallpaper in the communal dining room.

Bad things happen in there and I'm not talking about the food. Once, I felt myself being sucked into the wallpaper, smothered by a fresco of lilies. I held on tight to the arms of the chair so I wouldn't disappear into a swamp of green foliage and screamed so loud that the carers came running. I told them I was fine, and it was just the wallpaper but still they insisted on taking me to my room and fetching the doctor. Like I say, they don't listen.

What was I saying? Oh yes, the chateau and what happened there. You don't get to almost a hundred without seeing plenty and a lot of it I'd like to forget, and then a lot of it I want to hold onto so badly that it hurts. Like my family, and my husband Eric who will be along shortly and is always late. Seven children we had together, all of them born into a free France because of women like me. And you know what happened after the war? I will tell you. We were shoved back inside our homes and told to breed like rabbits while the men trudged back and took over again. Do I sound bitter? Well, I am. I wanted to be a teacher, you know. Never happened. Pah! So much for dreams.

I still dream though. About it all. The things I did and saw in the dark days of occupation, and what we endured. The hunger and fear to name a few. Maybe it would be better, easier to forget or blank out the images, but the mind can be cruel, this I know. Then again, I owe it to her to remember her face, her smile, my best friend whose name I can't recall... it will come to me, it's right there on the edge of the forest where we found her.

I was one of those who searched and cried for her every day, long after her body was discovered. Her poor little body, battered, bruised and defiled. She was such a sweet girl and didn't deserve what they did and how I hated them for it. All of those who were involved. I've told my great-granddaughter this, I think. Yes, I'm sure I have.

I told her the chateau is cursed, it really is. And I am scared that history could repeat itself, but she bats away my worries and rolls her eyes then reminds me that some things are just coincidence, and the Nazis are gone, and people change and there's no such thing as curses.

I know all this for heaven's sake because I cursed those Sabers to hell and still they thrive. It's not the Germans she should be wary of though. It's her, the one who has married Hugo, and her evil brother.

Do you know Hugo? He was such a handsome young man and all the women set their cap at him, but he was never going to look at a villager, not unless it was between the sheets and in secret, the fools. Hugo was destined to marry from his own class and even though he dragged his feet, I have to say he did very well for himself and chose a wife that I would have picked for any one of my sons. A good woman – everyone said so. I met her a few times through church. She was beautiful, hair like jet and pale-blue eyes. She had an aura about her, like she radiated happiness. You could feel the love, for everyone around and especially her children. The poor children.

It was a pity she married a drunken philanderer like Hugo, a useless article who, from what my Antoinette says, hasn't changed over the years and true to form has messed up again. No wonder he had a terrible relationship with his own father. That Duc was a decent man and did his best to claw back what the estate had lost during the war years, continuing his own father's work. None of his challenges were helped by Hugo who sauntered through life as though it owed him a living, running off to Paris when he messed up, then back again when he had run out of money. And after the tragedy, sending that poor little mite away to boarding school in a foreign country was just cruel.

Guilt. That's what it was. We all said so. No smoke without fire which is an analogy in very poor taste, but it fits. He was up to no good and it bit him on his backside but maybe, on reflection the little one was better off away because men like him have nothing to offer. Still, the goings-on up at the chateau had something to do with the accident, I'm sure of it.

I must tell Antoinette about that night. Not the accident, what happened to my friend. You must concentrate. What if she and Fabienne are in danger? Because I wouldn't want to make an enemy of the Sabers. I'm sure it means something, that all these memories are flooding back and it's not a coincidence because some things happen for a reason: they are meant to be. Like Antoinette meeting Fabienne all those years ago and going to work there and never mind that she shares the...

Oh, Oh. Here comes the smelly one. It's tablet time and she is a stickler for punctuality. I will ask her for my writing things and then I can make notes, so I don't forget about... now what was I saying? Oh yes. I've got it.

They are throwing me a party for my one hundredth birthday and have asked me what kind of cake I would like. I love cake so I've asked for raspberry filling and maybe some chocolate too. I'm very excited about my party. You are invited too but you will have to wear some clothes. I have no idea why you came like that, and it won't go down well if anyone sees. There are some prudes here I can tell you, so next time, please get dressed. It's very distracting.

Now I must take my medication and Eric will be here soon. You slip away quietly before the smelly one notices you. Don't worry: it's our secret. Go, go, slip out through the window and I'll see you soon, then we can talk more. I will look forward to it.

7

MAC

Mac pulled his phone from his back pocket and sighed when he saw the name on the screen, before accepting the call from his mother.

'Mum, I can't really talk. I'm just about to go into the supermarket so can I ring you back later?' He hadn't even got out of his car, but his mum didn't do short phone calls so it was best to head her off at the pass before she got into her stride.

Clearly taking no notice, his mother was persistent. 'I hear Marie-France has been to see you. She thinks you looked peaky.'

'Peaky! No, I do not look peaky and before you even say it NO, I am not going round there to be fattened up and drooled over by Jacqueline, okay. And while you're on, why did you tell her to come and clean the house when you know I can't afford it? Especially when I'm not staying?' Mac had just about enough money in his account to get him through the next six months if he was frugal, very frugal.

'I will pay for her, stop worrying. It's all been arranged, and I told you, don't make hasty decisions. You can work from there, you have a laptop, Wi-Fi and electricity so what more do you need? And it will be far cheaper than renting somewhere of your own over here, unless you want to be one of those thirty-year-olds who never leave home.' His mum was always to the point if nothing else.

'Cheers, Mum. Is that your way of saying I'm not welcome at yours?'

A loud tut followed that remark. 'Oh, stop feeling sorry for yourself, Mac. You know you will always have a room here with me and Tom, but I thought we'd agreed that you were going to put the past behind you. So, pull your socks up, get onto your old contacts and find some work and have a little holiday at the same time. You need a break and what better place to relax and get your head straight. I'm not being harsh but the time for wallowing is over.'

'Yes, I know all that and I fully intend to look for some new contacts while I'm here, but you won't change my mind about the farm. If I sell it, I can put down a deposit and buy my own home in England, like I intended before she–' Mac stopped himself, even he knew he sounded like a broken record.

When she responded his mum's tone was softer. 'Okay, okay. I'm sorry for opening wounds but I am worried about you so for now, please enjoy being back there and let things play out. See how you feel once you've had time to catch your breath. These last few months have been a crappy time for all of us and a lot worse for you, so don't make decisions when your head is a mess. Let it untangle slowly, that's all I ask.'

Resting his head against the seat Mac closed his eyes and sighed. 'Okay, and I'm sorry for snapping. I know you're only trying to help, and it will be nice seeing Tante Marie-France around the place. I can practise my French when she's telling me one of her very long stories.'

'Ha ha, yes, Marie-France loves a bit of tittle-tattle but don't forget you have lots of friends there so you should look them up.

I'm sure they will be glad to see you again. Right, I will leave you to do your shopping and remember...'

'Don't buy fish from the supermarket on a Monday. Yes, Mum, I remember very well what Mémère used to say, and I will obey, now go. I'll text you later. Give my best to Tom and don't rent my room out just yet, okay?'

Once final goodbyes were said Mac signed off and headed into the supermarket, looking forward to sheltering in the cool interior because it was gearing up to be another scorcher. And maybe after he'd bought some supplies, he might take his mum's advice and see if there were any familiar faces knocking about. Checking his watch, he saw that it was almost twelve and at that time of day there was one place he could almost guarantee seeing some of his old friends, the village bar and tabac.

He was enjoying the ambience of the quintessential street-front location, rickety wooden chairs set around ridiculously small tables beneath a jaunty yellow canopy that fluttered in the breeze. Unfortunately, one beer and two coffees in, Mac was about to give up and go home.

The shops opposite had already pulled down their blinds for the day, the butcher, baker and pharmacist heading home for lunch on what was obviously a slow day in Cholet when he spotted a familiar face heading along the pavement across the street. Seeing her immediately made him smile. Crazy Antoinette. She had always been the boss of their ragtag tribe that consisted of mostly farmers' kids and rural dwellers whose parents had failed them miserably by choosing to live out in the sticks.

When they were old enough to roam alone, they'd been happy with the small park or the woods and stream where they all congregated and spent lazy summer days. Then, as they hit their mischievous teenage years, they looked for fun elsewhere, usually in a bottle of cider, or a pilfered packet of cigarettes and then, when hormones began to rage, the inevitable occurred.

Antoinette was the mother hen of the group and he'd been grateful that whenever he showed up for the summer, she made sure he was included. The first time he'd been allowed to go to the park it had been with Jaqueline who had latched onto Mac like a limpet since they were little and saw him as her trophy, so woe betide anyone who tried to take him away. She was no match for Antoinette though, whose steely-eyed look made everyone wilt. She took command in any situation, like when Patric accidently set fire to a tree and Honoré fell off her bike and broke her wrist. It was always the leader of the gang who sorted everyone out and thankfully, in his case, managed to extract him from the clutches of Jacqueline.

Mac watched as his strawberry-blonde friend approached, her spiralled locks flowing behind as she strode confidently along the pavement. There was something bold yet not brash about Antoinette, like she always knew where she was headed, be it at the front of a group of kids on rickety bikes as they bounced along bumpy tracks or in life. She had made them all feel a bit more adventurous but at the same time safe, and as a wave of nostalgia took him by surprise Mac realised that he'd missed her.

Arms waving in the hope of catching Antoinette's attention Mac resorted to a whistle that he regretted instantly when the piercing sound cut through the sleepy midday vibe, drawing contemptuous looks from other passers-by and the couple at the next table. His discomfort was immediately salved when Antoinette stopped, spotted him and smiled before placing her thumb and forefinger in her mouth and replying to his call. Mac laughed out loud as she raced towards him, remembering how they had all practised the whistle that they used as their secret call sign, back in the day.

Before he knew it, she was there, arms outstretched then enveloping him in a bear hug, deceptively strong for such a willowy woman who was as long-limbed as he. Once she was done, she clung onto his arms, taking him in as she spoke. 'Hello stranger and where the hell have you been? I thought you had abandoned us. I am so sorry I didn't come to your grandfather's funeral, but I was on a little holiday to see my aunt. Claude was a good man, and we will all miss him.'

'Hey, it's fine and I'd never abandon you all. I've just been...' Mac stopped himself before he told any more lies or laid himself bare because he wasn't ready to finish his sentence with *busy wrecking my life*. 'Have you had lunch? I'm starving and we can catch up, unless you need to be somewhere. We could eat here or go to mine; I've just done a shop so have plenty.' Mac cringed and thought he sounded desperate and like a bumbling teenager all over again.

Antoinette smiled. 'I would love to have lunch with you. But not here, let's go to yours. It's been ages since I've been to La Fleurie. Do you still have the climbing rope in the garden? We had such fun on there, didn't we? I wouldn't mind seeing if I can still get to the top. Come on, where are you parked? I'm starving.'

Mac pointed as she took his arm and they headed down the street, her chattering on. He couldn't ignore the swell of happiness inside, or the fact it was something he'd not felt for a long time.

Antoinette laid the table while Mac brought over the food that was still in its supermarket wrapping, owing to his guest insisting she was going to eat her own arm if he didn't hurry up. It was all flooding back to him, the little things most of all. Like Antoinette was always hungry and would never leave home without food of some description and never ever turned down an invitation to stay for dinner. And that she always put you at your ease, made things seem natural, no standing on ceremony for her. And she never stopped talking. Going from one subject with bullet speed, always asking questions and half answering yours while her eyes noticed everything.

Dragging out a chair she seated herself at the table and began slicing the bread, firing questions at him one after another. 'So, your grandparents left this to your mum, but she's passed it straight to you. How nice is that! I bet you've got loads of ideas to do it up, and it will be brilliant having you here again. I hope you'll be back a bit more often now... hey, we can have a house-warming party. Get everyone together. What do you think?'

Mac took the seat opposite and poured them both a glass of wine. He would have answered had he been able to get a word in but as was usually the case, Antoinette rattled on, for which he was glad.

'You should have messaged that you were coming, but now I think about it I haven't seen you on Facebook for ages. You've not unfriended me, have you? So, tell me about your mum and her new husband. Is he nice? I'm glad she found someone after your dad... or do you not want to talk about him?'

Seeing her pause to take a sip, Mac took the opportunity to speak. 'Tom's a really nice guy and no, I don't mind talking about my dad, not anymore, although there's not a lot to say that you don't know really. He's a dick, a let-down, a cheat, too handy with his fists and I'm glad he's out of our lives once and for all. He was a waste of space when I was growing up and I don't miss him one bit. He lives in Spain now and I hope he stays there and leaves me alone.'

Mac raised his glass to Antoinette who responded in the same way. 'Well, that was nice and simple. Good wine, by the way. I'm glad she found a nice guy in the end. So, what about you? How come you've been such a stranger these past few years? I know your mum used to visit all the time especially after your grandma passed away. I did ask after you, but she said you were busy with work.'

Unease crept over Mac. He knew what Antoinette was getting at so held up his hands. 'I know what you're thinking. That I should have visited more but I *was* busy with work because I'd hooked a new client, a really big contract. I did fly over a few times for long weekends but you're right, I should have made more of an effort and if I could turn back the clock I'd do a lot of things very differently, that's a fact.'

'Hey, don't beat yourself up too much. It happens. People have busy lives and these days families can be spread all over the world. I only see some of mine once a year, but we get by with phone calls…' It was then that Antoinette's expression changed from understanding to concern. 'You did ring him, didn't you?'

At this Mac bridled because he wasn't a complete bastard. 'Yes of course I did. I got the Wi-Fi fitted and bought them a smartphone so we could video call every week right up until… until Mémère died. After that, as you probably know, Grandpère went downhill. I came over a couple of times with Mum and I visited him in hospital during the last few months, but he was out of it a lot of the time.'

Antoinette leant across the table and gave his hand a squeeze. 'Sorry, Mac, I've upset you, I can tell. It must have been awful, not being round the corner. He will have known you were there though, I'm sure.'

At this Mac shook his head and willed the tears misting his eyes not to fall. 'That's the thing though, at the end he was awake, and he was calling for me, Mum said. That's why she rang and told me I had to come quickly but I didn't answer my phone and when I did… let's put it this way, I was being a stupid selfish bastard. I never got to say goodbye or see him one more time and he wanted me there. I'll never forgive myself for that and sometimes I don't think Mum will either. She says all the right things, that he would have understood, and he only wanted the best for me, but she was there at the end, alone and watching the clock. Saw my granddad take his last breath. Nothing anyone can say will change that and I hate myself for it.'

Antoinette remained silent, as though she was thinking what best to say or allowing Mac to get a grip, so instead, she poured them both another glass of wine. When she did speak it was to ask another question. 'I can imagine that it is hard to come to terms with, but what did you mean, you were being stupid and selfish?'

Before he answered Mac drank more of his wine and took a moment to decide if he really wanted to lay himself bare and give Antoinette the full version of his tragic story and more to the point, if he had the strength to do so. It would only open wounds that had barely begun to heal and the last thing he wanted was his final visit to La Fleurie marred by *her* memory. Then again, *she* was the reason he'd been backed into a corner and one way or another, people would want to know why he was going to sell up and move on.

Straightening his back, exhaling as he did so, Mac decided to get it over with. 'Top and bottom of it is this. I was in a relationship with someone who took me for a ride and even when I knew all this, I still couldn't accept it and ran after her like a desperate fool. I think I was in denial and deranged. That's my only excuse.'

Antoinette leant back in her chair and folded her arms. 'Ah, I see. The woman I saw on your profile, the blonde?'

If she didn't spot that Mac's face had fallen, he certainly felt it. Just a mention, that was all it took to bring everything flooding back and normally he would have clammed up or changed the subject, but Antoinette wasn't the type to be fobbed off. Shifting uncomfortably in his seat he watched as she spread butter on her bread and then sliced a corner from the wedge of pâté, her knowing eyes finally resting on him, and before she took a bite, came a command. 'Come on, don't be shy. Tell me all about it. What did she do?'

Puffing out his exasperation at himself more than anything he was also worried that once he'd told her everything she might – most likely would – regard him as a total moron. In the end Mac conceded defeat. 'I think it's more a case of what she didn't do, because when I say she took me for a complete fool and ruined my life, I'm not joking or being dramatic.'

At this Antoinette raised an eyebrow. 'Well, you know what they say about sharing your problems and I am a good listener and your friend, so, let's see if I can help.'

'Okay, but I have a feeling you'll want to slap me or throw me in the stream when you hear what I've done so don't say I didn't warn you.' Mac had suddenly lost his appetite and pushed away his plate whereas Antoinette chewed her food and waited, seemingly untroubled by his warning.

'She's called Ankie, and I thought she was the one, the real thing, we were the real thing when actually she was a cold-hearted con artist who ripped me and a load of other blokes off. Which kind of makes me feel better that I wasn't the only mug in Manchester, or wherever she cast her net and believe me she liked to go fishing, a lot!'

Taking a long gulp of his wine, Mac then topped up his glass for Dutch courage, the irony of his last thought not lost on him. He needed to explain though, so that when the *'à vendre'* sign went up outside La Fleurie his friends would understand why he had to sell, and that he wasn't a cold-hearted guy with no respect for his heritage, just a complete and utter pillock.

8

MAC AND ANKIE

They had met online, friends of friends on Facebook. Ankie was Danish but lived in Edinburgh where she worked in a bar. She lived life to the full and had ditched her education to travel through Europe and found herself in Scotland. Mac had been instantly attracted to Ankie's spirit and sense of humour but initially, her looks. What could he say? He was a testosterone-fuelled young man and she was a hot, Danish blonde bombshell and after a couple of months chatting, she mentioned she was going to be in Liverpool with friends. Mac immediately asked if she'd like to meet up and was overjoyed when she agreed and more than willing to drive the thirty-five miles to see a virtual stranger. But it had been well worth it, and he'd stayed in her hotel room for the whole weekend and as much as he tried to be casual when they said goodbye, he was smitten.

After that they saw each other whenever they could but Ankie preferred to come to Manchester and get away from the flat she shared with three other girls. She wouldn't take the train fare when he offered but money was tight, so their time together was curtailed due to her stubborn pride. While they were apart,

Mac reminded himself of the teenager he once was, lovesick over Tara-Jane who was the most adored and hottest girl in Year 10.

During one of their weekends together in which she and Mac made the most of his new and very modern apartment, Ankie confided in him the reason she was always strapped for cash. Her mum and Bram, her younger brother, were back in Copenhagen and lived in a tough neighbourhood and since her dad had left, Ankie sent money home to help tide them over.

'Mum works so hard, two jobs, so she can keep a roof over Bram's head and now Dad has run off with his tart, there is just about enough money to survive. I suppose I should go home but their flat is tiny and I'd have to sleep on the sofa, so I do what I can from here. But if Mum asks, I'll go back in a heartbeat.'

No way did Mac want Ankie going back to Copenhagen so from then on insisted he paid for her fare down to Manchester, saying he wanted to help and see her more often. It took some persuading but eventually she saw sense. He had a good job as a freelance graphic designer so could also afford to treat Ankie to the things she missed out on. Mac could see she had a kind heart and thought it was a shame that she worked so hard yet had little to show for it. She loved the surprise presents he would send north, flowers, a gift voucher for her favourite clothes store with the message *'treat yourself'*. Tickets to the movie she wanted to see but knew he would hate, a McDonald's breakfast delivered by Uber when she'd done a long shift the night before.

Six months passed and he was on his way home, stuck in traffic on the Mancunian Way when his car phone rang and at the other end was a tearful Ankie, sobbing and hiccupping her way through a garbled conversation. 'Mac, I am in a big mess.'

'Why, what's wrong? Just calm down and tell me. That's it, deep breaths.'

'They have kicked me out of my flat because I missed paying

my share of the rent and already, they have found a new girl to take my room. What am I going to do? I have nowhere to go and can't even get back to my mum's because I sent her my wages to pay for Bram's school trip. I had to, otherwise he'd be the poor kid everyone laughed at...'

'Ankie, it's okay. We will sort this. Look, why don't you come and stay here for a few days until you decide what you want to do?'

More sobs came down the line until she gained control. 'Are you sure? But I don't have any money for the train...' She didn't even have to finish the sentence because Mac was already pulling off the bypass and as soon as he'd parked up, grabbed his phone and booked her a ticket.

'It's done. You should get a notification any second. I'll meet you at Piccadilly later. Text me when you're on the train, okay?' He'd thought he was so clever, a bona fide hero when in fact he'd just sealed his own fate and invited a serial con-woman to stay.

Six months later Ankie was still there, and Mac was the happiest guy in East Manchester. Determined to pay at least some of her way, she got a part-time job in a bar in the Northern Quarter and for the rest of the time enjoyed being a semi-kept woman and making Mac's apartment look like a home and not a lad's pad. They were a proper couple and he saw her as his partner, referred to her as such even though she laughed and called him old-fashioned. Mac liked being the serious one in the relationship so brushed off her teasing and thought he had it made.

The only problem was that nobody else did. Regardless of how much he praised her, her physical attributes, her sense of humour, nobody else could see what lay beneath, the kind, loving woman he believed was 'the one'.

Jack, Mac's best mate since school, couldn't take to her and neither could his wife who wasn't keen on her flirty ways and continental casualness. It had been one of those pivotal moments in a friendship when Jack warned Mac that there was a difference between 'open-minded and free-living' and 'borderline slapper and loose cannon'.

Okay, so Ankie was loud and could drink his friends under the table, and she liked to flaunt what she had but at the end of the night she went home with him, to what he now classed as their bed in their flat. His mother was another who couldn't stand Ankie and after taking it upon herself to troll through her social media accounts, his mum declared her a floozy or as they say in France, *une fille de joie*. For a while Mac took the huff with his mum and with Jack and his wife and focused his attention on Ankie.

Due to Mac's diligence, Ankie was oblivious to the opinions of her detractors while at the same time he ignored the niggling voice when he watched her on her phone, engrossed in conversation with one of her many friends or when she sometimes disappeared for the whole day when she wasn't working. He'd believed her when she said she'd been exploring or had taken a long bus ride out into the sticks to get some fresh air; it was an adventure and he shouldn't worry because she was home, safe, with him.

Mac pushed any irritating niggles to the back of his mind and put the comments made by his friends down to jealousy but then his granddad got sick and was taken to hospital, the three days he spent in France were torture. His mum was out of her mind with worry and wanted him to stay longer.

'You can work from here, Mac. You have your laptop and your phone, that's all you need so why do you have to rush back to Manchester? To be with *her* I suppose.' They were in the hospital corridor and now that his granddad had stabilised, Mac saw no reason to stay.

'Mum, it's okay for you and Tom. You're both retired and can do whatever you want and he's coming over at the weekend, so you'll have company and yes, if I'm honest I do want to go back and see Ankie. It's not a crime, you know.' Mac looked through the sheet of glass and into the ward. In the first bed lay his frail granddad, the body of what looked like a boy under a thin green blanket, and he couldn't quite believe that his hero, the only male role model he'd ever had was possibly facing the end of his life. Torn. That's how Mac felt right at that moment. Wanting to get back to Ankie who was terrible at answering messages and whose phone, more often than not, went to voicemail. Then knowing he should stay by his granddad's bed.

'I'm only two hours away by plane if you need me urgently and I promise I'll come back in a fortnight, okay? Just let me sort a few things out at home and I'll be here before you know it. Grandpère is a tough cookie and no matter what they say he's going to pull through.' Mac heard the lie in every word he said and had never felt so ashamed, or so desperate to get back to Ankie.

Nodding her agreement, his mum wiped away tears and gave him a hug before turning and going back to the ward. Her silence spoke volumes as did the uncharacteristic weakness of her embrace.

Exactly one week later his whole world imploded. He was suffering from man-flu so when he got in from work, knowing Ankie was on a late shift and wouldn't be home till after midnight he took two paracetamols and went straight to bed. When he woke at three in the morning and realised she hadn't come home, he immediately rang her phone which went to voicemail. His texts went unanswered. In desperation he messaged one of her colleagues and for a second was relieved to see the dots as a message came back.

It said that Ankie hadn't turned up for her shift.

Panic ensued and in the midst of it, Mac looked up from the bed and noticed that her dressing gown was missing from the back of the door and her slippers weren't by the chair in the corner of the room where she always left them. Throwing back the duvet, the urgency of needing to pee overriding anything, he headed to the bathroom and while he did what he had to do, Mac looked around for her dressing gown. It wasn't on the back of that door either. And worse, her new electric toothbrush and the fancy whitening toothpaste she'd lusted after, and he had bought from Amazon as a surprise wasn't on the shelf under the mirror. Flinging open the cabinet Mac's heart rate raised another notch when he saw her pills and toiletries were missing. This caused him to turn and race straight back to the bedroom.

Here, Mac focused on the wardrobe door and was annoyed with himself for even contemplating what his wildly beating heart feared. She wouldn't do this to him and there would be a simple explanation as to where Ankie was and when he opened the double doors her clothes would be hanging there like always.

It was one of those images that would stay in his mind forever and flashed up each time he'd opened the doors since: a rack full of empty hangers, a huge gap, the same as the hole in his heart where Ankie used to be.

After he'd run around the apartment, desperately pulling open drawers in search for stuff that belonged to her, he then started to notice things that belonged to him were also missing. His iPad, Bose speaker, brand-new BlitzWolf headphones. She'd even taken Alexa, and as he raced back to the bedroom and yanked open the drawer where he kept his few items of jewellery there was a very good chance the apartments above and below would have heard him scream 'NOOOOOOOOOOOO'.

When he saw the watch, a twenty-first birthday gift from his grandparents, was gone, the other items paled because that was his family treasure, an heirloom he would have passed down to one of his children, the imaginary family he was going to have with Ankie. If he thought that was bad, the days that followed were about to become a nightmare.

Mac had finished part of his tale and needed a break before he told Antoinette the rest, part two of the shame and humiliation of Mac the Mug. 'Shall I make us some coffee? I don't want any more wine otherwise I'll be sobbing into my glass and completely embarrass myself.'

When Antoinette gave him a nod, he stood and made his way towards the kitchen where he flicked on the kettle while she followed on behind, leaning against the counter while he fussed with cups.

'I'm so sorry, Mac. She sounds like a piece of work and the fact you were so into her must be a killer. I bet I'm not the only one to say this, but it is good she is no longer part of your life and now you can move on and find someone new.' Antoinette smiled, a mischievous look in her eye.

Reading the signs and knowing her well enough to curtail her enthusiasm before it took hold, Mac made sure Antoinette knew exactly where he stood on that matter. 'That is the last thing on my mind after the mess she left me in so don't get any ideas, okay!'

Another cheeky smile followed, but at least she was taking some of what he said seriously. 'Okay, spoilsport, but what do you mean, in a mess? She broke your heart, right... Did you have a breakdown or something?'

'No, not in the way you mean but I did lose my mind and as much as I'm cringing right now, a hell of a lot of money too. In fact, she wiped me out financially.'

Antoinette's eyes were like saucers, and he felt her concern when she rested one hand on his arm and accepted her coffee with the other. 'Oh no. How?'

Mac took his mug and with a flick of the head indicated they should go back to the lounge. He felt weary, as though his problems and past mistakes were weighing him down. Or was it just the midday wine making him drowsy? They took their places back at the table in the corner of the room and wanting to get it over with he resumed his story. 'Okay, long story short. I'm sure you've heard of women meeting con men online and ending up getting rinsed of all their savings, well, I'm the man who got rinsed by a woman.'

'My God, how the hell did she do it?'

'By copying all the details of my debit and credit cards so she could use them online and go on a huge spending spree. And I was too trusting and left my banking secure key where she could find it; and I allowed her to use my online accounts for stores... need I go on?'

Antoinette shook her head, one hand resting on her heart. 'No, I get it. Dare I ask how much she took?'

'All of my savings that was going to be a deposit on a house. Ten grand on credit cards that she took out in my name, another five on mine and about three more treating herself to whatever the fuck she fancied.' Mac's voice was pure acid, the bitterness he felt leaking out of him. 'To make it all worse, I had some kind of meltdown, it was like I had brain freeze. Probably the equivalent of writer's block, so I couldn't work. The ideas just dried up in my head and I sat in the apartment like a zombie. And then I had my epiphany, a eureka moment, and decided to go and find her and when I did, she'd tell me it was all a huge mistake and someone made her do it and she'd give me all my money and stuff back. That's how fucked up I was.'

'So, you went to Copenhagen?' Antoinette looked like this was the most interesting story she'd heard in years.

'Yes. She'd shown me photos of a bar where she used to work that was supposed to be round the corner from where her mum lived so I figured it was a good place to start. Find the bar, find her mum's place, find Ankie or at least get her mum to send her a message. Anything was better than sitting there wallowing.' Mac knew what question was coming next so answered it for Antoinette.

'No, I didn't find her. They'd never heard of her at the bar and neither had any of the others I asked in. It was a wild goose chase, and do you want to know what the worst part of that trip was?' A shake of the head from Antoinette, and then the killer truth.

'That while I was wandering around Copenhagen like a complete twat, I ignored the calls and messages from my mum. They were telling me to get to the hospital quick because Grandpère was asking for me and he didn't have long. It wasn't until I was heading back to the airport that I saw them and by the time I'd figured out the quickest way to get there, and taken the TGV train, I got there too late. Because I was selfish and obsessed, I never got to say goodbye to Grandpère. I hate myself for that and I always will.' Mac swallowed and dug his nails into the palm of his hand and forbade himself to cry while Antoinette stared, her eyes awash with tears which she dabbed away before she spoke.

'Mac, I am truly sorry. I don't know what to say apart from this: I knew your grandpère a long time, ever since we became friends – what... when we were about ten? – and he was a wise man. My papa says so too. And I think he would have understood about love and how it makes us do crazy things and even though he couldn't give you the advice you really needed right then, and I have no idea what he would have said to make it right, one thing I do know for sure is that he loved you with all his heart and he would forgive you, of all people, anything.'

At that Mac leant forward and rested his elbows on the table and covered his face to hide the shame and grief written across it. No doubt reading his mood, Antoinette attempted to lift it. 'Mac, no more for today. It's upsetting you too much and you haven't eaten anything so come on, have some lunch and I will attempt to cheer you up. I MEAN IT! Eat or I will ring Marie-France and tell her you are sick then she will ring your mother and...'

Dropping his hand-mask, Mac admitted defeat. 'Okay, okay... no more memory lane but I doubt you can cheer me up. I'm going to be your official best depressing friend forever.'

Antoinette let out a loud 'Ha' then pushed the pâté towards him and pointed, watching as he spread a generous amount on his bread then continued to prove him wrong. 'Right, misery man, you fill your face and then you can drop me at Papa's and later, you are invited to the chateau for dinner with me and Fabienne. I might get a few of the gang together and make a night of it. What do you say?'

Mac was about to take a bite of his bread but paused when he heard a name that made his heart flutter, something he thought was a thing of the past since his butterfly wings had been clipped. 'Fabienne is here, in Cholet?'

Nobody could have looked more pleased with themselves than Antoinette right then and she took great delight in Mac's reaction. 'Well, fancy that! Are you blushing, Mac? I told you I'd cheer you up!'

Mac rolled his eyes and took a bite of his food, not rising to Antoinette's teasing but knew already that he would accept her invitation to dinner. Fabienne was back. It had been nine years since they last saw each other, their special summer together. Not that he'd been counting or anything like that. Antoinette was scrutinising him and clearly had more to say on the matter.

'You know something... this is fate, I am sure of it. You have a broken heart that needs fixing and my Fabienne has troubles of her own and she needs a knight in shining armour to help her.'

Antoinette was teasing and from the wicked smile, loving every minute while Mac was concerned. 'Why, what's wrong with Fabienne?'

'You eat, I will explain. Go on, you are going to look like a skinny girl if we don't fatten you up then Jacqueline will suck on your bones after she has gobbled you all up.' At this Antoinette dissolved into hysteria at her own joke while Mac shuddered and did as he was told, already counting the hours until dinner.

9

RENÉ

She was nervous. He could tell by the way Veronique fussed with the arrangement of petit fours, moving the pink next to the lemon, pushing the chocolate one forward as if to tempt him with his favourite. There was a slight flush to her cheeks and the dark circles under her eyes had been covered by too much make-up, far too heavy for the sweltering heat of a Paris summer.

'Damn. I've forgotten the sugar. Where is my head today? One moment.' She was gone in a flash, a fuchsia-clad bundle of nerves skittering towards the kitchen in her last-season dress and down-at-heel heels.

While he waited, René relaxed in the apartment that he'd secretly coveted ever since the day he stepped inside, five years before, on his sister's rather rushed wedding day. A drunken spur-of-the-moment proposal from Hugo meant that Veronique whisked into action, giving him no time to change his mind. She'd insisted on being married in Paris, in a civil ceremony and then on to a restaurant to celebrate.

A few of Hugo's friends had been scraped together to make up a wedding party that was bolstered by his tight-lipped daughter and her much less restrained, mouthy best friend. The groom had somehow managed to stump up for his bride's dress from Balenciaga and the reception at Le Train Bleu where he must have quailed every time Veronique asked the waiter to bring more champagne for the dozen guests.

Afterwards, the family went back to the apartment. René knew of its existence but had only heard it described by Veronique. However, her words hadn't done justice to the setting or the magnificent Renaissance building, with its peach stone and elegant frontage. Once inside it was like stepping into the set of a period drama. He walked up the winding stone staircase lined with an intricately crafted iron banister and when he lifted his head, the domed window so high above flooded each step with light.

But it was the interior of the apartment that truly took his breath away and never had he been more riddled with jealousy than at that moment – well, perhaps once, but that was over a person, not objects. Despite the nationalistic streak that ran through his core or perhaps in reality, more to the far right, when he was faced with the epitome of bourgeoisie wealth it stirred up such a conflict of emotions. Because René could see himself there, in an apartment adorned with heavy velvet drapes and luxurious flock wallpaper, all faded but due to the quality standing the test of time. The whole place oozed impeccable taste, passed down by those with far more of it than Hugo and it irked René that a man such as he could have inherited something he did not deserve.

While Veronique had her new husband fetch more champagne, René had taken in his surroundings and couldn't help imagining himself there, with a glass of cognac, relaxing on the brocade chaise watching the sun set over Parisian rooftops. Even though there was a tinge of damp in the corridors and a hint of mothballs in his bedroom, there was something about the place that reeked of the upper classes. Yes, it went against everything he believed in, having such wealth handed on a plate, and owning it was beyond his wildest dreams and this, along with his intense hatred of the Chevalier/Bombelle dynasty fired up his most spiteful inner demons.

René would kill for it. And he'd done his homework during the train ride up to Paris because while there wasn't much he didn't know about Chateau de Chevalier, the apartment and its location was a different matter. Immediately, he'd realised what a little gem it was. Set in Le Marais, a fashionable area lined with crooked medieval architecture and narrow cobbled streets where, in total contrast, it also boasted the modern art museum at Centre Pompidou. Then there was the Hôtel de Ville, the macabre site of executions during the revolution transformed in more recent times into a winter skating rink. Known for hosting a vibrant artistic community it was no surprise that it also housed the Picasso Museum and as far as René could see the only blot on the landscape was the mention of a thriving Jewish and gay community. But to have all this, he could learn to overlook the deviants.

Hearing Veronique clip-clopping her way towards him René dragged his mind away from the unsavoury and swept the room, his eyes falling on antiques and paintings that he knew were worth a pretty penny and not for the first time, contemplated what he could get for them on the black market.

Veronique's too bright voice curtailed his contemplative mood. 'Here we are, sugar. I had to search because Hugo and I don't partake anymore.' As his sister passed the silver sugar basin, chatting as she did about the heat and the tourists, René patiently answered her questions jovially, enjoying watching his little mouse blink and twitch while he waited to pounce.

'Was it busy on the TGV? I hated the journey here last time. First Class was fully booked so we had to manage with seats next to some dreadful people.' Veronique poured the coffee and as she did René spotted her hand shook, ever so slightly.

A loud tut told his sister he had little sympathy as did his next words. 'Well, had you not sacked Gregoire then you could have travelled back in style and privacy so you shouldn't complain. Does Hugo miss his car and being chauffeured about?'

'Yes, he hates public transport but, let's face it, where does he go in Paris that requires being driven? To the tabac, or that ridiculous club. We didn't need it so that was that and yes, I take your point about the train so next time I will ensure we book well in advance. However, I can't see us returning to Chevalier for a while so that is the least of my concerns.' The telephone ringing in the hall interrupted them and Veronique excused herself.

René wondered who the hell rang house phones anymore, and then focused on their transport situation allowing himself a sly smile because he secretly loved the fact that his brother-in-law had been banned from driving and even more that his days of swanning around in his vintage limousine had been curtailed by René's own hot-headed sister.

René despised the bourgeois Bombelle family and everything they stood for. Thinking they were the *classe supérieure* when in fact this generation in particular – and by that he meant feckless Hugo – was a fine example of bone-idle entitlement. At least the daughter had got off her bottom and worked for a living, not like the waster his Veronique had married.

It went back years, his deep-rooted hatred for the family and all it stood for which was why, for as long as he could remember, he had sought to bring them down, one way or another. Ironically, he and Hugo went back a long way, and even if the old fool still regarded their connection as friendship, it was as faux as the fur his desperate little sister wore in winter. Still, despite the odds she hadn't ended up in an asylum and she had surprised René by thinking for herself but even though she'd tried to convince him and everyone her marriage was for love, he knew it was borne from desperation.

Throughout her life Veronique had gone from one disastrous relationship to the other and you didn't have to be a psychiatrist to know that she was constantly searching for the very thing she'd craved as a child. Love, comfort, stability, kindness. Well, she'd been born into the wrong family for that. Luckily, he'd been there to steer her in the right direction and pick up the pieces more than once and as much as he knew she hated that, and him, he derived such a tremendous kick out of her relief when he saved the day. He enjoyed it even more when, like now, she was working herself up into a state before she asked him for help. Had he not had a cup and saucer in the right and a chocolate petit four in the left, he would have rubbed his hands together in glee.

Veronique had returned and taken her seat opposite. 'And where is good old Hugo? I have booked us a table for dinner later... my treat.' Of course it was. As if *they* could afford to dine at Les Ombres but he couldn't resist rubbing their noses in it.

Nor could he resist the offer of the guest room for the night. Him being there would irk Hugo, unsettle him and even though René would have very much liked a hotel and the company of an escort for the evening, in all honesty he enjoyed tormenting his hosts more.

'He's at his members' club so he won't be long. I think he's meeting with his financial adviser.' Veronique sipped her coffee and winced when René let out a huge guffaw.

'His financial adviser who needs shooting. Would you like me to arrange it? That's hilarious. What on earth are they discussing? How to sell one of his vital organs? Oh no, that's not possible because they are all pickled.' René shook his head at the ridiculousness of his sister's comment but when she slammed down her cup and saucer, he realised she didn't see the funny side.

'I'm so glad you find our situation humorous, René, and it must be giving you an immense amount of pleasure watching me squirm because I gather you've worked out why I invited you.'

Sarcasm came naturally to René. 'Veronique, I am wounded. I thought you missed me.'

'Hell would have to freeze over before that happened, I assure you.'

This he liked, a bit of verbal sparring before she got down to business and his one raised eyebrow was accompanied by a smirk. 'So, go on. What is the real reason you suggested a sleepover with your big brother... would you like a cuddle for old times' sake?'

Before she stood and fled the room, Veronique's faced flushed puce and her eyes filled with tears. Her reaction caught René off guard because she rarely showed her feelings even to him, no matter how desperate she was. Good, this was good. Her highly charged emotional state told him she really needed his help. Standing, he brushed the creases from his suit and went to find her. Curiosity was killing him.

She was on the balcony, leaning against the decorative iron balustrade staring across the rooftops of the second arrondissement from where you caught a glimpse of the Eiffel Tower standing tall and proud, like René, who towered a foot above his petite sister. Seeing the tears on her cheeks he felt a certain amount of relish at being the cause of them. While he waited for her to compose herself, two turtle doves flew down onto the rail of the balcony next door.

'Vermin! I thought they had culled them all?'

A tut from his sister. 'No, they stopped it and I am glad. They were Mama's favourite bird. Did you know that?'

René bridled, because he did not. 'No, why would I?'

She continued to stare into nowhere, refusing to look at him, ignoring his question. Taking out his cigarettes and lighter he followed her line of sight, pulling a Gauloises from the packet and lit it as he spoke. Time to play the game. 'I'm sorry if I upset you, Veronique. It was not my intention but you know me, I have a warped sense of humour. Am I forgiven?'

'No, not this time, René. And please do not smoke next to me. You know how I hate it.'

At this René bridled again. 'Then step away: you know how I hate pious non-smokers.' When she stayed put, he took it as a deliberate act of defiance. She preferred to inhale toxic fumes than follow his command. *Interesting.*

Her sigh, one of exasperation rather than sadness surprised him as did the tone of her voice. 'It's always the same, isn't it? This stupid dance we do, this silly game of charades accompanied by sound, and do you know something, René?' She turned for a second and regarded him. The clue to what she was thinking came in the form of a withering look before she resumed her stance.

Not giving him time to respond she lifted her face and spoke to the sky and the birds and the sun. 'I cannot bear hearing your voice or watching you in action. I despise you and my life, and I've had enough. Of all of it and everyone. I'm tired of cat and mouse; of pretending what happened didn't; of you no doubt believing the things you have done to me, and others, are your God-given right or for the common good.'

Veronique then averted her gaze from the heavens to what was happening below: busy Parisians getting on with their lives while above, someone was admitting to theirs falling apart. René noticed with interest that Veronique's knuckles were white from where she gripped the iron rail and only one thought occurred as his tearful sister continued. *She really is ripe for the picking.*

'I am weary of being manipulated and beholden and talked about and derided and being made to feel insignificant and, God, being so unhappy. There. I am sure all of that has made your day and now your poisonous mind can work overtime calculating how to take advantage of my outburst and frame of mind. I'll give you a few minutes to digest all that and go pour us a drink. Then we can get down to business.' Veronique pushed away from the balustrade; her action abrupt.

Avoiding eye contact she didn't even bother to wipe her face as she departed and while René listened to her heels click on the hall tiles, he remained on the balcony, inhaling deeply, enjoying the kick from nicotine and his sister's little speech.

He found her in the *salon*, once more looking out across Paris. The light that cascaded through the wide windows did her no favours, highlighting the lines around her eyes that he would bet weren't the result of laughter, and the dark rings made her face seem hollow, just like her life. *What a waste.*

There was a glass of pastis waiting on the stand and he wondered if she'd spat in it. He wouldn't have blamed her. Taking a seat on the chaise, from where he had a view of her back, René began to turn the screw. 'So, now we've had the histrionics, shall we get down to why you invited me here? Hugo will be back soon and I'm running out of patience.'

Veronique turned and then drained her glass and placed it on the armoire by her side before taking the seat opposite him. She was calmer and seemed unperturbed by his jibe but maybe she really was used to it by now.

'I want out of this marriage but I'm not going empty-handed and currently there is nothing in the pot. I'm not prepared to wait around while Hugo and Fabienne thrash it out, so I need you and your certain skills and connections to make sure I have a nest egg waiting for me when I leave. Then I will divorce him. I doubt I will get a cent, so I have to prepare.'

René's interest was piqued but he wanted her to show her hand so remained impassive. 'How exactly?'

'First, let me explain what happened at the chateau with the lawyers and then you'll understand better what I'm proposing.' Veronique sat bolt upright, tense, like a deer stranded in the middle of a field, vulnerable, eyes wide, realising they were caught in the sights of a hunter, his aim trained solely on her.

Relaxing into his seat, René crossed his legs and smiled. 'Go ahead, sister dear. I'm all ears.'

Veronique was refilling their glasses after filling René in on the debacle at the chateau. He had no idea things were as bad as she described, and the direness of Hugo's predicament had brought him immense pleasure. Although there was one thing he didn't quite understand.

'This puzzles me: why did you object so vehemently to the sale of this place? It would certainly solve your problems. Surely half of Hugo's share would set you up quite nicely.'

Veronique passed him his glass. Her hand had lost its quiver. Was that her unburdening or the alcohol?

'Because I do not trust Hugo with one euro, let alone half of whatever this place is worth and once he'd paid his debts God only knows how much would be left to split with me. And anyway, this is our home, the one that reminds me the least of Paloma and no way am I ever going to live at the chateau. I couldn't bear it. Anyway, following my protestations Fabienne dug her heels in and then Hugo came up with his counter-offer which would still leave me back to square one. So, for now, we stand firm and at least have a roof over our heads.'

He was impressed with his sister. She had used her brains

for a change. 'I understand. So, what are your other options? How will you raise enough capital to escape Hugo's clutches?'

Veronique wasted no time and as she sat forward in her seat, lowered her voice. 'I have thought of two ways to raise money, but both are risky.' She paused, as though trying to remember her lines, wanting to get the pitch for her new life just right. 'I am certain, from the accounts that I saw the other day that Hugo has at least managed to keep up the insurance payments on here and the chateau, so, in the case of the latter, I am proposing a fire that will burn the whole decrepit place to the ground.'

René raised an eyebrow and allowed her a slight smile which was more of a reaction to the idea of Chevalier being nothing more than a pile of dust and wiped off the planet. Yet he still wanted to hear more. 'And the other option?'

'Look around you. This place is full of antiques that you could sell on through the black market, am I correct?' A curt nod from René then she continued. 'But emptying this place and moving it is risky and a logistical nightmare, without some nosey parker asking questions. However, what is in the safe is smaller and still valuable so, if there was a robbery, we could split the proceeds fifty-fifty. There isn't a safe at the chateau, which is why the jewellery of Fabienne's mother and grandmother is stored here. Everything inside belongs to her. My stupid, vain husband likes to wear the last of his wealth on his arm and finger. Although I suppose the robbers could demand his Cartier watch and that ugly signet ring. They'd be doing me another favour by taking that.'

'Have you seen it, the jewellery? It is definitely in there?'

Veronique nodded. 'Yes, there's a black velvet box but it is locked. Fabienne has the key. I see it every time he takes out our passports. That's where he keeps them and copies of his ridiculous will.'

'How much is it worth? The jewellery.'

'Hugo said a few hundred thousand. Enough for me to get away and start again and you can do what you want with your share. If we don't act quickly, I have a feeling Fabienne will be forced to sell it anyway, or Hugo will be so desperate he might go against her wishes and pawn the lot. Nothing would surprise me about him, not now.'

René paused for a moment before stating the obvious. 'I'm no safe-cracker, Veronique and as far as I know none of my associates are either. So how do you suggest I get in there? Oh, I know, I could check the advertisement section of *Le Figaro* and see if there are any bank robbers offering their services, or maybe Facebook has a safe-cracker group. I could ask there.'

Again, Veronique didn't rise to his baiting. 'It's far simpler than that. I propose we stage an armed robbery where my husband is made to open the safe by an intruder. Obviously, he will be terrified and do as they say. We will need to discuss the finer details of both ideas if you agree to go ahead... unless you have a better option.'

René stood and walked over to the drinks tray and unscrewed the bottle of Ricard, taking his time to pour, making Veronique wait for his answer. In truth he thought both proposals were viable but the one that excited him the most was the first because nothing would give him more pleasure than erasing Chevalier. It would be revenge for his great-grandfather and what the wartime Duc had done. The story had been drummed into him, passed down via his father, about who had *La Resistance* in their pockets and pointed the finger at a collaborator. The Duc might as well have tied the noose himself so now it was René's turn to make someone pay the price.

The sound of a key in the door alerted them to Hugo's presence so before the doddering fool entered the room René raised his glass towards his sister. 'We have a deal. To *liberté* and revenge.'

And although Veronique raised her eyes, no doubt at his mention of revenge, her body visibly relaxed seconds before she painted a fake smile on her face and greeted her husband. René watched on and while shaking hands with his brother-in-law, who pretended to be pleased to see him, ruefully acknowledged the guile of his sibling who was wasted in so many ways.

Oh, she's good, she's very, very good. But not as good as me.

10

FABIENNE

Fabienne's sandals slapped on the stone floor as she rushed towards the kitchen, shivering slightly in the cool corridor that was in complete contrast to the blistering heat outside. She'd only had time to dry the fringe of her short, raven hair that was still damp from the shower and consequently, drips of water ran down between her shoulder blades making her cheesecloth dress stick to her skin.

When she entered the kitchen Antoinette was busy preparing dinner but took a moment to appraise her friend's transformation while at the same time, Fabienne did her best to ignore the suggestive smile and tease that followed. 'Ooh la la. Mademoiselle looks very chic. Is it new?'

Fabienne joined Antoinette at the table and helped fill bowls with nibbles. 'No, it's not and I haven't made an effort. It's going to be humid this evening so I thought a dress would be nice and cool. You know, like the one you're wearing.'

The nudge from her friend made Fabienne spill pistachios all over the tabletop. 'You can't fool me and anyway, I admit to wanting to look super-hot for Joel. What's wrong with that?

And I'm sure Mac will appreciate your crinkly boho creation that, come to think of it, would benefit from the iron.'

'It's supposed to be like this. It's the look.'

A loud tut told her that Antoinette disagreed. 'And you have burnt your shoulders. Do you need cream? I will fetch some.'

Fabienne sighed as Antoinette scuttled off. Sometimes her best friend behaved like her nanny. It got worse when Antoinette was on a matchmaking mission – and she was on one now, Fabienne could tell. Ever since she'd zoomed up the drive and dropped the bombshell about Mac, no matter how many times Fabienne had denied being pleased or excited or just a teeny bit curious, her words had fallen on deaf ears.

Earlier, as she pulled shopping bags from the boot, Antoinette was animated, hurriedly telling Fabienne the news. 'You are NOT going to believe who I bumped into in the village. Go on, guess. Okay I'll tell you. It was Mac.'

Fabienne had stopped mid-dig, her attention drawn from weeding yet unable to get a word in edgeways as Antoinette rushed up the steps, talking ten to the dozen. 'I had lunch with him earlier today and wait till I tell you all about his ex-girlfriend who is a complete monster... come on, let's go get a drink and I will explain then you'll have to get changed, he'll be here soon. I can't have him seeing you like that. Hurry up! I said seven thirty; you've got an hour. Oh, and I bought pizza for dinner, nice and easy. Even I don't ruin pizza.'

Finally, Fabienne managed to speak. 'He's coming here, for dinner?' Why didn't you ring and warn me before... and where on earth have you been till now?'

Antoinette stopped and tutted. 'Because I had to go to the *maison de retraite* and see Eglantine. They rang because she was kicking up a fuss about her shoes, so I picked her up, took her to town and let her choose some more. They are more hideous than the brown ones she picked last time. Anyway, you know what she's like. I had my hands full, especially when she started telling me all about the naked man who came to visit her.'

At this they both chuckled while Antoinette shook her head as she spoke. 'Honestly, I love my grandmère dearly but she's getting worse with these stories.' She turned to go up the steps then halted. 'So, are you going to stand there looking stupid or pack up? We need to get ready. Oh, and I've invited my Joel and Rudy and Caprice. I bet Mac will be relieved that my brother is engaged. We don't want any more punch-ups over you.'

Fabienne cringed as she remembered the scuffle between Rudy and Mac many years before, when they were hormonal teenagers, two gangly fifteen-year-olds throwing punches and insults – both ended up with bruises, one black eye, one bloody nose. Shy Fabienne had been horrified, and via Antoinette had made it clear she wasn't interested in either of them so insisted they made friends. However, secretly, her fourteen-year-old heart already belonged to Mac.

The logistics of being schooled in England and having a father who insisted on spending Christmas in Paris and term holidays visiting friends who had nannies and children to keep his daughter occupied, didn't help. Then university, new friendships and longed for independence, meant Fabienne and Mac crossed paths for shorter periods, sometimes only days, once a few hours. And had they both not been so ridiculously shy that they could not make use of pens and paper and phones and their wily mutual friend who'd have been happy to broker a deal, perhaps they wouldn't have waited until she was twenty and he twenty-one to 'finally get it together' as Antoinette so quaintly put it. It had been the best summer of her life, only to end in tears and heartbreak. She'd tried hard to forget and hoped Antoinette had too. No such luck.

'FABIENNE! For goodness' sake, snap out of it.' Antoinette was at the door looking cross.

'Yes, yes, I'm coming.' As Miss Matchmaker disappeared inside, Fabienne, the skin on her arms tingling from being too long in the sun, did as she was told. Not just that, she really did look a state. Hot and sweaty from weeding the flower beds, her denim dungarees were covered in soil and her feet were grey from the dust of the driveway. Flip-flops weren't the best footwear for gardening, but it was so hot she couldn't bear wearing her work boots.

Snapping into action she had thrown her tools into the wicker trug, and as she raced up the stairs had tried to convince herself that she wasn't excited to see Mac again, not excited at all.

They were seated on the terrace shaded from the sun by the looming rear wall of the chateau. It was the perfect place to escape the heat and at the same time take in the rather overgrown lawn and flower beds and the surrounding woodland.

Rudy and Caprice were holding hands and chatting to Joel. Antoinette kept checking her watch while Fabienne was trying not to show impatience as she waited for one of the silver bells in the corridor behind them to ring. When one finally sounded, signalling that someone was at the door Antoinette leapt to her feet and with one hand intimated that Fabienne should remain where she was.

Minutes later she reappeared and behind her was Mac, looking shy and holding a bottle which was swiftly liberated by Antoinette. And as much as she hadn't wanted it to, had forbidden it in fact, Fabienne's heart skipped a beat when he searched her out.

Same brown hair, swept back off his angular face, square

jaw set firm, dark eyes like giant buttons. He hadn't changed a bit. Not in the nine years since their perfect summer had ended when she flew to New York to begin her internship at a Brooklyn gallery, and he headed back to Manchester to start his MA. After all those years of waiting for the right time, when it came their moment had been all too short but even so, Fabienne had fallen for Mac, and even though she tried not to show it, guarding her heart and clinging onto pride, she had been devastated.

They had been so sensible about it all. They were going to be on opposite sides of the Atlantic. It would be stupid to make promises they might not keep. They were too young to commit. So, they made a pact to stay in touch. Maybe meet up when they were both in France. Fabienne had made all the moves, Mac had responded with enthusiasm, but gradually their new lives swallowed up any good intentions and they drifted apart. Could they have tried harder? Had she given up too easily?

Pushing that thought away, Fabienne strode towards him, smiling, welcoming, confident; no longer the shy, unsure teenager who used to sneak glances at the English boy who had a funny accent and flitted from one language to the other; and neither was she the young woman who would have stayed, found a job in Manchester, if only he'd asked her.

'Mac, I'm so happy to see you. It's been a long time.' They embraced in the usual French way, her having to stretch upwards to kiss each cheek while their hands connected, his on her bare arms, hers on his shoulders. Old friends, behaving maturely, putting the past behind them. *That's all it is,* she told herself until a voice whispered in her ear: *Who are you kidding?*

It was dusk and Antoinette was searching for matches to light the candles while Fabienne loaded plates into the dishwasher. The evening was going well, lots of reminiscing, especially about Mac's grandparents who always welcomed a gaggle of dirty, hungry kids into their home then sent them off again fed and watered. Rudy seemed to have forgotten that Mac was once his arch-enemy but maybe that was because he was happy with Caprice who wouldn't have been pleased to hear all about her fiancé fighting over the woman seated opposite.

Closing the dishwasher door Fabienne covered the leftover pizza slices with a tea towel and then went to the fridge. 'Shall I take the dessert outside? I'm too full, but the others might want some.'

Returning with the matches Antoinette lowered her voice. 'Yes, I want some but never mind that now; what do you think of Mac? He's still gorgeous, isn't he?'

'Excuse me, but should you be saying things like that when you are with Joel?' Fabienne carefully slid the apple tart from the shelf and took it over to the table.

'He can't hear and I'm only stating a fact. So go on, what do you think?'

'Okay, I cannot deny he has certain charms, but I am not getting into some stupid holiday fling with him ever again so please, don't interfere or get any ideas, full stop. I mean it, Antoinette.' Fabienne went to find plates and ignored the fact that she was being ignored.

'I can tell he still likes you. His face lit up earlier today when I said you were here, and I've been watching him watching you and he's smitten. And I told you everything I know about his situation, and nothing is definite yet. He didn't say he was leaving. So, what are you going to do about it?'

Placing everything on a tray, Fabienne sighed. 'I am going to take this lot outside and feed our guests while you light the candles, okay!'

'You are so boring, you know that, really boring!' Antoinette trotted on behind, grumbling and tutting, and couldn't see the smile on Fabienne's face as she basked in her friend's words. *Smitten, surely not.*

The candles in the jars were burning low and Rudy and Caprice were heading home and once the goodbyes were over with, Antoinette went into action. Fabienne likened it to driving a bulldozer across the lawn because the freckle-faced interferer couldn't have been more unsubtle if she'd tried.

'Come along, Joel, you can help me tidy up, no, Fabienne, stay here with Mac. You have lots of catching up to do so we will leave you in peace. I'll make coffee and liberate some calvados from the *cave*, back soon. Be good.' Theatrical winking and head jerking in Joel's direction formed Antoinette's finale before she disappeared inside.

'Well, that wasn't awkward at all.' Mac smiled and took a sip of his wine.

'No, my toes definitely aren't curling right now but, I suppose she's right because we have been dancing around each other all night, and I'd rather we were just honest and open, otherwise it's awkward. Don't you think?' Fabienne had no idea where that had come from because she was only thinking it and then bam, out it came. Still, she was quite pleased with herself because she sounded a lot more in control than she felt.

Mac caught her off guard when he took the lead. 'Yeah, you're right so here goes. I'm sorry we lost touch and it was my fault. You made all the moves and as usual I was the weak link who should have made more effort. There's no excuse so I won't even try to make one up. But I did think about you especially when I popped back to see my grandparents but even then, I had to focus on them... See, I'm making excuses already.'

Fabienne wanted to be angry with him, tell him how much

he'd hurt her when he took longer and longer to reply to her emails and their jokey WhatsApp chats faded away. She hated Facebook and hardly used it anyway but the first time she saw a photo of Mac with another woman, it was too much to bear so she unfollowed him immediately and resolutely refrained from even having a sneaky peep now and then. It was for the best. Until now.

'This is what I mean... there's no point going over it all. What's done is done and we should focus on now, this lovely evening and friends being back together and anyway, from what Antoinette tells me you've had enough women trouble to last a lifetime.' There, that was easy. And it meant they could move on, to where and what she had no idea.

'Ah, she told you. Yep, I messed up. Got well and truly kicked in the teeth. But what about you? I hear you've got a fight on your hands with your dad. Antoinette gave me the bare facts earlier.'

Fabienne looked down at her wine glass and swirled the contents, the red liquid spinning like her mind. She was sad that Mac was in a mess, but at the same time glad that whoever the woman was had exited his life, for his sake and Fabienne's own selfish reasons. It was best to focus on the chateau, though, and steer away from matters concerning the heart.

'Oh yes. Papa has messed up big time but I'm not giving up without a fight. I love this place so much. It's my life, my future and the place where I feel closest to my mother and brother. Everywhere, each room, the gardens, hold memories of them and I cannot bear the thought of letting them go.' A familiar swell of anger churned inside and this, combined with the weight of loss that never seemed to ease fuelled such passion.

Sometimes Fabienne didn't know whether to scream or cry. Right there and then she wanted to cry, which was not a good look. *Stop this silliness right now. You're tired, had too much sun and wine and now he's here, making you overemotional. Drink coffee. You'll be fine.*

As if sensing her mood Mac stepped in. 'Well, if it's any consolation my dad turned out to be a total loser. It was a pity he waited so long to finally clear off and do us all a favour.'

Glad of the distraction Fabienne focused on Mac's news. 'So they're not together anymore? I think I only ever saw your dad once; it was always you and your mum here for the summer. I remember asking you where he was, and you said he was too busy with his business to take holidays. Come to think of it, you never spoke about him much at all.'

Mac shrugged. 'That's because there was nothing to say really. He was a part-time dad, someone who was around but never in the way I wanted a dad to be. His excuse for not coming to watch me play football or to parents' evenings was that he was busy because *'someone needs to pay the bills'*. Turns out he'd been really busy, with other women for most of their marriage.'

Fabienne could see the anger in Mac's face and the talk of infidelity prodded an uncomfortable truth that she had kept buried for many years, her secret. It prompted a question. 'Did it hurt your mum badly when she found out? I always liked your mum. She's a nice lady so I hope it didn't.'

At this Mac smiled. 'Yeah, she's the best and no, she told me she'd always known he was having affairs but could never prove it. I was so shocked, and I couldn't understand why she'd stayed especially because he could be a nasty piece of work, one of those cowardly blokes who hit women. And then, when she explained I wished I hadn't asked.'

'She stayed for you, didn't she?'

Mac nodded. 'Even though she missed her parents, she had no desire to return to Cholet, even though they hoped she would. She had a job she loved in the school kitchens, a nice home and I was happy and settled in a family unit. She told me she made do, how awful is that? I wish I'd have known because I'd have begged her to leave. We'd have been okay, just the two of us but no way was she going to walk away and struggle. In her head, it was all about me. Getting me to university and a good career and being with my dad made all that easier.'

'She's happy now though?' Fabienne willed Mac to say she was.

'Definitely. Tom's a decent bloke and he'll look after her.'

Then a thought. 'So, where's your dad?'

At this Mac rolled his eyes. 'Living with the woman he was having an affair with. They split everything fifty-fifty in the divorce and Mum bought herself a nice little house, then a few months later she met Tom. I've never seen her so content. As for my dad, I have nothing to do with him. I'm not interested, just like he wasn't interested in me.'

'And that's why she gave you La Fleurie. It's your turn to find happiness after what happened... you know, with that woman.' Fabienne saw the discomfort sweep across Mac's face so swiftly changed tack and tried to see where his head was at, filling in the bits that Antoinette hadn't found out.

'Anyway, we are focusing on the future and good things, so you need to tell me your plans for La Fleurie. Are you going to do it up? I bet there are some lovely old bits and bobs in there so don't go crazy throwing stuff out. I could have a look at it for you if you like, you know, cast a professional eye over it. There might be some little treasures in there.'

Mac seemed to brighten instantly. 'That would be great, I'd appreciate it... but what about you? Antoinette said you had big plans for this place, but we ran out of time because she had to go and see her grandma.'

Fabienne was about to explain when Antoinette and Joel appeared and not wanting to bring the mood down with her woes and business plans, she had a better idea. 'Why don't you come over tomorrow, if you haven't got anything on, and I can show you around and explain, and I'd like you to see the gallery that we've put together. There are some lovely old photos of the town I think you'd like.'

'I'd like that and I'm free all day. Shall we say about ten?'

Fabienne nodded as their conversation was interrupted by Antoinette who placed the tray on the table, the aroma of coffee filling the night air that was turning chilly.

For once, she didn't make everyone cringe with one of her jokey innuendoes and played it straight. 'Who's for coffee and Calvados?'

Mac asked for coffee as he was driving while Fabienne ignored her earlier advice, chancing one more drink. 'I'll never sleep if I drink coffee, so just a small Calvados, please.'

Antoinette poured and then passed the glass of golden liquid to her friend. 'Here you go, and Joel, you can have a big mug of coffee because I assure you, you won't be getting any sleep tonight so drink up.'

Shaking her head Fabienne caught the look in Mac's eye as he laughed and instead of chastising Antoinette, chose instead to enjoy the moment, one she never thought she'd experience again. Mac was there, after all these years and, maybe, this might be their time. Finally, the stars had aligned, and they were together, in the same place, with the chance to start a new life. He had his grandparents' cottage where he could, if he wanted, put down roots. And if she could only find a way to save the chateau, she would stay too. This was where she belonged and something told her, a feeling, a whisper in the air, that it was where Mac belonged too.

11

VERONIQUE

The clock was placed directly in front of her eyes so that checking the time required zero effort and allowed her to remain on her side, fully clothed in yesterday's dress and underwear, marking the hours at they dragged by while she was barely able to function. It was always the same when the fog of depression gripped her but this, this was thicker and greyer than ever before and the weight of it made it hard to breathe, or was that panic? Most likely.

There was a cup of cold tea by the clock and a little tag hung over the side, dangling and forlorn. How could Earl Grey tea make her weepy? Then again so had the lone pigeon on the windowsill, and the photo of her mother next to the lamp. She had heard Hugo shuffle in around an hour ago, then the clatter of china as he placed the cup and saucer on the bedside table. She hadn't acknowledged him, and kept her eyes firmly closed, hearing his tut of irritation before he shuffled out of the room.

The hands of time told her it was two in the afternoon while her stomach grumbled and told her she hadn't eaten. She ignored this because just the thought of dragging herself off the bed to get something made her even more weary, so she stayed put. And waited. And thought. And remembered.

The previous evening, during a lavish dinner at Les Ombres, Veronique had felt the knot of anxiety loosen because for the first time in so long, she could see a way out. Her only regret was that her escape had meant including René.

The following morning while Hugo slept in, René suggested he and Veronique went out for breakfast and afterwards they took a stroll around Square du Temple, a beautiful park where the residents of Le Marais took time out. Here, they passed benches filled with Parisians reading, chatting or unwittingly watching two people discussing a crime not yet committed and where it seemed René had already made one decision.

'I've given your ideas some thought, and it has to be one or the other: either burn Chevalier to the ground or we take the contents of the safe because it will look too suspicious if we do both. Even the police aren't that stupid and insurance companies less so.'

The morning sun warmed Veronique's skin but failed to reach her insides that were immediately chilled by his words. It was true, it was all a huge risk and they had to avoid suspicion at all costs. She'd given both plans so much thought. Lying in bed going over and over all scenarios and the thing that had niggled most, kept her awake all night was the risk of someone dying in the fire. As much as Fabienne and the jumped-up housekeeper were an immense irritation, nothing was worth that so even though, for many reasons she favoured the total eradication of Chevalier, it was with some trepidation she asked René. 'Which one have you decided on?'

'The safe.' René was succinct.

Veronique was in no position to argue, even though in some ways this was the trickier option. 'What if Hugh won't open the safe? He can be stubborn, you know that.'

René smiled, his veneers gleaming in the sun. 'Then you will.'

She thought she was going to faint. 'Me... I won't be there... you will have to do it while I'm out. Surely you can't expect me to be part of it.'

'For fuck's sake, woman. Of course you will be there. It's the best way to ensure success. If Hugo refuses to save the life of his dear wife, then we will see if his dear wife will save him and of course, you will. Won't you?' René walked on through the gardens, passing the children's playground without a glance. Veronique forced herself to do the same.

Catching him up she grabbed the sleeve of his jacket, panic dictating her actions that otherwise would have been far more reserved around her brother. 'I don't think I will have the nerve, René, to go through with a charade like that. Surely you can manage without me. I could give you the code. You could open it yourself.'

When he stopped and turned to face her, the thrum of skateboard wheels in the park behind keeping time with the pulse in her temple, the contempt on René's face told Veronique two things: she had walked straight into one of his games and there was no way out.

'Don't be ridiculous, Veronique. If I do that it will be obvious you told me and anyway, did you think I was going to do all your dirty work, sister dear?' Her silence prompted him to continue. 'So, if you want this to work, if you want your money, then you will play your part exactly as I tell you. Otherwise, the deal is off. Go buy a box of matches and torch Chevalier yourself.'

When René grabbed her hand and pulled it from his jacket, Veronique resisted the urge to wipe her skin on her dress. Instead, she tried to match his brisk pace, Sister Veronique the Obedient, mute, tearful, and horrified, trotting by his side. 'I *can't do it, I can't. Look what you've done. You are a stupid, stupid woman.'*

Her mind whirred while all around everyone seemed to be getting on with their lives, blading, see-sawing, book-reading, pram-pushing. *STOP that!*

Up ahead were two young men, out for a morning stroll, holding hands and chatting away and as soon as she saw them it focused her attention, her stomach flipped and her eyes slid to her brother who as she suspected, wore a sneer.

René Saber was his father's son all right, a vile individual who had been schooled by a master, the village collaborator, a fascist through and through. Veronique knew what would be going through her homophobic, racist brother's mind as he skirted around the two men like they carried the plague. His far-right views weren't a secret, or his allegiance to Marine Le Pen and her National Rally party. In fact it wouldn't have surprised Veronique if his own political ambitions had something to do with the generous donations he made to their campaigns.

Veronique abhorred his views and had heard enough of his drunken rants to last a lifetime. In fact that was exactly how she felt about her brother. He was abhorrent, just like all the men in her family had been and the sooner he was out of her sight the better which was why his next words brought her tormented heart and mind some comfort.

'Let's go back to the apartment so I can collect my things then head home before this place puts me in a worse mood. Only the Bombelles could choose to reside in such a deviant arrondissement... this place is riddled with subversives. Look, they are everywhere.' His voice was raised enough so that the young men would have heard his final comment, making Veronique cringe.

Never had she walked so fast in heels, but it was worth the pinch of leather just to be rid of René who, after he bade Hugo farewell, allowed Veronique to escort him down to the lobby. Here, in a hushed tone he told her he'd be in touch once he'd sourced what he needed for the job, and then they could make firm arrangements.

And still she waited and the hours passed – thirty-seven to be precise. With every tick of the clock Veronique descended further and further into her malaise, the fog thickening, sucking her in and clogging her lungs while the black clouds descended, pushing her deeper into the recesses of her mind, into the past where her greatest torment lay. Living in a home where the menfolk had lost sight of the truth, becoming incapable of kindness, blinkered by the desire for revenge that had been tempered in deep shame, twisting ignorant minds already warped by their tainted family history.

This was her inglorious birthright. The past was the monster that came to her in her dreams, leaving Veronique with a choice. Stay awake and face the world or sleep and face the things that haunted her. Decision made the room dim, one more shade.

Summoning enough energy to raise her body and pull open the drawer by her side, she grappled for the bottle of sleeping pills and unscrewed the lid. Swallowing down two, the bitterness of cold tea causing her to wince, Veronique flopped onto the pillow and closed her eyes. In the darkness she waited for them to appear, the monsters. Her father and René.

Hunger. In all her torturous dreams, it was the first thing Veronique felt. Not fear, or any of the other emotions she would have to go through, just terrible hunger. It had a sound, too, she could hear it through her skin. It came from the pit of her empty stomach, a churning, swirling bath of acid that growled like an animal.

A series of flickering memories had been clipped together to form a film reel that played over and over, always when she was at her lowest. They dragged her back and forced her to relive it all, her mistakes, her shame, her awakening. That day when she was hungry and she thought that for once, René was being kind when he offered her some food.

This was where it all really began, their charade, their dance, their uncomfortable truth. With the crust of bread. Before, René had never come right out and demanded something in return. He'd been taking for years, quietly, no fuss. And she'd let him because without her brother providing a distraction, her father's fists and attention would have focused on her. She wouldn't have survived their father, not alone. That was how twelve-year-old Veronique had regarded her life, as survival.

The pills began to work their magic, and as she slipped into the realm of sleep and opened the door on her nightmares, Veronique muttered words she'd said many times before: 'Be brave, close your eyes, it will be over soon.'

12

RENÉ AND VERONIQUE

**Cholet
1985**

Veronique was well aware of the pecking order and knew the rules because they'd been drummed into her, her brother and mother since forever. Papa, Denis Saber, was the boss and he reigned supreme. Women were of little consequence and there only to serve him in whatever way he desired and where his wife was concerned, she was put to good use. Veronique was regarded with derision, a secondary skivvy who was told frequently that she should have been a son because they were of value. That was Papa's opinion, anyway.

Papa had many opinions on a wide range of subjects and while she lay in bed at night, Veronique would listen to his hateful rantings and wonder what it would be like, to be riddled with such bitterness. It was as though it was eating him alive.

Mama had once explained that it was all due to the shame of being the son of a collaborator. This was the only good thing about the dreams because in them, Mama's voice came through clearly. Oh, how she loved to hear it, and see the face of the only person that until then, had shown her a glimmer of love. Mama always saved her last ounce of everything for Veronique no matter how weary or hungry she was. A portion of food, an encouraging smile as Veronique set off for school, a chaste hug when she returned, bones hugging bones. Stepping in front of a raised fist, and later, shushing and apologising. *'I am sorry m'petite, I am sorry for bringing you to this world, I am sorry, I am so sorry.'*

Veronique would cling to her mama and understood what she was trying to say because so many times she too had wished Mama had not brought her into this life, even if she had been born a boy. Sometimes, to help Veronique sleep, her mama would lie by her side and tell her stories of the sea. *The Little Mermaid* was her favourite and as she drifted away on the waves, she would make her mama a promise: 'One day we will run away, Mama. I will get a job in a shop and save all my money so we can live by the sea in a little house on the beach, just the two of us, without Papa and René. We will be happy there...'

Dreams were so hard to hold onto, though, especially on the farm when she was frozen to the bone, outside in winter, a fine drizzle soaking her clothes. Even years later, through the fog of pills and wine, she could feel, see, hear and smell it all.

Mama rested the bucket on the fence and on the other side the pigs snorted and squealed for their breakfast while sparrows hovered overhead, waiting for their chance. Veronique loved birds, especially robins. 'What is your favourite bird, Mama?'

A soft smile lit up her pinched face. 'Ah, that is easy. I love turtle doves because they symbolise love and fidelity. I once went to Paris and saw so many there, many moons ago.'

Veronique's feet were cold in her boots, the animal growled

in her stomach while the stench of the pigs and woodsmoke pervaded her nose and filtered into her dreams. She was surprised to hear her mama had any time for love and fidelity but was impressed she had been to Paris and asked who with. 'Was it Papa?'

And then Mama's face became sad. 'No, *cherie,* it was not Papa.'

Seeing her lost in thought as she scattered pig feed, and not being able to avoid the new purple bruise on her cheekbone prompted Veronique to ask a question she'd never asked before. 'Mama, why is Papa a bad person?'

For a second Mama's hand stilled, then she threw the grain and with her now free hand stroked the hair of her daughter, sighing before she answered. 'Because his father was a bad person, too, *cherie*. And thanks to him, your papa did not have a happy life. The Saber name was dragged through the mud, just like that,' her mama nodded to the brown mush before them, 'and he cannot forgive or forget so he takes his anger out on us.'

'But Mama, why did you marry a bad person who is angry all the time? Was Papa nice when you met him?' Veronique was curious, and desperate for her mother to give her father a different face, of someone kind, then she could hope he might one day return.

'No, *cherie*. He was not nice, not really but he pretended to be for a while because he needed a wife and an heir, or perhaps someone on hand to take his temper out on. I met him at the shop in Angers where I worked and had no idea of his family history or that his heart was black. I was a fool, and I realised my mistake too late. It is as simple as that.'

Even for a nine-year-old it was easy to put the pieces of Mama's life together, but it was her father's that intrigued her the most. 'Why was my grandfather a bad person? What did he do?'

Her mother looked down and held Veronique's stare. 'I will tell you, but you must promise never to mention it to Papa, or anyone. Do you understand? Not even René because he believes every word your father says so do not trust him. Do you promise, *cherie*?'

Veronique nodded, struck mute by the sheer anticipation of what she was about to hear. She'd been entranced by the tale, told only once by her mother but in the years that followed, she'd listened from her room to her father's drunken rambling version. It was much different.

According to her mama, at the end of the war her papa was almost seven. His papa was the *Maire* of Cholet and they'd lived in one of the best houses in the village and before the Nazis came, life had been good. His papa had made a choice and embraced the arrival of the conquering army and also, their ideology, believing wholeheartedly that they were there to stay, a new order that he wanted to be part of. Things didn't work out quite the way he and Hitler planned.

Everyone knew that Maire Saber had his own interests at heart, but they were powerless to stand against him and terrified of the Nazis who had taken over their lives so they toed the line. But it was the terrible death of one of their own, a young woman who had worked at the chateau, that stirred the hate they already felt for their *Maire* into a frenzy.

Nineteen-year-old Mademoiselle Doré's broken body was found below the arches of the railway bridge. The search party were sickened by what they found, as was the doctor who examined the corpse that had been ravaged by hungry animals. And on further investigation, he discovered that she had suffered much worse before she died.

The villagers pointed the finger at the soldiers who patrolled the woods and the chateau close to where she was found. Her parents begged the police to investigate but they answered to the all-powerful Maire Saber who stood firm and proud beside the *kommandant* when he addressed the citizens of Cholet.

At the front of the crowd stood Mademoiselle Doré's distraught parents, their young son sleeping in his mother's arms, oblivious to the horrors around him. Everyone listened in silent horror to the *kommandant*'s lies, while one of their countrymen nodded in agreement.

'The dead woman was a member of *La Resistance* and was caught spying on the chateau where my soldiers are billeted. She resisted arrest, was pursued through the woods and, while trying to jump from the bridge to avoid capture, was shot.'

The crowd gasped while Madame Doré sobbed gently into her son's hair as the *kommandant* made one more thing very clear. 'This woman was a criminal and criminals will be hunted down and dealt with. Anyone found to be harbouring or supporting members of *La Resistance* will be treated the same way. Let her death be a warning to you all.'

Of course, nobody dared to speak out, but they knew what the soldiers, or someone, had done to a young woman who was fighting to free France. The doctor made it known how he had voiced his concerns to Maire Saber and insisted that he investigate Mademoiselle Doré's rape and murder. He refused. His excuse was that he was protecting the people of Cholet who needed to get on with life under Nazi occupation, and that his compliance kept them safe. Nobody believed a word. They just hated him even more.

If Veronique was traumatised by her mother's telling of the old tale, she could only imagine how the residents of Cholet must have felt living through it. 'You see, Papa was there, the day *La Resistance* came to take away his father and then a pack of vengeful women, they called them *les tondeuse*, took his mother to the market square and for all to see, they cut off her hair. It was a punishment for entertaining the officers her husband invited to dinner. For betraying *La Resistance*, for the men and women who were tortured and executed.'

Veronique was horrified but managed to mutter a question. 'So, what happened to the *Maire*, my grandfather?'

Mama lowered her voice, the expression on her face grave. 'Oh, his punishment was far worse. They, *La Resistance*, took revenge for the comrades they had lost, one of them being Mademoiselle Doré, and hung him from a tree in the woods near to where she was found. So, you see, this is why Papa is bitter. Worse than vinegar, like acid.'

Veronique's young mind was able to understand this simple justice and she too lowered her voice when she spoke. 'I think they were right, to punish him because he did bad things, don't you, Mama?'

Her mother dropped the bucket to her side and held the handle, taking Veronique's hand with her other and stared at the house where her husband lay in bed, sleeping off the wine from the night before. 'I do, *cherie* but unfortunately, good or bad, not everyone gets what they deserve.'

Later that night, Veronique had gone over it all in her head and tried to find some sympathy for her cruel father and his family. Maire Saber's legacy had lived on through his only son who was vilified throughout his childhood, mocked and scorned, shunned and shamed for his father's collaboration. Madame Saber and her child ended up homeless and grateful to be offered shelter with her in-laws who owned a pig farm on the edge of Cholet. It was a fall from grace that his mother never recovered from. Traumatised by her ordeal she became a recluse who withered away, of no use to anyone, not even her damaged son.

This was how Veronique's mother told the tale whereas from her father's lips it was a different story. His father was a hero. A man whose politics were the stuff that France could have thrived on, led by the Reich. Had he lived, he would have been a great man of the time. Instead, he had died at the hands of a band of convicts and liberals, Jews and Marxists, and Denis knew exactly who had pointed the finger at his papa.

It was le Duc de Chevalier, the much-loved Gaston Bombelle who might as well have tied the noose himself. A man who had spent the war years in Paris, funding *La Resistance,* who was reputed to have sheltered British spies and was bitter that his precious chateau had been given over to the Germans. Maire Saber had given the *kommandant* the key to his ancestral home. The Nazis had stolen his paintings and family heirlooms which he considered his birthright, and he wanted revenge.

While Veronique believed her mama's version of events, René soaked up the alternative and agreed with his papa, especially when the drunken slob slid the bottle of wine across the table to his son, winking that he should fill a glass as a reward for his compliance and Saber solidarity.

Mama said that René was merely weak, because it was easier to cast faceless men and women from the past as villains rather than face up to what his father had become and the true reason they were consigned to living in poverty in a fly-infested pig farm, far enough away from villagers whose memories never seemed to fade. And far enough so that nobody heard what went on behind the walls of the Saber home.

So, after she'd learned the truth whenever Denis lost it – his mind, his temper, a few francs from his pockets that told him a thief was at large – Veronique understood why he beat his defenceless family until he passed out. It didn't make it better, though, and just like the residents of Cholet, she could not forgive.

Later, after, she would sob in her bed or listen to her mother doing the same in the next room, but when it was his turn, René never cried. He bore what was meted out, as though it was a rite of passage, challenging pain and humiliation. Instead of giving in to tears, he seethed and cursed, and swore that one day he would rise up, take back what was lost, restore the Saber name and avenge his grandfather. Hearing these words told Veronique one thing, that the minds of the Saber men were warped and she could not allow them to poison her brain too.

Maybe it was inevitable, that René would turn into his father. Maybe it had always been there, in the genes that swam through the blood of Saber men who believed what they were told, indoctrinated from a young age, learning behaviours that became ingrained in their psyche. Or had their souls always been bad? Veronique had hoped that René might break the mould. She'd even prayed for him in church but to no avail because when he became a teenager, he also became her predator.

René was stocky and strong too. He towered above their father who as the years began to take their toll, relied on his son more around the farm. And where René was concerned, he wasn't quite so handy with his fists either. He and René had always been fed first, and what they left was shared between Veronique and her mama. It was never enough. Around this time, when she was twelve and he turned sixteen there was a change in atmosphere at the farm, as though the balance of power was shifting. As the weeks passed it was clear that her brother was becoming a man, from the stubble above his lip, the hairs on his chest, and the lowering of his voice. But there was something else. He watched her, through eyes that she didn't recognise anymore.

They had always shared a bedroom, and as children the warmth of their bodies saw them through the coldest, bleakest winter nights when René would crawl into her bed and shiver by her side. But when René slid out of his bed in the dark and into hers, wrapping his arms around her that first time while she was half asleep, it wasn't cold. It was the height of summer, unbearably humid and he didn't need to keep warm. He needed her.

Fear, such terrible fear gripped Veronique, freezing her to the spot where she lay while revulsion swept over her skin in all the places he touched her, groping, rubbing a hard part of his body against hers, grunting like one of their pigs. When it stopped, he returned to his bed and slept almost immediately. Veronique stayed awake all night.

And so it began, the cycle of René taking what he wanted and who was she to stop him? She didn't dare say no, and who could she ask for help? Certainly not her father, or her mother who seemed always to be sick these days. She could never defend them against her husband, so would have no chance against her lustful sixteen-year-old son.

Veronique had no option other than to learn to accept certain 'things'. The hardest to bear was the loss of her mother who, after collapsing in the yard was taken to the hospital. Papa showed no emotion as they all stood around the bed and listened to the doctor explain that she was unlikely to return home. The thing that was eating her from the inside about to set her free. The kind nurse who showed them out of the ward whispered that it would be a mercy and Veronique agreed, for another reason entirely.

Once her mother found *liberté,* Veronique's only solace came during the hours she spent in school. It wasn't the most pleasant of environments, strict, run by nuns but at least there she was safe and enjoyed one hot meal a day before the drudgery of the farm began. During lessons she tried hard but wasn't particularly bright and spent most of the time dreaming of escape, turning sixteen and working in an office, a shop, anywhere other than being trapped in a house with two *disgusting* pigs while outside, the stench of a whole herd stuck to her skin.

Sister Mary Marguerite, whose eyebrows were one mass of black fluff that joined in the middle and had the shadow of a beard that the braver pupils giggled about, said that *'girls like her'* needed to try harder, the sneer on her face mirrored in those of her classmates.

Veronique didn't know for sure why she was so different or dare ask what happened to all the other girls like her, so she had to work it out herself. In bible lessons with the nuns and even at mass, Veronique had often wondered why children should be punished for the sins of the father, yet in other teachings, sinners were forgiven. But she wasn't a sinner. She tried so hard to be good because only an idiot would invite more trouble into their lives. She also wondered why such a benevolent God who was supposed to love everyone, especially the little children of the world, could be so cruel to send an army of even crueller brides down to earth to make her life even more of a misery. And why would Christ, the kind-looking man who did such nice things, marry women like Sister Mary Marguerite?

It defied logic, all of it. Instead of worrying about the brides, Veronique tried to work out what she'd done wrong. The only thing it could be, she thought, was being a Saber, and because her father got into fights in the bar in town, or maybe people had seen the bruises on her mama's face. All this *and* being the scruffiest smelliest girl in school it was no wonder she had no real friends and lived in isolation, in her heart and in her home.

But Veronique had something most of them didn't: beauty. And in later years she would realise why Sister Mary Marguerite despised her so much. She didn't see that she was the proverbial rose amongst the thorns, the sandy-haired girl with the velvet soft skin and clear green eyes, set in an elfin face that boasted a cute, upturned nose, and kissable rosebud lips, but others did.

One evening, as her father and brother ate their evening meal, the elder slurping and dribbling, he didn't notice when René slid the last crust of bread from the table and hid it under his jumper. He then passed Veronique his plate so she could take it to the sink, a hunk of cheese left uneaten. When he winked and gave her a smile, she took it as kindness. There was no more cheese, and she was hungry. The dregs of thin soup she'd scraped from the pan and her bowl wouldn't sustain her and it was a long wait until lunchtime at school the next day. The hens hadn't been laying so in the morning the last of the eggs would go to her father and brother. Stuffing the cheese in her mouth, she chewed it quickly and swallowed, already looking forward to the bread later.

As always, her father disappeared after their meal, taking the bottle of wine from the table. He could always afford alcohol and plenty of it. As she watched him stagger across the yard to see his precious pigs who he thought more of than his children, she saw a figure appear through the gate. A young man riding a bike. She recognised him from the village but didn't know his name.

'René, someone is here. Are you expecting anyone?'

Her brother came to the window and smirked. 'Ah, Davide, he is on time. He has brought me my bicycle.'

Veronique gasped. 'A bicycle. How can you afford a bicycle, René? Does Papa know... where did you get the money?'

When he turned to face her, she immediately saw that he was angry. 'It is nothing to do with him. Now go to your room and stay there while I discuss business, go. Now!'

Startled by his anger she turned to go but was stopped by René's hand on her arm. 'Here, I forgot, would you like this?' He pulled the crust of bread from under his jumper and held it towards her.

Nodding, she went to take it, but he snatched it away. 'You will have to repay me, and if you do, I will share my food with you every night, is that a deal?'

'How can I repay you, René, and for one piece of bread?' A knock on the door prevented him from answering properly.

'Here, take it. I will explain soon. Go.' René passed her the bread and nodded towards the bedroom door then waited until she had obeyed.

From inside, Veronique strained her ears at the conversation going on in the kitchen as she tore the dry bread with her teeth, wishing she had a glass of water to wash it down. She'd just finished the last mouthful when she was surprised to see the door handle turn and René appeared, Davide behind him.

When the stranger entered the room Veronique saw he was nervous, his spotty face flushed yet he couldn't take his eyes off her which caused her to look away and seek out those of her brother. She never forgot how René looked at her that evening and, in that moment, Veronique knew how she was to pay for the bread.

'Davide wants to spend some time with you so be nice and remember our deal. I will be outside.' He then turned to the man-boy hovering at the end of the bed. 'Be quick. My father will be back soon.'

When Davide had managed to drag his eyes from Veronique, he had given a curt nod before René left the room without a backward glance, closing the door firmly behind him.

The ceiling of the Paris apartment above had a crack running from one corner of the room to the middle and it was this that

Veronique focused on when she opened heavy eyelids, her vision blurred by sleep and the effects of chemicals.

The phone ringing had woken her and as she tapped the eiderdown, trying to locate her mobile, she was released from the grip of a monster and one of her worst nightmares. Finally, her fingers connected with the smooth cover of her phone which she held in front of her eyes and waited until she could read the name on the screen.

Of course, it would be him. Who else could have the ability to plague her sleeping and waking hours? So without relish, she swiped left and listened to the voice at the other end, René.

13

MAC

The sounds that woke him at 4.30am and prevented him from getting a wink of sleep were nothing like those that usually wakened him in his flat in Manchester.

That was all part of the magic, though, exchanging the rumble of lorry engines on their way into the city and raucous schoolkids getting off the bus for the cacophony of birdsong beyond the window of the cottage. You could set your clock by it.

When Mac was six, his grandfather had presented him with a tiny handbook that had the photographs of all the garden birds. He soon learned the names and calls of doves, sparrows, blackbirds and once, he'd spotted a goldfinch.

Back then, as Mac lay in his bed, he would try to identify each chirp, and would listen in the darkness to the sounds of the woods. The night-time noises were more random: a screech from the barn owl or the fox calling to his mate and the cry of cubs hidden in the undergrowth. Usually, Mac had been too exhausted from the excitement of being at La Fleurie to keep his eyes open for long and drifted off. But he'd been glad of his early morning alarm because it heralded the start of another brand-new day with his grandparents.

The only problem was twenty-three years later, as Mac lay on his bed, arms crossed behind his head, there was nobody sleeping in the two other rooms, no rattle of a kettle and the clunk from the pipes as Mémère filled it with water, then the hoot when it boiled. Grandpère wouldn't clomp downstairs at 6am and take his breakfast on the little table at the front of the house. The aroma of coffee wouldn't waft upwards and into his room and the voices of two people he missed so badly would never be heard from his open windows again.

Forcing that image away, Mac occupied his overactive mind with thoughts of Fabienne and how they'd left things the previous evening when she'd walked him to his car. Nothing had happened, apart from making firm arrangements for the following day and a goodnight hug, friendly, non-lingering. But that was fine, easier all round because it really wasn't the time to even contemplate rekindling what they once had; it would be foolish, asking for trouble.

Not that he wasn't tempted because he was, very much so; but he had other things on his mind like selling La Fleurie. And then he'd be heading back to Manchester. There'd be no point coming back to Cholet once the cottage was gone and therefore it was unlikely that he'd see Fabienne again. Glancing at his phone he saw it was 5.35am and knowing he'd just keep going over things in his mind, he decided to do something productive, like sorting out some of his grandparents' things. He'd not even opened the door of their bedroom yet.

Come on, get on with it, they'd not want you to be like this.

Pushing back the blankets, Mac left his warm bed and padded over to the window, the wooden floor beneath his feet cool. Looking down onto the garden at the beds he needed to tidy, he pictured his grandpère and beside him, a young boy learning how to prepare the soil and plant the bulbs for Mémère. It would have been Easter, a special time in France. Church, chocolate eggs, more church and a family feast.

Smiling at the memory he looked up and over the gate and lane beyond, to the fields of wheat and the rooftops of Cholet, just about visible through an early morning mist. It was a beautiful setting, and his friends back home would give their right arms for a home like this, a holiday bolthole, somewhere to escape and with that thought came that wave of shame that he was even considering letting it go.

Turning, he left his bedroom and passed the door to his mum's old room and then came to the last door along at the top of the landing. He stopped outside his grandparents' room and before he chickened out, turned the handle and stepped inside.

It was dark, lit only by a crack of light that invaded through a chipped corner of one of the shutters. The room smelled musty, of old books, tobacco, and the sweet aroma of burnt wood. A singed log resting on ash made him wonder when the fire had last been lit. Had his grandpère been cold, all alone in his bed? *No, he'd have been fine, warm and cosy, not lonely at all. He had Tante Marie-France to keep an eye on him.*

Ignoring the sharp prod of conscience, Mac went over to the window, turned the catch and pulled open the glass, and then unhooked the shutters allowing the morning sun to rush inside, bringing with it the scent of wild flowers and the dewy grass below.

When he turned back to face the room Mac took it all in. The flowered wallpaper was faded by time and woodsmoke, yet you could still pick out the lemon-yellow flowers, huge bulbous blooms hanging onto loopy green vines. The white iron bedstead covered in a quilted blue eiderdown was surrounded by ancient walnut furniture, an armoire and a cavernous wardrobe whose veneer still shone like glass. There were two matching cabinets on either side of the bed and on one, a bible and a travel clock in a pale-pink velvet case, circa 1960. Mac remembered that it folded shut and snapped like a crocodile. Mémère loved it.

He walked over, sat on the bed and held the clock in his hands, feeling the smooth peach-soft exterior. Noticing it had stopped at 2.23, he wound it up, turning the gold screw carefully. After setting the time, a guess as minutes had passed since he checked his phone, he listened to it tick and unable to resist the urge, Mac pushed the case closed. SNAP. It made him smile.

Going to his grandpère's side, he knew immediately what was missing: spectacles and pipe. He took them everywhere and the first thing his grandpère did before he left the room was stick his pipe in his mouth and put on his specs. He must have taken them to hospital and Mac suddenly felt an overwhelming hope that they had been returned. The only thing that remained on the cabinet, apart from the little blue lamp with the fringed shade, was a notebook and threaded inside the spine was a pencil. Frowning, Mac pondered whether he should open it, thinking it could be a private diary. Then again if Tante Marie-France had been up here cleaning, he'd bet his next meal that she'd had a nosey inside so without another thought he picked it up and turned the page.

It was the handwriting that set him off, the whoosh of love came from nowhere and took him by surprise when he saw the familiar loopy scrawl and then the words on the first page. Mac read them through out-of-focus eyes, and whispered the message as he translated...

For my grandson Mackenzie, this is all you need to know about La Fleurie. One day it will belong to you, it is your birthright. Don't forget about the treasure, go find it. Be a good boy, a good man. Be happy.

With love, your grandfather.

Mac only just managed the final word before he broke down and sobbed, staring at the words, so glad that they were written in pencil because the tears that dropped onto the page would have smudged ink.

The writing was faded and there was no date on the page, but the paper was worn and hinted at being turned many times. He read the words again, this time in French, hearing Grandpère's voice echoed in his own, as though he was seated by his side once more.

Pour mon petit-fils Mackenzie
C'est tout ce que tu a besoin de savoir
La Fleurie tu appartient
C'est ton droit de naissance
Je t'ai laissé un trésor
Va la trouver
Sois un bon garçon, un homme bien, sois heureuse
Avec amour,
Ton grandpère

Once composed, he became curious, so Mac wiped his eyes then carefully flipped the page and saw that it held a drawing of what looked like a floor plan, of the house and the outbuildings and on closer examination he saw that it was marked with crosses and notes. *Bless him*, thought Mac, on seeing that his grandpère had taken the time to tell him where the gas pipes, electric and water were connected, just in case.

As he turned each page Mac realised that he'd been left not only the house, but instructions of how to care for it. Dates of when the roof had been repaired and by whom, useful phone numbers, like the man who emptied the septic tank, and the one that made him laugh out loud was a detailed list of every bottle of wine in the cellar, a funny star squiggle denoting the ones he should save, the grand cru from Burgundy. And then a note *'do not tell anyone about the still but make me some eau de vie and drink a toast, to us'*. Mac chuckled and thought back to the days when Grandpère and his friends would gather in one of the outbuildings and distil the giant tubs of fruit they'd been saving all year. The still was home-made and he knew exactly where it was, covered in sacking in the corner of the *cave*. Their secret.

The vegetable plot had also been meticulously detailed – each row, when to rotate, how to get rid of slugs and two notes; one reminding Mac to store the potatoes in the *cave,* in the darkest corner, and another to plant using the moon cycle.

Again, tears stung his eyes, remembering how his grandpère swore by it, explaining how vital the moon was, its gravity pulling at the earth, causing rises and falls in sea levels, the tides governed by an orb, hundreds and thousands of miles away, high in the sky. For the animals, especially the birds, it was essential to navigation and migration and when planting, the old way was always the best.

Leaning on the pillows propped against the rails of the headboard, Mac was overcome by love for his granddad. It had drained him so he closed his eyes that were burning from lack of sleep and the salt of his tears. And, as his body relaxed, he listened to the sounds of the house waking up. The floorboards creaked and birds pecked the roof tiles above his head, the tap, tap, tap of their beaks keeping time with the cogs in his mind, clicking over and taking him back to a day in spring, when he was fifteen. He and his grandpère were pulling a cart laden with saplings through the woods and as they walked, he told Mac that they had a very important job to do.

Cholet
2008

Mac was already tired from pulling the cart whose wheels

squeaked and wobbled as they turned on the narrow, bumpy track. His legs ached but no way would he admit it. Mac still wanted to work as hard as Grandpère, be just like him so he wouldn't give up and anyway, the sight of the picnic box and bottles of water spurred him on, knowing that soon they would rest, drink and eat one of Mémère's wonderful feasts.

Even though it was cool under the shade of the trees that, as tradition dictated, they named as they passed – oak, pine, beech, chestnut – Mac was getting hot. The underarms of his T-shirt were sweaty, like those of proper working men. Not like his dad, who he'd never seen lift a finger, whose hands were smooth and lily-white.

Not wanting to think of his dad, who Mac was glad had stayed at home instead of coming on holiday with his family, again, he glanced backwards at the truck that carried rows of saplings, a water barrel and sack of lime powder. They made him curious, and a bit concerned that they would have to dig a lot of holes for fifty trees. That's how many there were, he'd counted.

'Grandpère, why are we taking all these to the woods? It's not like we need any more, is it?'

A sly smile crept over the elder's face and after a tap of his nose, came a mysterious answer. 'These are very special trees, and we have to plant them in a place where they will be safe, two metres apart, deep in the forest, away from prying eyes and at the best time of year, and now is the right time.'

'Because of the moon?' Mac had always loved hearing about the old ways of farming.

'Yes, and can you remember why?'

Mac recited what he'd been told. 'When the light of the moon is strongest, it increases the moisture in the soil making seeds swell and sap flow.'

To this, he received a satisfied nod from the wisest man in the world. 'Good boy. And look. At last we are here.'

They stopped to much relief from Mac who looked around, seeing only that the narrow track had ended and to the left, a large clearing that was enclosed by a wire mesh fence. 'What is it, a garden? We've never been here before, have we?'

Grandpère laughed at this, then became mysterious again. 'When you were younger. We passed through during a walk. We were talking about the animals that lived in the woods and you were scared when I told you about the wild boars who snuffle for food in the earth and have tusks that can kill a man. I had to put you on my shoulders after that; you were tired and upset so may not remember.'

'I'm not surprised I was upset... you can be a bit brutal sometimes, like when you explained what happened to Lulu the pig. I was so glad I wasn't here when the slaughterman came.' Mac had been horrified when he asked where Lulu had gone, the little piglet he'd watched grow, and his grandpère had told him.

Mémère had been so cross with her husband, for making Mac cry, reminding him that he was used to the ways of the country and that he needed to tread carefully with those who were not. She'd given him the scrawniest leg off the chicken and a small slice of gateau for dinner as punishment. That, Mac remembered.

Looking back to the clearing, he changed the subject. 'So, are we going to put the saplings in there?'

Grandpère rested his hands on his hips and surveyed the ground. 'We are. And it is going to be our secret forest where one day, if we are lucky and patient, we will find treasure.'

Mac's mouth opened as wide as his eyes; his words wrapped in a gasp. 'Treasure, really, like gold?'

Grandpère's bushy eyebrows were raised, accompanied by a

knowing look and mischievous smile. 'Better than gold, black diamonds.'

Already totally sold on the idea of treasure, Mac had questions fizzing around his brain. 'So, is that why you've made the fence, to protect the treasure? But why are we planting the trees on top, and why can't we dig for it now?'

Grandpère just did the throaty laugh that Mac was used to. 'Come on, let's get started and I will explain it all to you as we work but remember, it is our secret. We don't tell anyone in the village, or your friends, is that a deal?'

Mac nodded, then one more question. 'But I can tell Mum, and Mémère, can't I?'

Grandpère rubbed his chin and thought for a moment before sighing. 'Okay, we will let them into the secret. But nobody else.' Once they'd shaken on it, calloused hands gripping those unblemished by years of toil, they dragged the cart towards the fence and began work.

They knelt side by side, digging holes in the earth, warmed by the spring sun while his grandpère explained that for over a year, he'd been coming to the clearing, preparing the soil with lime, so it contained enough calcium and reached the correct acidity. Then he'd built the fence around the plot to protect the young trees from wild boars and other animals.

Mac was tired and hungry so asked if they could stop to eat and rest, and after receiving a nod, the wild farmers brushed themselves down and took a break but not before they had rolled two logs into place at right angles under a beech. Perched on his log seat and in between mouthfuls Mac had lots more questions. 'So where are the diamonds, Grandpère?'

'They are in the roots of those trees. I put them there, tiny spores that you cannot see with the eye but over the next few years they will grow. Nature will make the magic and in exchange for processing the nutrients in the soil, the spores will take sugar from the tree roots and turn it into treasure… they will become truffles.'

Mac's confusion must have shown on his face so once he'd eaten his sandwich, Grandpère took a slurp of wine from the bottle before explaining why what they were doing must remain a secret.

'Truffles are fungi, like the mushrooms you are so fond of. Many years ago, before I was born, even before the great war, the Loire produced the most black winter truffles in the world, thousands of tons that were sent far and wide. The soil and climate in this area provides the perfect conditions to grow them but sadly, after the ground was trampled and burned during the war the industry did not recover and now, we don't grow so many. And do you know what this means?'

Mac shook his head because he had no idea so listened intently while he ate his crisps.

'It means they are very valuable and when they are fully grown, they sell for hundreds of euros and they are going to be our treasure, or more importantly, your treasure.'

In his heart, Mac had been a bit disappointed when he realised there weren't any real diamonds in the soil, but he didn't want to upset his grandpère who had already worked so hard, germinating the seeds in his greenhouse, impregnating the spores, potting and watering the saplings and preparing the land for planting.

So, trying to sound enthusiastic, and not ungrateful or dubious, Mac asked, 'When will the truffles be ready? Do they grow like vegetables?' He already had visions of digging them up in summer, like the potatoes they grew at La Fleurie. And going to Argos to buy a brand-new PlayStation with the profits.

When his grandpère began to chuckle, Mac kind of knew he wasn't getting a PlayStation anytime soon. 'Yes, they grow like vegetables, but it could take seven, maybe as long as twelve years before they are a decent size and that's if we get any at all. It depends on many things; luck, hungry animals, mother nature. And in the meantime, I will have to keep the trees pruned and low: that way the nutrients will help the truffles grow.'

'Twelve years! I'll be well old by then. And how do we know if there are any there and when to dig them up?' Mac really couldn't imagine waiting that long for some magical mushroom things to grow big enough to sell for hundreds of euros and had already begun to lose faith and interest in the secret forest.

'Fruit flies, that's how I will know. When the tiny insects congregate on the surface of the soil. Or I might find a truffle dog or maybe I could train one.' A period of thoughtfulness elapsed, allowing man and boy to finish their food.

Mac knew his mémère had forbidden any more dogs after she lost her beloved Coco, so his grandpère was definitely on a loser there. He also knew that he could have been hanging out with his friends rather than digging holes. Still, respect for his grandpère and not wanting to hurt his feelings helped him muster some enthusiasm for what Mémère would say was a load of nonsense. He could hear her voice, and lots of tuts and head shaking when they told her. Mémère had no time for her husband's daydreaming.

Thinking it was best to get it over with, Mac stood. 'Well let's get on with it then. I'll pass the saplings over the fence and place them by the holes and then we can start planting.' He held out his hand then heaved his crazy grandpère upwards, receiving a pat on the back once creaky bones were straightened.

It had been late when they finished watering the saplings and even if Mac didn't really believe in the magic of nature, he did hope the fragile stems would survive and grow because planting them, giving them a chance of life, was something he and his grandpère had done together. Before they left they had shaken hands, congratulating one another on a job well done, both hands covered in dirt, soil under their fingernails, man and boy sealing a memory. As they made their way home, the wobbly creaky cart bouncing along the track behind them, both exhausted and looking forward to their dinner, Mac glanced at the man beside him and smiled.

If nothing else it had been a special day, hard work but one where he'd learned something new and spent time with his hero. The gang in the village would be there the next day and for the first time ever, Mac had the weirdest sensation and a troubling thought. That with every inch the saplings grew, marking time, a year closer to when they would bear fruit or whatever a truffle was, his grandpère would be getting older. And Mac didn't want that. He wanted him to live forever. Then La Fleurie came into view and the sight of it, and the promise of his mémère's cooking settled him. He was being silly, there was time, plenty and plenty of time.

Whenever Mac returned, he visited the secret forest with his grandpère to inspect the saplings where they would walk along the rows, pruning if the season allowed, speculating about the day they would dig for treasure. Five years later, the leaves that sprouted each spring were abundant, green and healthy and even though the little saplings didn't resemble mighty oaks their narrow trunks were strong, but there were no fruit flies burrowing into the soil, no sign that it had worked.

And as Mac's hope faded that somewhere underground were black specks of treasure, and as life pulled him away from La Fleurie he forgot all about the secret forest and their special day. He also forgot about his moment of clarity, his glimmer of mortality and slowly La Fleurie lost its grip, other things and other people captured his heart, and even the memories of those special summers couldn't lure him back. And now, it was too late.

A sharp sound brought Mac back from the past and as he opened his eyes, he saw that one of the shutters had slammed closed, so yawning, he slid from the bed, his dream already smudged, vague and fading fast. He knew it was about his grandpère and the day they went to the woods but the details were overtaken by a need for the loo and some breakfast. After securing the shutter, Mac picked up the notebook, intending to take it downstairs so he could read it while he ate. Then he had to get ready, thoughts of returning to the chateau at the forefront of his mind. A quick glance at the pink clock told him it was almost seven and his heart quickened. Only three hours until he saw Fabienne again.

14

FABIENNE

They were part way through the tour of the long gallery and to her immense satisfaction Mac had seemed genuinely interested in her collection and very complimentary of her and Antoinette's curating skills, even joking that Fabienne was a natural-born guide.

'Well, there's only one person who knows the collection like me, and that's Antoinette. She spends hours up here, dusting, checking, and just admiring the artefacts. She swears blind she's seen a ghost, once very early in the morning and a couple of times late at night.

'See the tall windows at each end? Well, the sun rises beyond that one,' Fabienne pointed to the east window and then turned, her finger indicating the west wing, 'and it sets there and on a clear night the moon floods the whole gallery, turning it blue. It looks beautiful, very atmospheric so I'm not surprised she thinks she saw something, but it was probably just shadows, clouds passing over the moon, something like that. Anyway, she's always up here ghost-hunting so I leave her to it.'

Mac looked upwards to the huge domed window above that allowed a view of a blue sky dotted by white clouds. 'So, I take it

Antoinette isn't scared of ghosts or being in this huge place all alone?'

'No, not at all. She's often here alone while I'm in London or Paris and you know Antoinette, she's not scared of anything or anyone.' Fabienne had stopped by the three enormous portraits that kept watch over the gallery.

'And what about you? Do you believe in ghosts? It doesn't sound like you do, which as far as I'm concerned is probably a good thing when you're staying here.'

At this question her heart sunk because nothing was further from the truth. But Fabienne kept her answer vague, not wanting to bare her soul: it wasn't the time for that. 'Oh, I do believe, with all my heart and it would make my day if I saw the spirit of one of my ancestors gliding through the ballroom or making bread in the kitchen. When I was little, I used to see people who I thought were real, a woman who looked like a maid, and a cat – of all things – that would leap through the walls then disappear.'

'I did used to wonder if La Fleurie was haunted but it's always been such a comforting place to be. I was more wrapped up in the stories my granddad told me about The Resistance hiding in the woods and the wild boars that would eat me if I wandered off alone.'

At this Fabienne laughed because she could imagine Monsieur Doré telling his grandson tales. He was a lovely man who always welcomed people into his home yet had a mischievous air about him. Pointing upwards, she nodded to the subject of the three paintings in front of them. 'Well, I bet if anyone can tell a good tale it would be these handsome devils.'

When Mac raised his eyebrows and gave her a startled look, they couldn't contain a giggle. 'I mean seriously, the artist did them no favours, did he? The poor sods. And I'm sorry to disrespect your ancestors but thank God the gene pool found some new members before you came along.'

Laughing, Fabienne whacked his arm. 'I'll take that as a compliment but it's safe to say our interpretation of beauty isn't quite the same as the Pre-Raphaelites'. But in defence of the artist, he created these from photographs. They're not the originals.'

'Really, how come?'

Fabienne sighed. 'My great-grandfather was an art dealer in Paris and was well connected and amongst his friends who frequented the Montparnasse district, a vibrant artistic community, were such painters as Modigliani, Picasso, Cocteau, Chagall, the list goes on. He had amassed an impressive collection of paintings and statues, reputed to be worth millions nowadays, and they were displayed here, on the walls and in the rooms of Chevalier. I'll show you some of the photographs next, of the parties and guests who would come to stay here for the summer and weekends, the beautiful, talented avant-garde of society who I am sure would have raised eyebrows amongst the residents of Cholet.'

Mac sounded impressed. 'Wow, so your grandfather rubbed shoulders with Picasso. I love his paintings. And Monet and Matisse. I like Monet the best.'

For some reason, Mac appreciating art made Fabienne happy, and she hoped that he would also understand the tragedy of the story that surrounded the original paintings. 'Well, wait till I tell you what happened next. When the Nazis invaded, they pillaged thousands of pieces of art from homes across France and unfortunately, Chevalier was no exception. My great-grandfather was naïve and didn't believe the Nazis would be interested in art, only land, so ignored advice from his good friend Jacques Jacquard, who the year before in August 1939 had ordered the removal of four thousand artworks from the Louvre. The operation was secret, and the pieces were distributed across France and hidden for safekeeping. When the Nazis entered the Louvre in September 1940, all they found were empty rooms. We were not so lucky.'

'That's awful. How much did they take and why were they so intent on taking artwork?' Mac looked around at the gallery and Fabienne filled in the blanks.

'Hitler was bitter after being twice refused entry to the Academy of Fine Arts in Vienna, and he also despised modern artists for being degenerate so was intent on confiscating that which he found abhorrent. The rest he knew was worth a fortune. When my grandfather heard the propaganda, he realised his mistake and ordered everything to be removed and arranged for it to be sent south to a convent where it would be stored and kept safe. The nuns there had connections to his wife's family. It was early November, and they hoped to use the cover of darkness to smuggle everything away. The staff loaded our treasures into two huge trucks – one had the paintings, the other contained furniture, rugs, vases and objects you see around the chateau – but someone betrayed us to the Nazis. One truck got away, setting off first and taking an alternative route via the rear of the estate but the soldiers arrived as the last of the paintings were being loaded. They took everything and then, took over the chateau for the duration of the occupation.'

Mac looked incredulous and then pointed to the portraits on the wall. 'But what about these, and the others I've seen on the way up? How come they didn't take them?'

The answer was easy. 'They are all reproductions, painted by unknown artists commissioned by my great-grandfather after the war. He never forgave himself for not acting sooner so tried to scrape together a collection that resembled what we lost. And there's an even more tragic reason he wanted to restore the chateau to its former glory.'

Fabienne paused, it always made her feel sad when she thought of poor Ophélie. 'During the occupation, my great-grandparents did what they could to help La Resistance and in my grandmother's case, this involved passing messages to the agents who worked in Paris. Nobody would suspect a refined lady taking coffee at La Flore, or so they thought. Unfortunately, she was arrested on suspicion of being a collaborator by the Gestapo and held for many days in the cells. Here, she became unwell and after my great-grandfather kicked up an unholy fuss, calling in every favour he was owed, she was finally released without charge. Whatever she contracted in the cells led to pneumonia and she never recovered. Ophélie died shortly after and left my great-grandfather with a broken heart. She adored Chevalier and once the war was over, he vowed to restore it in her memory.'

Mac looked as sombre as Fabienne felt. 'That really is tragic. Poor Ophélie, and your great-granddad, too. But it looks like he did a great job, and got some of his things back.'

'Yes, he did. The antiques were returned after the war but they are nowhere near as valuable as the artwork that was stolen. In fact, you see the frames that the portraits hang in? Well they are probably worth more than the painting itself.'

'No way, how come?'

'Because recently there has been a huge increase in value and interest in vintage frames. Even if you separate one from a watercolour or a mirror, it can still be extremely sought after and valuable. At the auctioneers we are seeing customers who are more interested in the stamps and markings on the back of a frame than what it contains.'

'Is that how you can tell if they are valuable?'

Pointing to the portraits, Fabienne explained further. 'Yes, there are many clues if you know where to look. For example, these paintings were commissioned in 1949 and the frames were made by a specialist atelier, hand carved and gilded. As are the others. If we were to remove them, you would see the marks of the craftsmen who created the frame and I already know their value. So now do you see why selling the collection is a fool's errand?'

Mac nodded, his expression one of concern. 'I do. It's a no-win situation because if you sell what you have it won't raise enough cash to restore this place and at the same time, the ambience of the chateau will be lost, and you'll have nothing to exhibit.'

'Precisely, and for some reason my father is unable to grasp this very simple point. Anyway, enough of all that. Let me show you some photographs of how things used to be, before leaky roofs and buckets took over our lives. We can't even use the turret rooms at either end because the floorboards are so rotten. It's such a shame.' Fabienne had wanted this to be a fun day, not one where her father, Veronique and the disrepair of the chateau cast their shadows, so inclining her head towards the other side of the gallery, she attempted to cheer herself up with tales of actresses and musicians streaking across the lawn and the fountain being filled with champagne.

They'd spent another half an hour looking through the photo albums that contained grainy images from times gone by, but sadly none of La Fleurie, and were moving on to the journals when Mac had an idea. 'There's a chest at the cottage full of old photographs and stuff that my grandma kept. They might be of some interest to you. Old newspapers and magazines and my mum's school reports. You're welcome to take a look if you want.'

'I'd like that. Me and Antoinette were thinking of collating an up-to-date history of Chevalier and the town by starting our own journal because the housekeeping one ended during the war. It's a shame because it was a lovely tradition... look.' She flipped open a page that was dated 1806. 'See, the housekeeper kept details of everyone who worked here, what they were paid, and then there's the book-keeping which is fascinating in itself because it's like a window on their lives, you know, how much they spent on food and what they ate. We love looking through them.'

Fabienne was tracing the words and figures meticulously written in ink, lost in a world she could only imagine and when she looked up, caught Mac staring at her. 'You think I'm a nerd, don't you?'

When he answered his face was serious, his words seemed sincere. 'No, not at all. I can see your passion and it's making me think about La Fleurie and the part its played in my life, and all the people who lived there before. Even though this place and your history is on a grander scale than the cottage, it still comes down to the same thing, doesn't it? That all this is part of your life and heritage and La Fleurie is part of mine.'

Fabienne was overwhelmed and quite joyous that Mac got it. 'Exactly. You see, when I touch these old books, or one of the beautiful vases in the *salon* or even one of the pans, or the copper kettle on the range, I know that others have done so before me. Their hands have rested there, and those hands belonged to the body and mind of a person who saw and loved and lived, and they have a story to tell. That's why I can't let it go. I must find a way, for them. There's a famous poem, one of my favourites by Lamartine that sums it up so well: "Inanimate objects, do you have a soul which sticks to our soul and forces it to love?" That's how I feel, like all this has stuck to my soul.'

Suddenly consumed by emotion, maybe the stress of the battle with her father or the sleepless nights worrying about money, Fabienne felt the unmistakable threat of tears and Mac had also fallen silent, probably embarrassed by her poetry recital and rather impassioned speech. And being so close to him wasn't helping either because it was still there, the pull of his magnet. She was as drawn to him then as she'd always been, and it had been a struggle not to reach out and touch his hand. So, when she heard the slap of shoes on stone and Antoinette appeared in the gallery, relief flooded her body.

'Hey, there you are. Thought you were up to no good when I couldn't find you downstairs.' Antoinette was clearly determined in her quest to reunite Mac and Fabienne, whose relief had been replaced by the urge to throttle her friend.

'I've been showing Mac our collection and explaining about the journals, if you must know.'

'Oh, really, is that all. How very disappointing. Anyway, I have made you both some lunch and left it in the kitchen. I'm meeting Joel and then I'm going to see Eglantine so wish me luck.'

Fabienne couldn't even look at Mac so focused on her friend. 'Thank you and please give your grandma my love and tell her I will come to visit with you next time. I love to hear her stories.'

At this Antoinette rolled her eyes. 'Yes, she's very entertaining unless the naked man has been to see her. That is simply too much information from your grandma. So, with the thought of naked bodies in mind I will leave you both alone. Be good, or bad, whatever takes your fancy, and I will see you later.' A very exaggerated wink preceded her departure where she turned quickly and headed towards the stairs, her hand waving a backwards goodbye.

Plucking up the courage to face Mac, Fabienne saw that he found the whole thing amusing which relaxed her slightly. 'So, shall we take the elephant downstairs for lunch or tie him up against the table? Honestly, Antoinette really knows how to make me cringe.'

'Hey, it's fine, we both know what she's like and I'm starving so let's go, and forget about the elephant; he's not hungry anyway.' Mac was closing the cover on the journal as he spoke.

On their way downstairs Fabienne's mind worked overtime, and read her own meaning into Mac's words, *'forget about the elephant; he's not hungry anyway.'* Was that a subtle hint or a message saying loud and clear that *them*, what they had, was best forgotten? And that thought stung; it stung like hell.

During their chicken salad lunch, eaten on the terrace, protected from the scorching rays of the midday sun by a battered old parasol, it had been a battle of the wills not to tell Mac to stop playing games and piss off back to his cottage while at the same time, cling onto every minute in his company.

And she was confused, too, because when they were on the gallery it had felt so comfortable, like he'd never been away, then the moments when they were centimetres apart and she sensed that all it would take was one touch, the right word. Words that she'd wanted to say now died on her tongue and those warm feelings inside had been extinguished by his throwaway comment. But once they were in the kitchen, fetching the food and wine, and while they ate, she'd caught him watching her again, and she wavered, sure it was still there, she knew it, saw it, felt it. That connection and ease they felt in each other's company.

So, either she was getting desperate and imagining it or he'd been joking about the elephant, and she'd taken what he said the wrong way. *You're oversensitive and overtired. Maybe that's all it is; he didn't mean it the way you took it.*

They were enjoying one of the bottles of wine that Antoinette had left to chill in the fridge where Fabienne had found the note saying, 'Have a drink, have fun, have sex, it will do you good' accompanied by a wonky, winking face. She'd felt herself go bright red as she scrunched it up before Mac could see but as the wine slowly began to relax her, Fabienne saw the funny side and possibly the sense in Antoinette's words.

Nevertheless, it was imperative not to make a fool of herself with Mac and then ruin their reunion and not only that, she really couldn't bear any more drama in her life so instead, she concentrated on what he was telling her about one of his finds, a notebook that belonged to his grandfather.

'It looks like he's been making notes since grandma died which tells me he was preparing for the future. It makes me sad, knowing that he was alone and thinking about what would happen to him and the cottage.'

Fabienne was intrigued. 'Oh, bless him, but don't be too sad because lots of people do that, leave a list of instructions that are more personal than what's in their will and I think it's nice, comforting to know what they would have wanted.' She watched as Mac nodded and then curiosity got the better of her. 'What does it say?'

'Mostly it's warning me not to drink his best wine, who to call if I get a water leak and what I need to plant in spring. He was very meticulous.' Mac laughed and seeing him do so, she remembered how much fun they had that summer until her daydream bubble was popped by a question.

'I was going to ask you to look at it for me because there are some sections that I don't think I'll be able to translate properly, and Grandpère's writing isn't easy to decipher. My spoken French is much better than my written, but two entries caught my eye. One was titled *"Ton Histoire"* with a family tree and then the next one was titled *"Ma Soeur"*. I know Grandpère had a sister who died during the war, but he never spoke about it; nobody did, although she's mentioned in the diagram. It says she died in 1940.'

Fabienne's interest went up a notch. 'That was the year the Nazis invaded France, in May. It sticks in my mind because I know they took over Chevalier in November: it's in my family journals so I wonder if her death had something to do with them, the Nazis. Yes, I'd love to read the notebooks and translate for you, if you don't mind me seeing private stuff.'

'No, I don't mind at all. It's in the car so I'll get it later.'

Fabienne couldn't wait to get her hands on a piece of history and told him so before the focus turned back to her problems.

Mac poured them more wine as he spoke. 'Have you had any more ideas how you can raise funds for the renovation work?'

'No, not really. I have considered opening the grounds to the public so they can enjoy them, but I can hardly charge money to sit on grass that needs a good cut or have a picnic by the green, gungy lake. The flower gardens are in a terrible state too. The thing is, I'm getting desperate so any form of income right now would be better than nothing. I might have to bite the bullet and start selling stuff as much as it will kill me. Instead of a big, full-on restoration we might have to do it the hard and long way, room by room, which will take forever. And soon we will have to pay the government taxes, you know *habitation* and *foncière*, and on this place they are ridiculous.'

'It's really that bad?' Mac looked shocked.

'Oh yes. I will start with the ugliest things, the *objets* that I can bear to sell. I have jewellery in the safe in Paris, but that will be the very, very last resort because some of it belonged to my mother. And Antoinette is going to have to find a job soon because I can't expect her to carry on looking after Chevalier for nothing. So something will have to give and I'm out of ideas.'

'Well, I'll have a think, see if I can get my marketing brain in gear. I do a lot of ads in my job so if I can help with anything like that, just say the word. But there's one thing I don't understand?'

Fabienne batted away a wasp that was after her wine. 'Fire away.'

'After hearing how passionate you are about your family history, why were you willing to let the Paris apartment go? Does it not mean as much to you as this place?'

Fabienne fiddled with the stem of her glass as she tried to think of an answer, one that wouldn't mean opening old wounds so she started with the easy stuff. 'It's hard to explain because I absolutely love the apartment, the location, the building, the interior. I swear it's like stepping into a film set. I can even imagine it in black and white because most of the furniture and even some of the wallpaper and drapes have been there for over a hundred years. It is as special historically as this place but...' She paused, finding the words and looked up at Mac who waited.

'Maybe because I spent most of my time here with my mama and *petit*-Baptiste I am swayed. I have only vague memories of being in Paris with them; going to the park, to see the tower, feeling cooped up even though it's really big, but nothing like this place. Here is where I feel them both. I can see Baptiste toddling on the grass, my mother laying out a picnic for our lunch, hearing him crying from the nursery when he was teething, and they are buried in the family graveyard on the estate. I don't want to leave them behind, I suppose.'

Mac leant over and covered her free hand with his. 'I get it, I really do.'

It was this contact, the first since saying goodbye the previous evening, and the naturalness of feeling his skin so close to hers that prompted the need to share something private, a rare moment where she bared herself. 'And there's another reason, perhaps a spiteful selfish reason I wanted to sell the apartment – to take something from my father that he loves more than Chevalier and even me, to punish him for the way he's behaved.'

'Hey, I'm sure your dad loves you, in his own way, no matter how much you disagree.'

Fabienne shook her head and held onto Mac's hand, the force of her grip conveying the strength of feeling running through her body. 'No, he doesn't. My father loves only himself, and money and maybe for a time having a beautiful wife that everyone adored and admired. But once the shine wore off, he went back to his old ways. You know he's never had a job. He's a total snob who has lived off his inheritance and ridiculous investments made from the leather sofa in his members club. He sent me away because he couldn't face what he'd done to my mother, and because I look like her, he packed me off to another country. I have despised him for many years, ever since I found out what he was...'

Mac folded her hands in both of his and spoke softly, his words comforting her, bringing calm. 'You don't have to talk about it if you don't want, I can see it's upsetting you. You've gone pale, and your irises have gone almost black. They always do that when you're angry.'

That he'd noticed something, remembered even, wiped out the elephant, the image of it fading fast and now it was out of the room Fabienne knew that she was going to grasp the moment with both hands. 'No, I want to. I need to tell someone, something even Antoinette doesn't know.'

Had she not been enjoying the feel of his hands on hers she would have taken a sip of wine because slandering the Bombelle name didn't come easy to her. 'My mother and brother were killed on the bend, as you turn left out of the gates. My father never drives that way and would rather go the long route to town than pass by. But I used to go there all the time without anyone knowing and sit under the trees where it happened, hoping that I would feel them there or by some miracle, get the answers to why she crashed.

'Then when I was eighteen, my mémère gave me the letters that Mama had sent to her. She said I was old enough to know the truth about Papa and I think most of all, she wanted me to understand why they never got along. He cast her as the proverbial monster-in-law. I loved Mémère and she me; we were close, and I was glad there were no secrets between us especially before she died. When I came home to Chevalier, I searched Mama's room for the letters that she would have received in return, so I would have the full set, be able to read the flow of correspondence from one to the other. I found them in the most obvious place, somewhere I would hide for hours so I could be alone with the memory of her.'

'Where were they?'

Fabienne untangled her hands from Mac's but kept hold of one and felt his thumb stroke the side of hers. 'They were in the bottom of her wardrobe but now they are in mine. Come on, I'll show you.'

Mac didn't reply and without another word they went upstairs.

15

VERONIQUE

One week. One more week of purgatory before it was set to happen, and Veronique wasn't sure if she could bear the wait or the toll it was taking. Ever since his call, brief and to the point, she'd retreated to the bedroom. Hugo had retreated to his club. He was irritated by her; she knew that because her husband wasn't a man in touch with his feelings or those of anyone else. It was how he was, and it had suited her, being married to someone who understood the rule of give and take, the balancing act of a mutually beneficial relationship.

Turning on her side, Veronique curled into a ball and listened to the sounds of an empty apartment that in her addled brain she'd hoped to fill with friends – his not hers – and some laughter too. She had seen a new role for herself as the hostess, le Duc's vibrant new wife who would give grand dinner parties, slowly make some acquaintances, be accepted. It was fine at first, bearable, easy to fake being happily married especially when you'd landed on your feet and ended up in such beautiful, if shabby chic, surroundings. And then she realised the money had run out, and her fanciful notions were just that, and she was trapped.

Looking over to Hugo's side of the bed, unslept in for days, she wished that the photo of the couple on their wedding day was true, not as fake as the smile she had worn for the camera. She'd tried so hard to fall in love with him though, rewind the clock, skip past the stuff that had tainted her. She threw herself into being the best wife she could while deep down knowing she would never be good enough. She was not from the right stock and *'a girl like her'* would never really fit into his world. She would never be Paloma.

He'd always been elusive, emotionally bankrupt even when they were younger yet as much as she tried not to, she'd wanted him so badly, and not only his lifestyle. She'd harboured a ridiculous naïve notion that maybe she was different. That she was beautiful enough, even more beautiful than his wife, and had something special that would crack his code.

Oh Hugo, why couldn't you see? Why couldn't you be the one to save me?

Veronique looked at her wedding ring, the first she had ever worn and on the day she made her vows, apart from the ones that alluded to love, she really had meant them. They were binding her to something she'd longed for, craved. And in return for respectability and stability, financial security and freedom even though she didn't love him she would have stood by Hugo forever.

Veronique's hips ached from lying on the bed for hours on end so she flipped onto her back. The pain in her bones reminded her of aching feet, that day six years before when she'd walked through the streets of Montparnasse, looking for a cheap place to stay.

She'd ended yet another flagging relationship and had taken a train to Paris with enough money for a few days in a budget hotel. And after that she knew if she didn't find work she would have to call René. Tell him in a bright voice that she was making a surprise visit. And while she would hate having to fall on his mercy, again, Veronique despised him even more when she imagined the smirk on his face, and how much he would love playing the benevolent brother.

She'd stopped at a small café and ordered an espresso and a glass of water, one to revive flagging spirits, the other to last a while and allow her to rest. So, when the waiter brought her a martini and she followed the direction of his pointed finger, there, just behind the glass, like a gift from God, was Hugo.

Would she have approached him had she spotted him first? Definitely. Because her predicament warranted taking a chance. As it was, there'd been no need to go cap in hand. He could have ignored her but instead he made the first move. The martini was an invitation, and it told her that he'd left the past where it was and after she'd smiled and waved, he came over to her table.

As he brought her up to date with his life while she skirted around her own, Veronique read between the lines. Hugo was tired of rattling around the apartment; he also hated being companionless, the odd one out at dinner or a function and hadn't the energy or money for escorts. He'd admitted this quite freely: it was his way. More or less estranged from his bitter daughter who did her best to avoid and irritate him in equal measure, Hugo was ripe for the picking, Veronique saw. And thanks to his arrogant, steely heart, he could gloss over the past and her minor part in a terrible tragedy. As for his own, that was his conscience to bear. It was as though it had never happened even though they both knew it had, so why talk about it? And by not doing so they sealed a silent deal.

Two hours later she had seen through the bluster, taken in the crumpled jacket and the shirt in need of an iron, and the jaded look of a lonely man, a shadow of the cad she once knew, the randy old dog she'd been fed to by René, all those years before.

16

RENÉ AND VERONIQUE

**Cholet
1990s**

Veronique watched from the kitchen door as the white van carrying her father's body drove out of the yard while René smoked a cigarette and chatted to the *gendarme*. From their body language and her brother's relaxed demeanour, she suspected he was one of René's 'friends' who he paid to turn a blind eye to the nocturnal goings-on at the farm. Veronique wondered if her father should have done the same and not demanded a cut of René's black-market profits but deep down, she knew that's not what had got him killed.

What had caused her father's drunken body to be found face down, suffocated in a pile of mud and pig shit, his scalp and body chewed and mauled by the very animals he cared more about than his family, was simple. He had crossed the line where his sixteen-year-old daughter was concerned and nobody was allowed to do that, only René.

She'd known there would be trouble, that evening at dinner when they sat down to eat and her father eyed René's new leather jacket and then the full plate of food in front of Veronique. Then he had looked up at her, before casting a final, sly glance his son's way. He'd continued to smirk and guzzle wine all the way through the meal as they ate in silence, like always. Not that Veronique cared because she had nothing to say to either of them. So she focused on her food and ignored the way her father was focusing on her breasts. René noticed too, but said and did nothing.

It was later, as she sat on her bed reading, that the handle turned and her father appeared in the doorway and without saying a word, flicked out the light. Veronique had no time to scream or protest before she heard the shuffle of his feet and then a grunt as he hit the floor, and as her eyes became accustomed to the darkness, she watched the scuffle between father and son as fists flew and expletives filled the air. Knowing when he was beat, the elder gave in first and staggered from the room followed by René, calling him the worst names which later, as she huddled in bed and sobbed, Veronique found ironic.

When René finally came home, the sound of the kitchen door slamming and then the hum of the washing machine woke Veronique who waited, holding her breath. René entered the bedroom and slipped into his own bed, not uttering a word.

It was the feed man who discovered their father's body the following morning when he arrived with an early delivery. After he'd hammered on the door, she and René found him being sick beside his lorry in between telling them not to look in the pig pens and to ring the police.

Veronique repeated what René had told her to say to the respectful *gendarme* who seemed to believe every word. 'My father is a violent man and when he is drunk flies into a rage for the smallest of reasons. I hadn't prepared his dessert and he went crazy but before he could beat me like always, René fought him off, then locked him out while he sobered up.' Veronique trembled as she spoke, not from the shock of seeing her half-eaten father, more the fear of getting caught out and the wrath of René if she messed up.

The patient *gendarme* scribbled in his notepad as he asked another question. 'And were you together all night, mademoiselle?'

Veronique nodded as tears rolled down her face, not from sadness but the mere kindness in the young man's voice. 'Yes, my brother remained with me. We went to bed around ten after watching television, presuming Papa was sleeping it off in the barn, like always.'

And just as René had promised, the *gendarme* asked a few more perfunctory questions then with a polite nod, flipped the notebook closed and that was the end of that.

Around a week later, René arrived home and as he called for Veronique to come outside, she noticed that in his hands, he carried a wooden casket. Wordlessly she followed him over to the pig pens and watched as he undid the bottom, took out the bag of grey ashes and tipped them into the mud before turning to face Veronique, his tone cold as he spoke. 'I think that's where he belongs, don't you?'

All she could do, was nod her agreement. There was nothing more to say.

Over the following weeks René was busy, storing and then moving stolen goods from the barn in the van she'd helped him buy. The casket was on the shelf in the kitchen, and it was where René stored his money. Veronique could tell it gave him a kick.

The days seemed endless, where she went to school and did her best to ignore the nuns who told her she was average while the mirror in the bathroom told her she was anything but. The rest of the time she kept her eyes down and kept house, the one that now belonged to her and her brother equally. Life was calm and he'd asked for no more favours. René bought a new bed and slept in their father's room; there was plenty of food which he shared, but Veronique was always waiting for the axe to fall, the handle of her bedroom door to turn.

It was as she walked home from school in the pouring rain on the last day of the summer term, with the whole of her average life in front of her and not a clue what to do with it, that Veronique realised her mistake. Her father's sudden death had given her the perfect opportunity to rid herself of René. But when her big chance presented itself, she had thrown it away.

If she'd only told the *gendarme* what she knew, the truth about what happened then maybe they would have investigated her father's death and René would be in jail. And this made her so angry, with herself, life, everything. Her mama once said that not everyone got what they deserved, and this was definitely true because Mama certainly did not deserve Papa or the death she'd suffered. He, on the other hand, had been dealt the right card when he ended up face down swallowing shit.

Would Veronique get what she deserved? This thought caused her hours of worry because she fully expected to be punished by God for the things she'd done, the ones René told her to, acts that the nuns had said were a mortal sin. All she could do was accept her fate because there was no turning back the clock and what was done was done. Therefore, until she met her maker, Veronique decided she had to make the most of what life dealt her, within her capabilities and using whatever resources she had. Sins aside, she deserved a better life and somehow, she was going to get it.

Her opportunity came a few nights later when René brought up the subject of the farm. He'd bought steak, one each, a sure sign that he wanted something, and her stomach turned.

They were eating, each mouthful hard to swallow but she dared not waste it. He was drinking too much; she was waiting for the axe to fall when René just came out with it. 'It's time we talked about the future and the farm and what to do with you. Now you've left school you need a job.'

Veronique's heart thudded and her skin crawled while her mind was working overtime. 'Yes, I know. I will start looking on Monday.'

When René ignored her comment, it didn't bode well. Then he surprised her. 'I think we should sell this stinking place and buy somewhere in town, together. The English can't get enough of France and shitholes like this are being snapped up all over the place. Nobody else wants a pig farm and I certainly don't so, what do you think?'

In that second, Veronique experienced something new – having a sense of power – so for the first time in her life she decided to stand up to René and if she played her cards right, she was going to get what she deserved. 'But what if I don't want to sell? You can't make me.'

René looked like someone had slapped him, but he kept his temper, she saw him suck it and then his voice took on a conciliatory tone. 'No, I can't. But surely you don't want to stay here? Look, we won't get that much for it, but we can sell the pigs and if we pool our money at least we will have a decent roof over our heads. Otherwise, we will be in limbo because one can't sell without the other. You know how it goes.'

Veronique fell silent, her hands were shaking so badly that she had to stuff them between her knees, but she held her nerve, thinking, thinking, about her future. Should she agree to sell? She could escape with her share of the money, go away and start somewhere new. Then the voice of Sister Mary Marguerite reminded her of what happened to young girls who ran away to the city and Veronique's inner rebel instantly quailed. She thought of her mama and what she would have told her to do... and then an idea, so bright it shone and brought strength to her soul and voice.

'No, I do not want to stay here but I do not want to live in Cholet either. And I want to work in a shop, like Mama did, but not a boulangerie, one that sells gifts, pretty things that people buy for happy occasions and have them wrapped in beautiful paper.' Where it all came from she did not know, maybe in a recess of her mind, behind a door marked *Forbidden Dreams*.

For a moment René looked like he was going to start laughing but instead he placed his cutlery on his plate, sat back in his chair and tapped the fingers of his left hand on the table. The right was occupied with his glass of wine which he swigged. Alcohol could send René either way and tonight it made him mellow. 'A shop? Ah, that is interesting and very specific too. Have you anywhere in mind?'

Not sure if he was toying with her Veronique felt her cheeks colour but she did not back down. 'Maybe Châteaubriant. It is a busy town with lots of summer tourists, or Angers, anywhere but here in Cholet.'

René picked up his fork and speared a piece of meat and before he took a mouthful pronounced judgement. 'I think I have an idea which will benefit both of us. Leave it with me. Now eat. Your food is going cold.'

His acquiescence didn't comfort Veronique, in fact it had been too easy so rather than be made a fool of, she pushed the point. It was now or never. 'And there is one more thing, René.'

With an irritated sigh and a look to match, he asked, 'What?'

'If I agree to sell the farm, from now on, if you want anything, you get it yourself. Do not ask me to help you. Is that a deal? Do I have your word?' Beneath the table her legs shook, and she hoped the tremor wouldn't reach her body because he would like that. Forcing her spine and arms to remain rigid she waited.

When René gave a curt nod, his words were so unexpected she had to hold in a gasp. 'It's a deal. Now eat. Don't waste good food.'

Doing as she was told Veronique picked up her knife and fork and with a bowed head, not in deference but so she could hide the tears of relief, she began to eat her meal, the first free dinner in a long while.

It turned out that Angers was too pricey, so they settled for Châteaubriant where, with the proceeds of the farm, Veronique and René bought a run-down shop close to the centre. There was living accommodation above, two bedrooms, *salon,* tiny kitchen and a very disgusting bathroom. With the pig money, they made the property habitable and presentable and stocked the front of the shop with all the things on Veronique's wish list while in the storeroom at the back, René oversaw his own little empire, filling their father's casket with rolls of cash.

She wasn't surprised that his compliance came at a cost. However, this time she wasn't a commodity, the shop was. The perfect front, a place to launder money, a home, a respectable face for all to see as she wrapped gifts in beautiful tissue and paper and smiled at the tourists.

Five years it lasted, her happiness. René kept to his part of the bargain, and he even seemed nicer, not kind, more like amiable and that was enough. He got on with whatever his 'businesses' entailed and soon, he had found himself another place to live, leaving Veronique queen of her own little palace. He popped back now and then, unannounced and uninvited, bringing her a gift, a new microwave or an envelope of cash so she could treat herself but for the most part he let her be. He also took the casket and for that, more than the extras, she was glad.

And then one Wednesday, market day, twenty-two-year-old Veronique had left her assistant, Bernadette, in charge while she nipped out to buy some lunch and met a very good-looking guy in the queue for bread. His name was Alain.

Yes, she thought it was fate, the parallel between her mama's life and hers, but Veronique was convinced that the man she met at the market would be nothing like her papa. She was right. Alain was a decent person. She met his family; they were decent too. And they seemed to like her, welcome her into the fold. He had a good job driving milk containers and treated her with respect and kindness. He was so handsome, even more than Johnny Hallyday with the same sun-streaked hair and ice-blue eyes. They made a beautiful couple, and he was devoted to her, and she to him.

René wasn't keen, said he didn't trust him. Apparently, he was too good to be true so she should tread carefully because men were only after one thing. At this she'd rolled her eyes. She was doing well, had her own business and home; she was a good catch. She knew René was jealous so smothered her thoughts and his words that might poison her brain because nothing was going to ruin what she had with Alain.

She was telling one of her customers about the holiday they were taking to La Rochelle and that the shop would be closed for a week. René was in the storeroom behind when the woman, one of her regulars who came in for gifts for her very large family, passed a comment that made Veronique's heart sing.

Wiggling the third finger of her wedding hand, the lady winked and said, 'I think that soon we will be seeing a shiny ring on your finger, Veronique. Mark my words, you will be a madame before we know it.' Taking her purchase, she then made her way to the door, teasing as she left the shop. 'But do not let him whisk you away. Hold onto your independence because I like coming here for my gifts, so be your own woman and put him in order before you say yes.'

Veronique laughed and waved and promised to take her advice then for the rest of the day daydreamed about a white wedding and a life with Alain, and wondered if he really was going to propose while they were on holiday. It was the longest week, waiting to turn the sign on the shop to 'closed' and a sleepless night as she excitedly counted the hours until morning when Alain would be there to collect her.

All day she waited, on the window seat, never taking her eyes off the street below, willing him to appear. She was ready to go. She'd worn her best dress and new stockings, had her hair done at the salon and swept high, like an ash-blonde Audrey Hepburn. Her suitcase was packed, her shoes on the floor by her side. All she had to do was slip them on, grab her bags and coat, and go to Alain. He never came.

When she phoned his parents' home, they said they hadn't seen him. He'd not been to visit them for days and didn't answer his phone. Or were they lying? But why? She tried the company where he worked and they thought he'd left, didn't show up one day. They couldn't help, another dead end. So she went to his home, a tiny flat where the woman across the way confirmed he'd moved out. 'Gone,' she said, 'in a click of the finger, just like that.'

And then the postcard arrived, from Spain and on the back were handwritten words that were like a knife through her heart.

I have met someone new. I am sorry. Forget me. It is over. A

She had never experienced loss, not like this. It was different to when Mama went because Veronique had been happy when the angels took her away from the pain. The nurse had been right and at the funeral Veronique had remembered a poem. It said that truly loving someone meant letting them go, even when you wanted them to come back more than anything in the whole world. She had been glad to let Mama go. But losing Alain was like having her heart ripped out and, in its place, a raw bleeding gaping hole that was so painful the only way to ease it was to sleep.

René was furious that Alain had treated her so badly and said that if he ever saw him again, he would throw his body in a wood shredder like the farmers do with dead animals. His words brought no comfort so instead, he brought her pills to make the days easier and the nights as black as the pit inside her chest. How she welcomed the brown bottles that appeared by her bedside, as if by magic. They were her friend, and at last so was René but even he couldn't stop the sickness that came in the mornings and lasted most of the day, or halt the swell of her belly once Veronique realised she was expecting a baby. Or so she thought.

They were in the flat above the shop and René was pacing, determined to make Veronique decide. 'You can't keep it... Why would you want to have a child by a man who deserted you? And what would people think? You are respected, we are respected, finally getting somewhere. You and I are going places and you don't want to be hindered by a brat. Look at this place, remember the hovel it used to be. Can you not see this was just the start and we can have more of this?'

René was right, as usual. He had never trusted or liked Alain, and yes, the little flat was filled with new things, good quality furniture, a fancy television, the best cooker in the store, plush carpets throughout but possessions meant nothing, not when your heart was broken.

'Please René, don't be cruel, I can't bear it right now and what do you mean, "getting somewhere"? Yes, we have nice things, we are doing okay, and I am grateful.' Veronique flopped onto the sofa and kicked off her shoes, weary already, willing the night to come soon.

'I told you, do you not listen? This–' he waved his hands in a gesture that indicated their home and shop, 'has always been a stepping stone, a front, you know that. But I am making progress elsewhere and now, I have bigger fish on the hook just prime for reeling in.'

Veronique yawned and feigned interest because at least it was drawing attention away from the reason her trousers felt too tight. 'What fish? What are you talking about, René?'

'The details do not matter, just know that I have made some very lucrative deals and contacts in Nantes and recently closer to home, in Cholet. I'm telling you, Veronique, I am going to be rich, and I'll take you along for the ride but not with a baby hanging round your neck, so you have to decide what you are going to do. It is all arranged, and you can get it done tomorrow. I will pay for it. Otherwise, you are on your own.'

Veronique ignored his threat and couldn't hide her irritation when she heard the word *Cholet*, and she tutted loudly. 'What is it with that place and you? I thought we left it behind when we came here. Just forget about it. I hate it, you know that.'

When René slammed his hand on the table it rattled the ashtray and the glass of brandy, making Veronique pay attention. 'Because one day, I will take back what was ours and make those who hung our grandfather pay. It was because of them we lived like we did, had a father like Denis. And in the meantime, I will make as much money as I can out of the descendants of those who betrayed our family. Even that lot in Cholet who watched while our grandfather was hung, and they hacked our grandmother's hair. I will buy their useless farms and decrepit homes for a pittance and sell them to stupid English people who see beauty in that which I despise. And I will buy their land, build on it and slowly I will become the most powerful man in Cholet. Do you understand, Veronique? I will not stop until I am back on top, and in the Mairie where the Saber name belongs.'

She had heard his plans before and passed them off as drunken ramblings, but in the cold light of day she realised he meant every word. He was obsessed, bitter and vengeful. A potent combination. For a while she'd believed the beast had been tamed but he was evolving, she had seen it with her own eyes but been too in love and wrapped up with Alain to pay heed. Which was why she had to think, tread warily, keep René calm.

'Yes, I understand that you have my best interests at heart but for now please, let me sleep. I need to think, and I can't when you are shouting. I need to take one of my pills and rest. Then we will talk later.' Standing, she saw him nod his silent permission and without another word he left, and she breathed relief.

After taking two of her saviours, then dragging off her trousers and jumper she flopped onto the bed and pulled the covers over her body. Still, it tormented her, even on the edge of oblivion, the nagging voice that told her she had missed two chances to escape René, the brother who had rented her out. So many times, she had gone over it in her head, found reasons to excuse his behaviour, see some love buried in his actions, allowing herself to almost forgive if not entirely forget.

They had been unfortunate to be landed with a father like theirs, and René had suffered too. In his desperation and irritation at his circumstances, he found a way to get the things he craved, the small pleasures denied through poverty. A bicycle, a nice jacket, some new shoes, a van that would allow him to escape the farm and scrape a new life.

And he could have abandoned her when they sold the farm.

He could have cast her aside and let her flounder, a naïve sixteen-year-old alone in the world but instead he had made her dream come true, found the shop, a home. In the end, after taking it away, he'd given back her respectability.

'How many other seventeen-year-olds can say they own their own shop, eh, Veronique?' She could hear his voice, on the day he had passed her the key to the shop and allowed her to open the door. And on the first day of trading how she'd wished for Sister Mary Marguerite to see her behind the counter surrounded by beautiful things. She would say, 'What can a girl like me help you with today?'

René had given her all that, had showed her how to lift her head high and shake off the past and she should have listened to him about Alain. Resting her palm on her stomach, scrunching her body into a ball, Veronique imagined a life with a baby. One who would have no father, be the child of a mother who people would whisper about; a mother who had proved the nuns right about *girls like her*. When she felt the blanket of sadness being drawn over her body, starting at her feet and slowly reaching her mind, Veronique waited patiently for the darkness of sleep to take her away from the horror of what she knew she had to do the following day. She would have one more night with the baby that was curled inside her, and then it would be gone.

Two months later, Veronique and René were in his car, she was wearing the new outfit he'd given her money to buy with the instructions to make sure it was classy, from a good shop, because they needed to make an impression. He'd said it was time she stopped moping. 'Get your hair and nails done. Come with me to a dinner party. We will have some fun, mix with my new acquaintances and it will give me a chance to show off my beautiful sister.'

Veronique still needed the pills to get her through the night but during the day, if she kept busy and focused on her customers she managed to force away thoughts of everything that was missing from her life. As they rounded a bend, René glanced over and smiled. Veronique basked in the glow of his approval. It felt good; life was bearable. And since Alain, he had treated her differently, more as an equal, someone he actually liked, asking for her opinion on properties he'd seen. They even laughed together. Finally, Veronique saw a glimmer, a chink in the grey fog, some brightness on the horizon.

'So, tell me where we are going? You have been very secretive about your new friend.' They were approaching the outskirts of Cholet and Veronique hoped that they would follow the road on to Angers but when René took the turning towards the town, her heart sank.

'Don't worry, we're not going to go anywhere near our old place, so take that look off your face. Tonight, dear sister, we are dining with the nearest thing we French have to royalty and *voilà*, we have arrived, in more ways than one.' René turned right and would have heard Veronique's gasp when they passed through the enormous gates of Chateau de Chevalier.

'Oh my, René. How on earth have you managed this and why would you want to dine here, with these people? You hate them. And surely they know your name, that we are Sabers.' Veronique's panic was borne from her lack of confidence and if she had a driving licence she would have stolen René's car and zoomed straight back up the drive but instead, she had to listen to his laughter.

'My dear sister, have faith in your brother and confidence in yourself. Yes, there is history between the Bombelles and the Sabers but while this man will never forget, the one inside is the kind who will sell his soul at the poker table, who has no concept of loyalty or even how his snobbery and entitlement blinker him to his own foolishness. He is arrogant, a chancer, handsome and so very vain with it. Unfaithful to his beautiful wife, utterly fickle and a terrible businessman and ripe for the picking.'

As René's words washed over her, rather than be nervous about meeting their host she was intrigued. He sounded like a character in a film, one that everyone was supposed to hate but all the ladies loved. Finally, she was about to meet the latest member of the Bombelle family, the nemesis that had dogged the Saber family for half a century. So once she had smoothed down her ruby-red dress and checked her make-up in the mirror, Veronique turned to face her brother and smiled. 'Well, what are we waiting for? Let's go and enjoy our dinner because, dear brother, I am hungry.'

A moment passed between them and after receiving a curt nod and a smile, one that reached René's eyes, she unbuckled her belt and got out of the car. Taking her brother's arm, Veronique went inside to meet Hugo Bombelle, le Duc de Chevalier.

17

MAC

Fabienne lay by his side and traced the lines of his biceps through his skin. He had no idea if, as she led him up the stairs, she was planning what had just happened, but once inside her bedroom it had felt so natural that he didn't want to ruin the moment by analysing it.

The bedroom windows were wide open, and he welcomed the breeze that billowed the voile and cooled their skin. Fabienne was on top of the sheets, he partially covered by a thin layer of cotton, and he smiled, remembering how she was always more comfortable with her nakedness than he. *Comfortable.* He liked that word because that was how he'd felt since the second he'd clapped eyes on her the day before and this was the same, as though they had never been apart. Her teasing voice cut through his thoughts, and he kissed the top of her head as she spoke.

'Why have you gone so skinny? You have always been slim, and I can see you keep fit but there is almost nothing left of you. I need to fatten you up, and make sure you don't run out of energy.' She lifted herself onto her elbow and waited for his reply which was easy.

'That is the result of months of worry and thinking I was going out of my mind, oh and losing every penny I had to a con artist.' Mac really didn't want to talk about all that, but he also didn't want her thinking he had worms, or an eating disorder.

'Ah, I see. Will you be able to get your money back? You didn't say.' Fabienne looked concerned.

'No, I'll not see that again. Even though it's being investigated by the police, as far as the bank is concerned I allowed someone else access to my online accounts and worse, left my banking details and secure key unprotected. I'm appealing but I doubt they'll change their minds.'

'It is awful. That you lost your savings – but at least you have a home here, and La Fleurie is so beautiful, a perfect picturesque cottage that just needs to be brought into the modern day. We must make some plans for it, and I need to check it out, make sure you haven't got any valuable antiques hiding in corners. Knowing you, you will take them all to the *déchetterie* and throw something valuable over the edge.' Fabienne stood and padded over to the door and unhooked her robe then wrapped it around her body. 'Two minutes, I need to use the bathroom.'

While he waited for her to return Mac's brain whirred. He had to tell her he was selling, get it over with otherwise she might read too much into what had just happened, think he was staying or would be a frequent visitor to Cholet. God, what had he done? He would explain, the second she came back and hearing the chain flush in the room next door, Mac realised he had about three to go.

When she returned, Fabienne took up position on the bed, her short dark hair ruffled, her suntanned face bare of make-up and she reminded him of a pixie, the ones in a book at the cottage, the kind he always imagined lived in the woods.

She flicked his arm with her finger and thumb. 'What are

you thinking about? You do that a lot, wander off, like you have stuff on your mind, and I need to know what is going on in your head. You have sad eyes, Mac and I hate that. I want to make you happy, like you used to be.'

Mac had no idea how she managed to read him so well and as he took her hands in his, he could see from the look on her face that she'd guessed something was wrong.

'Fabienne, I need to be honest with you about something. I was going to tell Antoinette and I've been trying to pluck up the courage to tell you. The thing is...'

When she placed her fingers over his lips and smiled, Mac was silenced, made to listen instead. 'You have come back to say goodbye to La Fleurie and put it up for sale. Yes, I know. You forget that this is a small town and who Antoinette is dating, and Joel's cousin works for the *notaire*. Remember the young woman who booked an appointment to value the house.' When she freed his lips, Mac tried to speak until her raised eyebrow and finger told him she hadn't finished.

'And I understand why you wish to redeem your stolen money, but I also think you would be incredibly foolish to rush into such a huge decision. Instead, you need time to think things through and discover your options, and spend the rest of the summer with me, in bed, making love. See, that seems like a much better plan already.'

When she raised her palms to the ceiling and shrugged her shoulders, her smug expression made him smile and pull her to him, the weight of their bodies falling onto the mattress where they lay. She waited while he thought.

Fabienne had made it all sound so easy, given him a get-out clause that would save him from making one of the toughest decisions of his life. And she wasn't even mad with him for holding back, keeping his motive for returning to himself and that was kind of special. She was special, but he'd always known that, deep down.

'I can't believe you knew... Actually that's wrong; I can't believe that I didn't realise that half of Cholet would know my plans. See, I've been away too long and let the city poison my brain as well as my lungs. But I'm going to need money soon. I am literally skint so we'd better get thinking about how I can keep the cottage. Oh and at the same time we need to save this place so no mean feat.' Even if he couldn't see her face, he knew she was smiling. When she pulled away and sat, he saw he was right.

'So, you'll stay, and we will fight the fight together, like the brave and loyal chevaliers who once guarded the chateau?'

Mac nodded and laughed. 'Yes, you crazy woman, we will be like the chevaliers and give it our best shot, or sword or bow and arrow. What have we got to lose? Apart from a few more kilos if I can't buy food or pay the bills but let's be positive, best foot forward and all that.'

'Yes, that, whatever it means. But do not worry about food. Antoinette has been preparing for a famine and we have two freezers full of the stuff, a vegetable patch that is heaving with produce and best of all, my father's *cave* that bizarrely is stocked with wine. Papa always did get his own priorities right, so, if we have to dig in, we won't starve or die of thirst. That I can promise.'

Mac wrapped his fingers around hers. 'I love how you make everything seem so easy and thank you for not hating me.'

Fabienne looked confused. 'Why would I hate you? That is the opposite of how I feel.'

A moment passed between them, a statement made and a question unasked, until Mac filled the gap. 'Because you are doing everything in your power to save your home and I'm thinking of selling La Fleurie. Then earlier, when you were telling me how you feel when you touch the things around this place, it was killing me inside. My grandparents' house is full of stuff they touched or collected and loved. I can still feel their presence through all their bits and bobs, like they are willing me to change my mind and if that wasn't enough, since I arrived in France all these memories have come flooding back. With every word you said, hearing the passion in your voice, I felt more and more like a traitor and that I was letting them down badly.'

Fabienne jiggled his hand, as if to shake some sense into him. 'No, you are not. You are a guy who has been through a bad time, lost his savings and if I must say, his pride and you are not a bad person for wanting to get that back. Yes, selling the cottage is a solution but from what you have just told me, and knowing you like I do, I think that if you rush you will regret it so take your time and let me help you find an alternative. At least we can say we tried, okay?'

'Okay, it's a deal.' Never had Mac felt more relieved to be thrown a lifeline, apart from when his mother had signed over La Fleurie to him but even then, a part of him screamed not to let it go.

Then, a thought occurred. 'I've just realised that before you lured me up here on false pretences then more or less threw me on the bed and ravished me, you were going to show me something. Or was that what you were getting at all along?'

Fabienne threw her head back and laughed. 'Half and half and anyway, I was only following Antoinette's orders – and she was right: having sex was just what I needed.'

'Oh my God, so now you are throwing men into bed on the strict orders of our mad friend? I'm totally insulted and when did she tell you this? You two are totally weird, you know that don't you?'

Fabienne had tears, and more when she confessed through

her laughter. 'She'd stuck her instructions on the wine bottle in the fridge and who am I to disobey?'

'Well in that case, I think it's my turn to do the ravishing, just to balance the books and save my manly pride.' And with that, he dragged the sheets over their heads, Fabienne gave a dramatic scream and then succumbed to her skinny lover's advances.

They had moved from the bed that looked like wild animals had rampaged on it, to the carpet and were seated beside a box that contained letters wrapped in a jumper. It smelled of Diorissimo that according to Fabienne was her mama's signature scent.

'I spray it on the wool now and then so that when I open the box or hold it close, she is there. I bought another bottle when the one in her bedroom dried out because in my dreams, when she talks to me or kisses me goodnight, that is what I can smell. She is near me once more.'

Mac had never heard anything so sad and was lost for words so instead he took the jumper from Fabienne and held it to his face and inhaled the essence of her mother, before passing it back as he listened to her story.

'These letters are correspondence between my mama and Mémère, written over a period that was very difficult for them both. I know every word and line, and I can feel it here.' She brought both her hands to her heart. 'When I read the words between a mother and a daughter, I know that one is suffering, the other is unable to help apart from be there, offer support and understanding. And even though I am so glad they had one another it somehow reminds me of what I missed. All the times since Mama and Mémère died when I have wanted to ask them a question, hear words of reassurance, tell them some wonderful news or know I had someone's arms to run to. Thank goodness I had Antoinette because without her, I would have been so alone.'

All Mac could think was that he wished he'd known, been there, and more than anything not let her down. All he could do now was listen so lowered his voice, respecting such a poignant moment. 'I'm sorry, Fabienne, that you felt like that. I truly am.'

At this she brightened. 'Hey, I survived, don't worry. So, to my mother's story and what I discovered in the letters. The rest, my mémère filled in once I'd read them.'

18

PALOMA

**Angers
1999**

She had known for a while that Hugo was unfaithful and that his so-called business meetings in Paris were an excuse to meet his mistress, or mistresses. She had no idea for sure how many there were and she had begun not to care. And while it killed her inside, and she hated him for it, Paloma put her children first and his infidelity to one side, focusing her attention on giving them a happy home at Chevalier.

He knew, she suspected, from the subtle sarcasm in her words when he headed off, briefcase in hand, barely able to kiss his children goodbye in his eagerness to escape. Paloma had given him tacit permission to do what he wanted in Paris, as long as Chevalier was respected as their family home, a place never to be sullied by his behaviour.

Paloma's mother had urged her to divorce him. He was a scoundrel who was never good enough for her daughter and a terrible role model for her grandchildren. Fabienne was coming up to four while Baptiste had just turned two and soon they would start to pick up on things. However, Paloma was adamant that as long as Hugo obeyed the rules and her children were happy, she could manage, for a while longer, until she decided what to do.

Paloma had returned to her parents' home in Angers for a family party to celebrate her father's birthday. Hugo remained at Chevalier, making vague excuses that were welcomed by Paloma who knew he wouldn't be missed, especially by her mother.

Fabienne was beyond excited to stay the weekend with her grandparents and see all her cousins on the Sunday for the celebration. She had a new party dress and patent pink shoes and didn't stop talking about it for days before. As they'd left the chateau that morning, Paloma noticed that their housekeeper had sorted the mail into two piles. Not having time to read them, she grabbed the envelopes bearing her name and stuffed them in her handbag, leaving those for Hugo where they were.

It wasn't until the following afternoon, as she and her mother sat by the fire and Fabienne and Baptiste played with their toys, that Paloma decided to read the letters and as she sorted through them, one envelope in particular caught her attention.

When Paloma removed the contents of the letter and pulled out the photographs inside, her hands began to shake and as she stood, whatever rage had taken over them swept through her body.

'My darling, what is wrong? What is it? Why are you shaking?' Paloma's mother was soon by her side but before she could see the photographs, her daughter flew into a rage and tore them to pieces, which she threw into the fire. Then she stood and watched them burn, tears coursing down her cheeks.

When finally, she spoke, Paloma's words were barely audible but laced with such anger and hatred that for a second mother didn't recognise daughter. 'How dare he! How dare he take his whores to our home... he has gone too far this time... how dare he insult me this way... under the noses of our staff... everyone will know, Mama. Everyone will be laughing at me.'

Her mother did her best to placate Paloma but never had she seen her daughter in such a rage, such a state and her next words chilled her bones. The scene that played out in the *salon* was one that a distraught mother and grandmother would go over a million times in the future, where she would ask herself if she could have done more to prevent a tragedy from unfolding.

'Come, Fabienne, Baptiste, we are going home. Quickly, get your shoes and coats, we must leave immediately.' Paloma went to the table where Fabienne was colouring and grabbed her hand and tried to hurry her along and when she resisted, all hell broke loose.

'No, Mama. It is Grandpère's party tomorrow and I want to stay.'

'Fabienne, do as you are told. NOW!' When Paloma raised her voice, so loud and angry it made everyone in the room jump, both children began to cry and when she pulled at her daughter's hand Fabienne screamed and cried the loudest, protesting as her feet dug into the carpet, resisting her mother's force.

'No, I am not going, you cannot make me, Mama. I hate you, Mama, I hate you.'

When Paloma let go of her daughter, shocked by such vehement words, she felt the hands of her own mother on her arm and for a second listened to common sense.

'Paloma, please, you are upset and distressing the children. You need to calm down, and you need a moment to think this through. So sit. No good will come of taking the children home, especially when you are in this state.' The words fell on deaf ears.

'Then I will go alone, catch him in the act because I bet you any money, the second we left, that whore was in his bed. Well, he is in for a shock. Mama, look after the children and I will ring you when I have kicked that man out of our home. I have had enough.' But when she turned to leave, Baptiste, who had been playing with his train set on the floor and was already in floods of tears, scrambled to his feet and grabbed his mother's legs and as much as Paloma tried to pry him away, he held on tight, screaming for her not to leave him.

At the end of her tether, while her mother tried to placate Baptiste and Fabienne who had hidden behind the sofa out of reach, Paloma made a decision that many would regret forever. Picking up Baptiste, she held him to her and comforted him and said it was okay, he could go too. Without saying goodbye to her daughter who refused to come out from her hiding place, Paloma grabbed her handbag and ignoring the impassioned pleas of her mother, raced from the room and the house.

The last time her mother saw her daughter and grandson, it was as one bundled the other into his car seat and then sped off, up the drive and out of sight. Hours later, she received a knock on the door and as soon as she saw the *gendarmes* on the steps, she knew something terrible had happened. And while Fabienne slept upstairs, dreaming of a party and cake and her new shoes, downstairs her grandparents listened in shock to gentle words of the *gendarme*. He explained about the fatal accident, that had occurred only metres from the gates of Chevalier and that sadly, both occupants of the car were dead. From that day on, there was only one person everyone blamed for the death of their beautiful Paloma and petit-Baptiste. Hugo Bombelle.

The story told, Mac watched as Fabienne folded the jumper around the letters and then placed them back in the box. There was one big question on his mind. 'Does your dad know that you have these letters and that you know about his affairs?'

Fabienne shook her head as she closed the lid on the box and reached over, putting it back inside the wardrobe before closing the door. 'No, I have never told anyone. After Mama died, I spent my time between here and my grandparents' home and everyone was very careful to protect me from the truth and hide the rift that was even bigger than before. I knew that they hated my father – any fool would have seen that – but I wasn't keen on him either, so I presumed they saw what I did. A cold man who didn't have any time for his remaining child.'

'Were you glad you found out, even though it would have been a massive shock when your grandma told you the truth? I remember the rage I felt when I found out what my dad was really like and how long it took to fade, but at the same time knowing the truth set me free because I didn't have to pretend to like him anymore.'

Fabienne leant against the wardrobe door and stretched her legs, smiling when Mac changed position and sat beside her, taking her hand in his as he listened. 'Oh yes. It was a terrible shock but as I pieced together the letters I was able to capture a time in my mother's life, see it clearly and it bound me to her even more. As a woman, I was able to understand it more than if I'd been a child and make sense of everything my grandmother told me because it haunted me for years.'

'So, you didn't remember her leaving with Baptiste?'

Fabienne rested her head against Mac's arm as she spoke. 'Yes, I remembered. I would have nightmares about it, the scene in the *salon* when I told my mother I hated her and refused to come from behind the *canapé* to say goodbye. Those were the last words I ever said to my beautiful Mama, and I could not make it right, so I blocked it out of my life, but not my dreams.'

Fabienne was crying so Mac pulled her close and held her while she sobbed and when she stopped, he let her talk. 'I know she will have forgiven me because that's what mothers do. Mémère told me that. After she told me the truth, I was so upset about it all, but most of all about the way I had behaved so Mémère reassured me. She said she'd forgiven Mama for not listening that day, for taking Baptiste with her and for getting killed but for a long while she'd been so angry with everyone and everything. It helped me, her honesty, and allowed me to forgive my four-year-old self.'

'And what about your dad, did you forgive him?' Mac knew he wouldn't have been able to, never in a million years and when she answered he could hear the anger in Fabienne's voice.

'No, never, and neither could Mémère or Grandpère. All Mama's family hate Papa and I don't blame them.' She brushed her tears away in an angry motion.

'Does he know you know?'

'I honestly don't know, and I don't care, just like he won't care either. Perhaps he suspects Mémère told me things, but he never had the decency to sit down with me and have an adult conversation. He swept it under the carpet, just like he swept me off to school as soon as he could. At the time I found out, I was getting ready to go to university and I couldn't wait to be away, and whenever I returned, we were even more like strangers.'

Mac stroked her arm as he spoke, wanting her to know that he understood the 'rubbish dad' thing. 'I do get it, what it's like to have a distant parent because my dad was the same and I have to really dredge my memory to think of something positive, but I was lucky, I had my mum and she made up for what he lacked. Now, I just think of my dad as this bloke who used to live with us, and he might as well be a stranger. That might sound harsh but it's true.'

'I knew you'd understand. That is the sum total of my relationship with Papa, we are strangers and, in a way, I'm glad I've never given him the opportunity to lie, or say my grandparents are liars, or even say something bad about Mama. I prefer not to speak of it, which is why I have never discussed it with Antoinette, only you. And let's face it, if he was entertaining women here, half of Cholet will have known about it and there's not a shred of gossip that Antoinette's great-grandmother does not know.'

Mac knew exactly what it felt like to be gossiped about, pitied and no doubt laughed at behind his back so didn't blame Fabienne one bit for wanting to move on, even if it was only publicly. One more question remained, and he had to ask it. 'Did the police ever find out what happened that night to cause the crash?'

'No. The *gendarmes* came straight here to tell Papa. He was upstairs, asleep. He'd given the housekeeper and cook the weekend off, saying he was quite able to look after himself. I suspect that it was so he could entertain his mistress in private but the *gendarmes* said he appeared to be by himself – no other vehicles in the drive – so maybe he'd also given his mistress the night off. We will never know.'

'It's awful though, that your mum was so close to home when it happened.' Mac could almost picture it, the bend just before the road straightened out and then a couple of hundred metres on to the gates of Chevalier.

'I know. They say she was driving too fast and the skid marks on the road indicate that she swerved and braked. Maybe it was to avoid a deer, or another car but if it was, nobody ever owned up. They wouldn't, would they?'

It was at that moment, as Mac shuddered at a scene from the past, they heard the sound of a car in the present as it came up the drive and then the toot of a horn, signalling Antoinette's return.

'Oh-oh, here's trouble. I hope you are prepared for her cheeky comments and embarrassing questions? We won't get away with this, you know.' Fabienne was already standing. 'I'm going to take a shower before I face the inquisition... Would you like to share?'

Taking her hand, Mac hauled himself off the floor and followed her to the bathroom. Ignoring the beady eyes of her ancestors who watched them from the walls, he closed the door on the ghosts of the past and as he stepped into the steaming shower and took Fabienne in his arms, held onto the future and allowed his troubles to be washed away.

19

VERONIQUE

She had been sat on a bench opposite the children's play park for over two hours, pretending to read a book she didn't really understand because it was in English – *Every Little Breath* by someone called Keri Beevis. It wasn't even hers. She'd plucked it from the shelf at the reading garden as she passed by and fully intended replacing it on her way home. The title was ironic, though, because for the last twenty-four hours the tightness in her chest was making every little breath almost impossible, so bad she thought she might die.

That's why she had summoned enough strength to get dressed, covering her unwashed body with the first thing she dragged from the armoire, her greasy hair with a straw hat, her hollow eyes with sunglasses before she passed Hugo reading his paper and left the apartment without a word.

The need for fresh air and to be away from her husband was as overwhelming as the anxiety that was eating her alive just as watching mothers with their babies was killing her slowly, with every unhealthy minute she sat and stared at them.

It wasn't the first time she'd done this, and it probably wouldn't be the last because Veronique knew exactly why she tormented herself. It was punishment. For her part in the deaths of one baby, one child, and one mother. It was also a way to vent the anger that swelled inside, hating on the woman who had spent the last ten minutes looking at her phone screen, ignoring the little girl who kept trying to show her the sandcastle she'd made. Or the mother who had been chatting to her friend and not seen her child's sun hat had fallen off, leaving its head exposed to the afternoon sun.

Veronique felt like going over there and giving them both a piece of her mind but resisted, accepting that once she unleashed the rage it might result in arrest. That's how much she hated those women right now, just like she hated herself.

Innocence. That was what she saw on the faces of the little ones who played in the park, and she soaked up their joy of such simple pleasures like picking buttercups, or sand running through their fingers, and swinging higher and higher, legs flapping as they tried to touch the sky. She must have been like that once, before her innocence was stolen. René must have been good too. It could have all been so different had they been born to someone and somewhere else.

She watched as a boy, maybe four years old, held the hand of his brother, a toddler, as they made their way to the sandpit and a rare flashback made Veronique's eyes sting with tears. She and René had laughed; there were glimmers of the sun through the leaves on the trees above her head, warming her face, shining light on a scene from the past. A sunny Sunday after mass and they'd somehow escaped the farm to run free in the greener fresher fields, darting through curtains of corn, laughing with her brother, playing hide and seek.

They had come to the orchards on the edge of Cholet where she and René climbed an apple tree, shaking the boughs to release the fruit, squealing with delight when the rosy reds thudded to the floor. René, to her right, had tried to climb to a higher bough but lost his footing and slipped and as his body tipped, she saw the fear on his face, eyes wide, the whites as big as the moon and his mouth shaped like an O. Instinctively, Veronique reached out her hand, gripping a branch with her other to steady herself. René only just managed to grasp on, his palm sweaty against hers as he managed to get a foothold and heave himself back up, his relief apparent.

She had been so happy to have saved her big brother, but her joy was quickly turned to hurt when he didn't thank her and seemed cross that he had made a mistake and needed her help. It had been a good day until that moment, when a cloud crossed the sun and cast a shadow on her brother's face. He took control, said they had to go home but not before telling her to collect the apples, shouting if she dropped one, calling her stupid and making her cry. Just like the little boy was doing, in the sandpit on the other side of the fence.

Veronique left the past behind to watch the present unfold and a mother who was berating the older child who had flicked sand in his brother's face. The wails and shouting went through Veronique like a saw through wood, slicing through the calm of another sunny day.

Turning the page of her book, keeping up yet another pretence, Veronique's nerves were further grated by the roar of an engine somewhere on the road beyond the park, some flash millionaire in his Ferrari showing off. That was another thing she hated, men and their obsession with fast, flashy cars and it was one of the reasons she had so enjoyed getting rid of Hugo's. The other went a lot deeper.

Never had she been more shocked, when she returned to Chevalier with Hugo as his wife and saw the vintage Vega parked in the garage. The sight of it rocked her to the core, knowing that he had kept it after what happened. *How could he?*

Again, behind her, another roar of the engine that dragged her mind further into the past, a place she was desperate to avoid because the present was bad enough. But as she observed from behind the safety of her sunglasses, and cursed the woman offering her son one of those dreadful blue, sugary drinks, she allowed the demons in. What the hell. They were everywhere anyway, in her home, in the park, in her past.

20

HUGO AND VERONIQUE

**Chateau de Chevalier
October 1999**

She had realised straight away what René was up to. He'd played his hand well, introducing his stunning sister to the scurrilous Duc and it hadn't taken much effort on Veronique's part to get him into bed. She knew it was wrong, but she didn't care, not anymore. She needed to fill the gaps Alain had left behind and if that meant having fun with a wealthy man who adored his young lover, then so be it. René's instructions were clear. Keep Hugo sweet and find out as much as she could so that he could capitalise on the information as and when he needed.

Veronique embraced it all, the thrill of an illicit affair, the gifts Hugo regularly bestowed, dining at the best restaurants in Nantes, often with René in tow so they avoided suspicion. But the thing that brought Veronique the most pleasure was the new-found camaraderie between her and her brother.

It wasn't even a chore because Hugo was handsome, refined, wickedly funny and wonderful in bed and not only that, Veronique loved her stolen moments at the chateau where she imagined life as a Duchesse. As she lay on the four-poster bed in a room that was decorated like a film set, she would smile and think of Sister Marguerite and how wrong she'd been about *girls like her*.

Whereas visits to Chevalier were rare, her trips north to Paris became a regular thing, made without René, where she spent weekends of pure indulgence paid for by Hugo. She adored the Parisian apartment and the lifestyle that went with it and soon, she wanted more, Veronique wanted it all. And when she told René, he had simply smiled and said, 'Then, dear sister, you shall have it.'

It was a dull October evening, a rare visit to Chevalier while Hugo's wife and children were at her parents for the weekend. He'd dismissed the staff and by dusk, after a day of drinking, they were all incredibly drunk. Veronique followed René and Hugo out of the drawing room and through the foyer, her heels clacking on the tiles as she tried to keep up.

They were best of friends, her brother and her lover, thick as thieves, always planning some moneymaking scheme, ways to get René into the Mairie because they weren't like the old brigade who held grudges – that was for fools, not forward-thinking businessmen like themselves. And as usual, their good-humoured rivalry and banter had resulted in a drunken, cheeky bet on the side. The subject had been René's new car, a top-of-the-range sporty Peugeot that he was adamant would beat Hugo's prestigious, vintage Facel Vega in a race.

Veronique sat on the steps to the chateau drinking champagne and when she shivered, Hugo rushed over and gave her his jacket, wrapping it around her shoulders, slurring his words and spilling whisky from the bottle as he waved his arms and gave instructions. 'We will decide this with timed laps around the estate... you know the road that runs around the edge. We will take turns and see who is fastest. Veronique, you can be the timekeeper.'

While Hugo passed Veronique his Cartier watch, René raised his glass and fumbled for his keys. 'I accept the challenge and will go first. Prepare to eat your words, my friend.'

Within seconds he was in his car and Hugo was counting down, then waving him off as dust and stones flicked across the drive. They could hear the roar of his engine as it powered along the country road and faded away, zooming around the far side of the estate out of earshot and then within minutes, from the other direction they heard the sound again as it returned along the road, only just making it through the gates at such high speed before roaring up the drive and coming to a halt.

Veronique stopped the timer. 'Four minutes, twenty-seven seconds is the time to beat. Well done brother, and good luck to my lover.'

They all laughed as Hugo placed the bottle of whisky on the steps and after kissing Veronique, ran towards his car and within seconds he too was racing down the drive and onto the road. René had just sat beside Veronique and started to pour himself more whisky when they heard the piercing screech of tyres and then the sickening sound of crushing metal. For a moment they both stared, then sprang to their feet and ran towards René's car.

Veronique was hyperventilating and utterly terrified of what they would find when they reached the road while her brother was already making plans. 'If he's dead we need to clear our things out of the chateau and make like we were never there, okay? And if he's not, he will be glad of a friend to help him clean up his mess.'

When they turned left onto the road, they saw no one, not until they rounded the bend where nothing would have prepared them for the sight that met their eyes. Standing in the middle of the road was Hugo, his hands on his head, staring at his wife's upturned car that was wedged into a tree, the roof completely crushed. Veronique was paralysed with horror, and it was only when René began shouting at her to get out and help Hugo that she forced her legs to move while her brother raced ahead. Veronique followed and as she passed the wreckage, smelt the petrol that was pumping out of the tank and saw the trail of yellow flames slowly building, getting taller. Before she could call out, there came a boom that caused them all to cower and then a whoosh of heat that billowed upwards, setting the trees above alight and completely engulfing the car.

Both Veronique and René supported Hugo who was shaking violently, rambling incoherently as they all looked towards the flames. 'It wasn't my fault, why is she here, I wasn't on the wrong side, I wasn't, not going too fast, you'll tell them won't you? Why isn't she in Angers, oh God, what if they find out it was me, what if they find out?'

Veronique couldn't speak, only stare at the burning car, her eyes locked on the yellow and orange flames that glowed from inside and flicked around the crumpled wreck. René was the only one who kept control and began to shake Veronique from her trance. 'Get in my car, now, turn it round and drive it back to the chateau. Hurry, you must go. I will bring Hugo. Hurry, Veronique, before someone comes along.'

When his words didn't make her move the slap that cracked against her cheek did and as she turned and ran, she could hear her brother cajoling Hugo. 'You must come with me, there's nothing you can do for her now so we have to hurry. Come on Hugo, she is gone but we can save you.'

Seconds later, after turning René's car and speeding back to the chateau, Veronique spotted Hugo's car as it raced up the drive, slowing when it passed by, allowing her brother to shout more orders through his window. 'Go inside and get our things, wash the glasses and put them away and collect the champagne bottles then throw them in my car; we will dispose of them. Nobody can know we were here; do you understand?'

After Veronique nodded, René drove Hugo's car around the side of the chateau towards the garage, out of sight. By the time she had done as he had instructed, placing their overnight things and a carrier bag of empty bottles at the front door, René was guiding Hugo inside, through the foyer towards the stairs, talking him through what he must say and do. 'Go to bed, say you were unwell, coming down with a cold so had some whisky and hot water to help you sleep. You have been alone all day, nobody was here with you. We will leave by the tradesmen's entrance, out along the track by the woods, to avoid anyone seeing us. I will ring you tomorrow; you will be fine. No one will ever know what you did.'

Veronique watched and listened as they took each stair slowly, Hugo muttering, agreeing to everything René said, sobbing, saying he was scared and couldn't go to jail. When she heard this and thought of the woman whose body was burning in a car only metres away, Veronique turned and picked up the bags and took them to the car where she waited for her brother, nausea and fear consuming her. Minutes later, René ran down the steps and almost leapt into the car, cursing her for not having the engine running before he flicked the switch and sped them away. Veronique couldn't bear to look at him or the chateau.

But it was as the car bounced along the track that led them off the estate, that René reminded her of exactly who he was and what she had become, again. 'In all my dreams it couldn't have worked out better than this... Do you realise what a gift today has been? I didn't think the letter would arrive until Monday but never mind, it worked; that's all that matters.'

Veronique didn't speak: her lips were numb.

He prattled on regardless. 'So, all we need to do is sit tight, keep our heads down and wait a while, until Hugo has grieved, and the mourning period is over and then we can move in. I can see it now. His new young wife, stepmother to two sad little children who adore their Uncle René, and you know what the best part of all is?' He looked at Veronique who was winding down her window, the swirling nausea rising upwards towards her throat. 'That he knows I know what he did, that he was responsible for killing his beautiful wife and if he wants me to keep his secret, he will be paying for it for the rest of his life.'

Even when Veronique stuck her head out of the window and threw up, the vomit splattering the paintwork of his shiny new car, René didn't stop laughing and laughing and laughing. The sound of it haunted her dreams for weeks, as did the screech of tyres and the crush of metal but if Veronique thought those nightmares were bad, she was about to learn two things that would make them a whole lot worse.

The news that Hugo's two-year-old son had also perished in the accident was the cause of Veronique's total breakdown. If it hadn't been for the intervention of Bernadette, who called an ambulance when she found her boss out cold on the floor of the apartment, Veronique may have done something more stupid than allowing René to control her life. As it was, a fortnight in hospital and some proper medication allowed Veronique to return to the flat above the shop, but not before telling René that he was no longer welcome, she was changing the locks and he was to leave her alone.

The hospital psychiatrist had suggested that Veronique

remove negative and toxic influences from her life and the second he said it, she knew that René was all those things, and worse. He agreed without a fuss and Veronique knew why, because he had to keep her sweet for when he resumed his master plan. He already had a new, fancy apartment on the other side of town where he took his girlfriends or whatever he called them. The only reason he turned up at the flat, after asking permission first, was to keep an eye on her while feigning interest in her health and she was done with all that fakery. She was also done with his stupid Hugo plan but had no intention of telling him that, not until she had to.

She eventually began working in the shop again, continued to go to therapy where she told the doctor all about what had happened to her as a child, but never what had happened at Chevalier and it did help, talking, someone listening. And she was doing okay, getting by until eight months after her hospitalisation, she had a visitor to the shop. It was Alain's mother, Hélène.

Completely distraught, in a rambling, desperate monologue interspersed with weeping and nose blowing, she told Veronique that nobody had seen her son for over a year, and he was officially a missing person. 'Do you not have any idea where he can be? Has he contacted you at all?'

Veronique was truly concerned and shocked that Alain would behave in such a way towards his family who he adored. Then again, she had thought he loved her too. 'I received a postcard, just once. It was from Spain, telling me we were over, and he had met someone else and that I should forget him.'

At this Hélène brightened. 'Do you still have it? I could show it to the police.'

Veronique shook her head and saw the light in Hélène's eyes dim. 'I threw it away. I couldn't bear to look at it. He broke my heart when he ended things.'

Yet she was so confused because for all this time she had thought Alain had simply met someone else, maybe moved to Spain or had run away on holiday with his new lover. 'Has he not contacted you at all, a phone call, a postcard?'

'Nothing. We thought he had gone on holiday with you but then you phoned and asked where he was. His sister said it would be woman trouble and that we should stay out of it but then we learned he didn't go to work and had left his flat. But when we broke in all his stuff was there.' Again, Hélène began to cry and while Veronique offered her a chair and sent Bernadette for a glass of water, the cold creep of dread made its way through her bones.

'Have the police got any clues at all? We were supposed to go on holiday, as I told you, and he was going to collect me and drive us to Rochelle in his car. Have they found that?'

'No, nothing at all. It has disappeared like Alain and now, he is just another missing person, the same as thousands of others and that is why I am visiting everyone I know, anyone who knew my Alain. I came here a while back but the young lady told me you were sick, so I waited. I hope you are better now.'

Veronique's heart broke once again, for herself, Alain and his mother. The visit had stirred up banished feelings, but seeing a member of his family again, holding the old woman's hands as she sobbed was like touching Alain, a connection to the two things she had lost.

Once Hélène had ran out of questions and made Veronique promise to get in touch if she ever heard from Alain, and promised the same in return, they said their goodbyes. The visit had taken its toll so after telling Bernadette to close the shop and take the rest of the day off, Veronique made her way upstairs to the sanctuary of the flat where, as always, she double-bolted the doors from the inside.

For the rest of the afternoon, she went over and over it all in her head, lying on the sofa, watching dusk fall and the shadows slide across the room, wishing so many things. That she had kept the card so she could have shown Hélène the writing, had her confirm it was Alain's hand that had written it. The fact she even suspected it was forged was as terrifying as the next thought... about who would want to make her think that Alain was in Spain and if he wasn't... where was he?

It was as she dredged her memory for clues that something rose from the murky depths of her depression. René had been incensed that Alain had left her but really, that wasn't how her brother's mind worked. The real René would have loved her to be abandoned and need him again; he wouldn't have cared about her broken heart. Instead, he had capitalised on it. Why hadn't she realised before, not been savvier? Ah, and then she got it, the pills that he so willingly provided, that clouded her mind and incapacitated her for days.

It was all so obvious. René had Hugo on the hook and was planning his next move and needed her help, which wouldn't have been possible if she was in love, or even married to Alain and certainly not if she was pregnant. And then the most horrendous thought and the thing that sent her rushing to the toilet where she deposited her lunch and her midday medication. The wood shredder.

It was a sick joke amongst the farming community and something that as a child she'd heard her father say many times. And then there was stuff René had stored in their barn at the farm. Car parts brought by the scrap man who owned the yard in the next town, who had the dreadful machine that René had once described over dinner, that crushed metal into cubes.

The truth hit Veronique in the stomach, harder than any punch she'd ever received from her father, more painful than hunger and what she'd had to do for a crust of bread. Had René disposed of Alain and his car? Or was he living in Spain with the woman he loved? From the bathroom floor, she prayed, squeezing her hands so tight her fingers hurt. 'Please God let him be in Spain, even if it means he loves another. Please don't let bits of him be scattered across a field, picked at by crows, turned into the soil.'

As she crawled into bed and lay there in the darkness Veronique sobbed for Alain, for her mother and a tiny little spark of life, snuffed out, someone she'd never even met. And then when she wore herself out from crying, the nightmares came in the form of Sister Mary Marguerite with teeth like fangs that ripped girls like her apart. And when she thought she was awake, dragging herself from the terror, she was met by another: her father stood at the bedroom door, flicking the light on, and off, on, and off. When she screamed into the night, asking for help, there was René, pulling her backwards into the darkness, holding tightly onto the strings that she tried to cut with blunt scissors, keeping her close and never letting go.

The following morning Veronique sat with a cup of coffee at the kitchen table, staring at the wall, trying to fathom what she should do. One thing was for sure: René would never admit to getting rid of Alain and she could never prove it. The other thing she was sure of was that she could not bear to look at him for one moment longer and had to get away but if she ran, it meant leaving behind her beautiful shop and leaving Bernadette in the lurch. Then again René needed a front so maybe she would be okay; he would make her the manager, whatever. Slowly a plan formed in her mind and Veronique knew that this was third time lucky, and she could not waste the chance to escape her brother.

Later that afternoon, while Veronique waited for her train, she rang René from the call box at the station all the while hugging her handbag to her side. It contained an envelope of cash, the entire contents of the business account that she'd withdrawn earlier that day, enough to tide her over while she looked for work.

He answered on the fifth ring. 'René Saber.'

'René, it's me. You need to listen and not interrupt because if you do, I will put the phone down and you will never hear from me again.' It was a test, he passed. 'Alain's mother came to the shop yesterday and told me he has been missing for a year and I suspect that you had something to do with it... Do not speak, René, I mean it. I know you won't admit to it, and I cannot prove it, but I am sure if I rang the police right now and mentioned your name they might be a tiny bit interested in all the things I have to say.'

Silence.

Veronique imagined him shaking with rage and knew that with her next announcement he might implode. 'I am going away, and I will not be back. I will not take part in whatever plan you have for Hugo, although I am sure you will enjoy extracting whatever you can from a grieving man with a secret to keep.' She heard a croak and warned him again. 'Shush, René, I haven't got to the best bit yet. In the shop there is a letter, signing my share over to you in return for what I have taken from the bank today, which is all the money from our business account, every single centime. It will be plenty to tide me over, at least enough to buy bread because you wouldn't want me to be hungry, would you, René?' She waited, a heartbeat and then he spoke, his veiled threat delivered as a statement that was laced with anger.

'You will regret this, Veronique.'

She smiled; there he was, the real René. 'Probably, but until that day comes, I will be free. Goodbye brother.'

Veronique had replaced the receiver and picked up her

suitcase and headed for the platform, eager to ride the train to Nice, to the sea, to freedom.

Veronique closed the book and stood. She'd had enough torment to last a lifetime so why was she submitting to more of it watching feckless mothers neglect their babies? She was merely indulging the demons that had doggedly followed her for years, always waiting in the wings to strike, eager to derail whatever happiness she found, feeding off her insecurities that wrecked relationships, her fragile state of mind and her terrible choices in men aiding their work.

Twice she had found herself in hospital where her next of kin was called, her kind and understanding brother who swept her up and ferried her home, taking good care of his fragile sister who always ran as soon as he forgot to close the cage door.

Once, when she had been beaten black and blue by a man like her father, thrown out into the night and one step away from becoming *one of those girls,* she had been so desperate to prove Sister Mary Marguerite wrong that she had rung René herself. He was her crutch, and she was his obsession and for both, the other was a drug neither could do without.

And on that day in Paris when she had bumped into Hugo, someone with his own demons who needed an angel who understood, Veronique thought she was being so clever. Hooking Hugo all by herself, surprising René with news of her new lover, thinking he would be impressed that in the end she had ended up exactly where he'd wanted her, all without his help.

How foolish she had been to presume that Hugo was still the wealthy man she had seduced all those years before, a man that René had already bled dry, manipulated and cast aside.

And as she walked through the Parisian sunshine, Veronique listened to the chatter of her faithful demons who followed on behind, making fun, asking her why then, was René so willing to help. What more could he want from Hugo, or her? And then as the apartment came into view, the demons screamed a word that almost stopped her heart.

Revenge.

21

FABIENNE

It was mid-morning, and they were all taking a break from tidying the flower beds before they tackled the murky green water in the fountain and later, the vegetable patch needed some TLC. They'd finished emptying the library days before and soon they would start the task of cleaning the shelves and cataloguing the books.

Mac was sunbathing, lying flat on his back, bare chested, his shorts slung low revealing a bony pelvis and the waistband of his boxers. Antoinette was sitting cross-legged on the grass shelling peas, bobbing to the music on her headphones while Fabienne was making a start on translating Mac's notebook.

Smiling as she looked from one to the other, Fabienne felt kind of blessed that despite her other worries, she had them in her world, two people who she could lean on and trust, even if one did like to make fun of her at every opportunity and the other had returned out of the blue and wham, just like that, had stolen her heart all over again.

She couldn't help it though: once she knew he was there in Cholet and had heard from Antoinette, via her very reliable network of informants, that he was thinking of selling up, she had no choice but to act.

Fabienne had known the second she saw him that she couldn't let him go again without a fight. This handsome, skinny man who had once been the shy, skinny boy who would crash into her life each summer then disappear, who she would dream about all year, fibbing to her schoolfriends that he was her boyfriend. Even the first time around, during their summer together she had been naïve, not really a woman even though she thought she was so worldly wise, but now, she had learnt a thing or two about life and men and how to use what she had to her advantage.

That night, after Mac had gone home and promised to return the following day, she had lain awake, pushing her own worries to one side while trying to work out how to make him stay, or to keep the cottage so it was an anchor, a reason to keep coming back for the summer. That would be a start. And then she would ring him every day while he was in England, make the effort to visit him, not just let him fade away like last time. She had a battle plan and, like her ancestors before her, would put it into action as soon as he arrived. And she did.

They'd been inseparable since, for almost a week he'd flitted back and forth from the cottage to the chateau, but that very morning, as the first rays of sun woke her from a fitful sleep that was littered by dreams and flickering snapshots of the past, the romanticism of the past few days morphed into a session of overthinking and obsessing that they'd rushed things. Her and Mac, diving into bed only hours after meeting again, feeling smug that she'd talked him around, hoping she could keep him prisoner in her chateau.

That was why, as she made coffee and lit the range to warm a batch of croissants she'd found in the freezer, she'd asked Antoinette, the font of all knowledge. Turning from the sink and resting her hand on her hip she first gave a loud tut and then made an ugly face, indicating she was bored before telling her what for.

'Will you please stop acting like a crusty old maid. Just live a bit, for goodness' sake. You thought you were being so sensible when you had your no-strings-attached summer of sex and boy, did you mess up, so let's face it, this time you need to grab him wherever is appropriate, or not, and hold onto him, like this.' She then did a weird action with her hand that was a cross between squeezing something very tightly and milking a cow.

Point taken.

Mac slipped back into Fabienne's life like he'd always been there, and Antoinette loved having him around to boss about and tease. Fabienne had resolved to embrace their second chance.

Her daydreaming session was then ruined by Mac who suddenly sat up and turned to face them. 'I've just had an idea about how you can bring some money into the chateau. It's not a quick fix but something to think about in the long term. It'll take a bit of planning and marketing but I can do that online, and the best thing is, it won't cost a penny.'

At this Fabienne's ears pricked up and she held her finger on the next line in the notebook so she wouldn't lose her place as Antoinette removed her headphones and both waited to hear his idea.

'Have you ever watched the programme in England called *Antiques Roadshow*?'

Fabienne didn't watch much television, but that show had been a favourite amongst her colleagues at the auction house. 'Yes, I have, why?'

'Well, that's what you could do here. Hold a yearly event where people bring their treasures for you to value. We could charge entry and maybe you could get some of your friends in the business to come along to help. It would be a great way of advertising the chateau too, get its name out there and you never know, someone might bring a gem and we could even get this place on the news. The Annual Chevalier Arts Fair. How does that sound?'

Fabienne loved this idea. 'I am sure my colleagues would help out, and they could stay here for the night free of charge. I keep promising they can come to visit.'

Mac was on a roll. 'And, if you made it into a kind of festival, utilised the grounds, we could have traders selling food and crafts, like that farm show we used to go to as kids at Angrie, do you remember?'

'Ah, yes, the olden days festival, where everyone dressed up and showed people how to make clogs and shear the sheep. I used to love it. My parents took me every year. There was a man on stilts, and the candy floss machine, and the crêpes, we always had those.' Antoinette looked miles away, dreaming of food.

Mac had more ideas. 'I've been to loads of outdoor summer events where they have everything, classic cars, a fairground…'

Antoinette interrupted and made them all jump with her memory. 'Donkeys! They always had donkey rides.'

'Okay, donkeys too… but I think it's got potential because anyone who is a trader has to pay a small fee, as do the people who come to enjoy all the stalls and have their antiques valued by mademoiselle here. So, what do you reckon?' Mac looked so pleased with himself and Fabienne thought it was a fabulous idea but one that would take too long to organise. They needed cash quickly, like yesterday.

Rather than burst his bubble she joined in the conversation, sharing ideas before Mac went inside to fetch her laptop so he could do some research and Antoinette carried on shelling peas.

While he was gone, she immersed herself in the past and read the notebook, turning to the page titled *Ton Histoire* and traced Mac's family tree. It was when she came to a name next to his grandfather's that her interest was piqued, and she quickly flipped to the page that read *Ma Soeur* – My Sister. Reading quickly, Fabienne soaked up old Monsieur Doré's words, clues to the past that sent goosebumps across her skin.

I can't remember much about my sister. She was much older than me and died in 1940. She was seventeen. I was only two years old, but my parents talked about her often, but not about how she died because I think the words would have been hard to say. I eventually heard the whole story from her closest friend, a stalwart of Cholet who lived through the days of the occupation. You must go and visit her, Eglantine Moreau, she will tell you more than I can about your great-aunt of whom you should be most proud but until then, here is what I know...

When Fabienne finished reading, she reached over and frantically tapped Antoinette's arm, indicating she should remove her headphones. It coincided with Mac's return, laptop in hand. Standing, her face flushed from excitement, she told them both what she had discovered.

'Oh, my goodness, you are not going to believe what I have just read in the notebook... Come on, come with me, this will blow your mind.' Before either Mac or Antoinette had a chance to ask, she was racing inside and up the stairs to the long gallery where, completely out of breath she stopped at the housekeeping journals and began to flick through the pages, watched by the others who were also gasping for breath.

'What on earth is it?' Antoinette peered over Fabienne's shoulder and Mac did the same.

'Hold on, let me look.' Her finger worked down the page, eyes scanning the names of the staff working at the chateau in the late thirties. 'Doré, Doré... *voilà*, there she is! I found her.' Stepping aside, Fabienne allowed them to look at the journal as she explained.

'Mac, how amazing is this… your great-aunt, your grandfather's older sister, used to work here as lady's maid to Duchesse Ophélie and according to the notebook, she was present the night the Nazis came and took the artwork. Can you believe that?' Fabienne was thrilled to have found a link between Mac's family history and her own and was eager to tell what she knew.

'The Nazis stormed the chateau and made all the staff leave. Whatever wasn't in the truck outside they took from the rooms themselves. Your great-aunt was distraught, knowing what they were doing and that she couldn't stop them. She adored Chevalier and la Duchesse Ophélie and felt it her job to protect it and them.'

Mac was looking at the entry and then turned to Fabienne. 'I remember going with Grandpère to the cemetery and visiting her grave. I was only young, and we only went the once. All I know is she was killed by the Germans, and he didn't speak about it.'

'Well, this is another amazing thing. In the book, he says that you should go and see her best friend, who lived through the occupation because she will be able to tell you all about what happened, and you'll never guess who that friend is.' Fabienne looked from Mac to Antoinette. 'It is your great-grandmother, Eglantine. Look, it's there, written by his hand.'

'Oh, my goodness, really?' Antoinette took the notebook from Fabienne. 'So, all those tales she told, they were true, not made-up rubbish. Well fancy that. I can't believe that we are all connected like this. I love it. I bloody love it.'

While her friend read, Fabienne asked Mac a question. 'And you know what your great-aunt's name was?'

The next voice came from Fabienne's loyal best friend, hushed and incredulous as she answered the question. 'Antoinette. Her name was the same as mine. How wonderful is that? Someone who loved Chevalier as much as I do once lived and worked here, just like me. Eglantine did tell me her friend worked here but I didn't pay attention and thought it might be in more recent times, as a cleaner or something. I feel so bad now.'

'Hey, don't be sad or beat yourself up. We both know that Eglantine hasn't much grasp on reality so I'm sure she won't be offended, or even remember. The fact you love her and go to see her so often is what counts.' Fabienne rubbed her friend's arm then flicked away tears from her own eyes. She was overwhelmed by the discovery, as was Antoinette.

Mac had a question of his own. 'I wonder if there's a photo of her somewhere, here or back at La Fleurie. I'd love to know what she looked like; wouldn't you?'

Fabienne was ahead of him and grabbed his arm, pulling him further down the corridor. 'I think there is. This one here, look.' She pointed to a grainy photo on one of the sideboards showing the whole household at the front of the chateau and in the centre sat the Duc and Duchesse de Chevalier, her great-grandparents.

The problem was there were five maids in the photo, all dressed the same in their black dresses covered by huge white pinafores, all attired in their best for the photo. 'She could be any one of those. It's easy to guess the others, like the *majordome*, that's what you would call a butler, and there's the cook and by her side the chef who they'd had brought from Paris, much to her disgust, I'm sure. And there's the chauffeur who I know is Gregoire. He once pointed himself out to me. Poor old Gregoire, it was so unfair of Veronique to sack him when she sold Papa's car, he's been here since he was a boy. Le Duc made him his chauffeur, look how smart he is.'

Antoinette agreed. 'It broke my heart when they sent him

away. He might have been ninety-five, but he still knew how to polish a car even if he was too old and batty to drive it.'

Fabienne saw Mac stifle a laugh at Antoinette's special way with words then asked their resident joker a question. 'Why don't we do what it says in the notebook and go and see Eglantine? Do you think your grandmère would like some visitors?'

At this Antoinette smiled. 'I think she would absolutely love it, but I warn you, she goes from being really interesting and funny to being completely gaga, but still funny with it. It depends on what day you catch her – so let's hope today is a good day.'

Without missing a beat, Fabienne grabbed the photo and then they all headed downstairs. Clutching the notebook and frame in one hand and Mac's in another, she listened to the voice that was whispering in her ear, *Keep the faith, mademoiselle. Let the past guide you. Everything is meant to be.*

22

EGLANTINE

The four of them were huddled around a small table in the visitors' lounge, while behind them, the usual crowd had gathered to watch the afternoon game shows that Eglantine despised. She was having much more fun taking a very, *very* long time choosing from the delightful array of colourful macarons in a fancy box.

She sensed they were all losing patience, and this notion was confirmed when the handsome skinny man made a suggestion. *He has nice eyes,* she thought, *like Clark Gable.* Eglantine let her finger hover while he spoke. 'Why don't you have the pink one because that's raspberry, and my favourite or I might just have to steal it when you're not looking.'

Eglantine was in a good mood because the chef had served a decent lunch for a change, so chose to ignore that she had been spoken to like a child and instead gave him a smile and took his advice.

After popping the pink one on her plate she bestowed a conspiratorial wink before having a bit of fun with him. 'Thank you, young man, and it's nice to see you with some clothes on for a change. Now, what is it you all want? I can tell you are here for a reason. Am I in trouble again?' Eglantine then adopted her best innocent expression as she continued, 'It wasn't me who rang the *gendarmes* about the tiger climbing the cherry tree, I swear.'

She noticed with glee that Mac was blushing underneath his dumbfounded expression while on her right Antoinette giggled. Eglantine popped the macaron in her mouth and as she chewed, turned her attention to the pretty young woman to her left. Even though her hair was cut short, like a pixie, she was still the image of her lovely mother but clearly felt the need to explain who she and skinny-man were, what they had found in a notebook and why, God and her patience willing, they were there.

'So, we were wondering if you could tell us anything about Mademoiselle Doré, Antoinette, your best friend. Do you remember her? We brought a photograph and wondered if she was in it. You might be able to point her out?'

At this Eglantine couldn't help but be affronted and crossed her arms over her chest. 'Of course I remember her. She was only here the other day and told me all about what was happening at Chevalier. She is such a good friend and visits quite often. Not like the other lot.'

Eglantine never missed a trick and noticed pixie-girl exchange a confused look with Antoinette who was already getting on her nerves by eyeing up the rest of the macarons so after deftly moving the box away from greedy-guts, Eglantine diverted everyone's attention.

'Show me then, the photograph.'

Pulling the frame from the carrier bag pixie-girl placed it on the table, waiting quite patiently while Eglantine found her glasses and wiped the lenses then, once they were placed firmly on her nose and adjusted for comfort, she focused on the photograph. Scouring the black-and-white image in front of her,

Eglantine traced with her finger the line of servants standing outside Chevalier, making a *hmm* sound as she scrutinised each one. When she spotted her dear friend's face it was like stepping back in time and the sheer sight of her caused Eglantine's heart to soar.

'There she is! That's my Antoinette there, next to the chauffeur. Her hair has come loose from her cap. See.'

Taking back the frame pixie-girl looked down at the face of Antoinette, smiling as she spoke. 'It's not the clearest of images but at least we have something to go on, a link to the past. I'm so glad I know which one she is.' After passing it across the table so the others could see she asked another question. 'What colour hair and eyes did she have? It's impossible to guess from the photo.'

In her mind Eglantine saw her friend so clearly. She had been perfect, and to her always would be. Captured in time, whole, unsullied, alive. 'Oh, she had the most beautiful hair the colour of copper. I was so envious. And green eyes, like the Bretons. She was Gallic through and through. Not a wishy-washy colour like yours.' Eglantine frowned as she directed her comment to her great-granddaughter who simply tutted.

Pixie-girl took back the frame and gazed at the image as she spoke. 'What else can you tell us about your friend? We would love to know more about her, especially Mac as she is his great-aunt.'

This revelation was a surprise to Eglantine and now she looked at him properly. Yes, she could see glimmers of her old friend Claude, in his gangly build, the cut of his jaw and the cheeky smile. The recognition of a face from the past, albeit vague and altered by time was followed by a wave of nostalgia. Feeling her mood soften, despite the annoying theme tune to *Open the Box* ringing in her ears, Eglantine became wistful and when she answered, struggled to smother the emotion welling inside.

'I miss her so much, you know. She was my very best friend. Bright as a button, funny and pretty and loyal, oh so very loyal. She adored la Duchesse and missed her incredibly when the Bombelles were in Paris. She even chose to live in when she could have easily cycled to and from work, but she simply loved being at the chateau. It was her world away from the everyday life we all knew. And she was in love, too, but I can't say who with because it's a secret.'

Pixie-girl nodded. Her expression, Eglantine noticed, was kind. 'Well, I wouldn't want you to betray her trust so perhaps you could tell us about the occupation. We know that Antoinette was there the night the Nazis came and stole the paintings, and that later, she was shot by the Germans who said she was a member of *La Resistance.* Is all this true?'

When her heart lurched and the past came rushing into the room like angry soldiers waving guns and barking orders, Eglantine had to push them back, stall for time before explaining about that dreadful night. 'Could we have more coffee? Ask that fat one over there who doesn't like me. She will bring some. It might go on ration again and we need to stock up because the stuff we drank back then was disgusting. Ersatz, that's what they called it, but it should have been called cats'...'

When Antoinette intervened, Eglantine found herself back in the room, the here and now, not the dark days of the occupation. 'Okay, Grandmère, we get the message. I'll go and bring some more coffee but please, try to stay on track and answer Fabienne's questions and NO swearing. I mean it.'

Once she'd given Eglantine a warning look, she shot off and pixie-girl took over, asking an easier question. 'Was Antoinette a member of *La Resistance,* Eglantine?'

Again, that feeling of dread returned, reminding her about

loose lips and that secrecy was imperative so Eglantine lowered her voice. 'We are not supposed to talk of such things. What if one of the Nazis are here, listening? See him, over there, the one with the yellow jumper.' Eglantine gave a slight nod and glared in the direction of an armchair that held the diminutive figure of a sleeping man. Her two guests glanced quickly and then back again, listening intently to what she had to say. 'I have my suspicions about him. He's got shifty eyes and has a penchant for saucisson and, this is most important, his son brings him wine each Sunday from Alsace. So, what does that tell you, hmm?'

Skinny-man looked unconvinced and gave her a reassuring smile as he whispered, 'I like German beer but that doesn't make me a Nazi, and Alsace is French now, so don't worry.'

'Well, it didn't used to be. And he could have German blood for all we know.' Eglantine was quite pleased with her counter-argument, however, skinny-man soldiered on.

'Okay, good point so let's keep our voices down just in case he is a spy. He's fast asleep, though, and the television is so loud I doubt he will hear anything, so don't worry too much.'

Eglantine didn't think the television was loud and decided to let that go but agreed about the spy thing so lowered her voice too. The last thing she wanted was to be arrested and tortured like some of her comrades had been. 'I was recruited to *La Resistance* early, at the start of the occupation. Our network code name was the Historians, and we worked the Shelbourne Line evacuating stranded servicemen and doing whatever was necessary to disrupt the Nazis. I would pass on any information I could to a woman called Yvette. She ran our network with a man named Vincent. Sometimes I carried messages for them to Nantes and Angers. It was a dangerous time, and I was scared for much of it, terrified of being taken in and tortured, but we had to do what we could.'

'And Antoinette.' Pixie-girl leant forward slightly.

'Yes, she too wanted to help. Once she was forced out of the chateau and took to spending hours in the woods, watching the soldiers who were staying there. It became an obsession and I told her not to go so often but she wouldn't listen. She said she had left something inside and if she had the chance, she was going to retrieve it. Antoinette and the others had to get out of the chateau in such a hurry because the Nazis were all over it but I said whatever it was, it wasn't worth risking her life for. I did ask, but she would not say. I have my suspicions, but it was for the best that I wasn't sure. Under torture you cannot give away secrets you do not know. So, she continued her treks to the woods and whatever she saw she reported to me, and I passed it on. How many trucks they had; the head count of soldiers; if they stored weapons there – any tiny shred of information was useful.'

Skinny-man asked the next question. 'Do you know what happened when she was killed? They must have caught her in the woods, spying.'

Normally Eglantine hated to talk or think about what happened to Antoinette because afterwards the anger and sadness stuck to her heart like glue, but it would be disrespectful to not speak of it. Her suffering could not be for nothing. 'Yes, they did but instead of taking her to the jail for questioning they– the soldiers did terrible things to her and, so she wouldn't tell, they shot her – said she ran away and resisted arrest – and then they threw her body off the bridge. They said she was going to jump but it was lies, all of it.'

The return of Antoinette with another pot of coffee gave Eglantine time to gather her emotions and the three of them sat in a moment of respectful silence before she found the strength to continue. 'Everyone knew what had happened, but the doctor was scared too. He dared not speak out and the *gendarmes* were at the beck and call of the Maire. I was so angry, and the bitterness ate at me, like an infection and I swore that somehow, I would avenge my beautiful friend because she did not deserve what they did to her. I can never forgive anyone who had a hand in it.'

Eglantine was trembling so reached over and took her great-granddaughter's hand, speaking directly to her. 'That's why your mother's middle name is Antoinette. It would have been her first but that husband of mine insisted we call her Hortense. It's such an ugly name but then again, it came to suit her as she grew. Babies are always beautiful.' Ignoring the affronted look, she continued. 'But I was so pleased when Hortense named you Antoinette because you do have my friend's beauty and spirit and that makes me glad and very proud. I want you to know that.' Eglantine stroked her great-granddaughter's face in a moment of tenderness that was quickly replaced by laughter when she added, 'Even though you are far too bossy and talk too much. Now, let's drink our coffee before the German wakes up and takes it. That lot stole everything, the greedy bas–'

'Grandmère, you promised no swearing!' Noticing Antoinette's raised eyebrows and in a rare moment of obedience and equity, Eglantine sucked in her annoyance and popped the remaining pink macaron on skinny-man's plate because he needed fattening up.

While they finished the pastries and macarons, Eglantine chatted on, enjoying having a captive audience who seemed happy to listen to her thoughts on random subjects that suddenly pinged into her head, all eager to get out at once. Like a trip she once took to Egypt where she wandered the desert on a camel and had an affair with a Bedouin chief who was the image of Lawrence of Arabia. The mystery of someone's toenail clippings that she found in her bed made Antoinette gag, but to be fair that's how she had felt when she found them.

Annoyingly, none of them had any idea what time her husband would be in later, but they were most interested in the juicy gossip, about the woman in the next room who was having an affair with the man who came in once a week to do physio. The noises that came from that room made Eglantine blush. And lastly, she described in great detail the jumper she was knitting for Antoinette, her granddaughter, not her best friend.

This piece of information made Eglantine sad because she would love to knit something for her dear friend, and it also restored their previous conversation when pixie-girl brought up the subject of secrets. 'You mentioned that she had a lover, and that you had suspicions about what she'd left behind… I don't suppose you could give us a clue, could you? We won't tell anyone. We promise. But it would be so wonderful to have a clearer picture of Antoinette's life so she can always be remembered.'

Eglantine looked from one to the other and then rested her eyes on pixie-girl.

'She was in love with Gregoire, the chauffeur. When France was invaded, he did what many young men did and fled to join *La Resistance* rather than be made to work for the Nazis. They were so in love. He was going to buy her a ring, she told me, and then when the time was right, he would ask her father if they could marry and perhaps le Duc, who thought very fondly of Gregoire, would let them rent a cottage on the estate. She was broken-hearted when he went but knew it was the right thing and vowed to wait for him. So, you see, when those Nazi pigs murdered her, not only did they take her away from me and her family, they took away her dreams and those of dear Gregoire.' The tears fell from Eglantine's eyes as she accepted a serviette from skinny-man who asked the next question.

'Do you think that's what she went back for? The ring.'

Eglantine nodded. 'Or maybe love letters, a photo of him. I

do not know. Like I said, before the occupation we were free with our secrets, shared everything with one another but then it all changed. It was best to keep things in here and here.' She tapped her head then her heart. 'But when the liberation came, that was the time to share, to expose the shameful secrets of those who had sold their soul, pass on all the things we knew so the deaths of our comrades could be avenged. That is why I made sure that one traitor in particular, was punished.'

Eglantine's visitors looked from one to the other, but it was her granddaughter who spoke first. 'Who was the traitor and what did you do?'

'Who do you think? Maire Saber and his wife. Antoinette told me that the day before the Nazis came, he had stopped by, apparently on the off-chance to enquire if the Duc was home. He needed to speak to him urgently, he said. Unfortunately, Saber had been a dinner guest of le Duc many times and had been shown the collection of paintings, and he saw exactly what was happening that day in the chateau, its contents being packed up.

'Antoinette said that he was asking so many questions. Where were they going and when. None of the staff left the chateau that day or night because they were so busy and all of them were totally devoted to le Duc. The only person who could have told the Nazis what was happening was Saber. And when Antoinette was murdered, he sided with the *kommandant*, refused to listen to her parents and even threatened the terrified doctor who examined her body. I had to do something.

'And that is why I pointed the finger at the traitor. All of Cholet despised him anyway. Everyone lived in fear of the Nazis. Many were accused of spying for *La Resistance* and dragged to the jail where they were interrogated and tortured. Such terrible things happened. Like reprisals. Men and women were sent to the firing squad, even children. You must look for the story of Guy Môquet and what happened to him in Châteaubriant, just down the road from here. Antoinette, surely you know this, did they tell you at school?'

'Yes, Grandmère, they did, and it is terrible and very sad. I will explain to Fabienne and Mac later, don't worry.'

Eglantine gave a jerk of her head then continued. 'Saber was a fascist through and through, always had been and made no secret about it on the run-up to the war. It was as though he thought his time had come. And I am sure with all my heart that the people of Cholet regretted his appointment. But it was too late, and he embraced the Nazi occupation. He was convinced that France belonged to the victorious Reich and wanted a seat at their table after the war. He dined with them, up at the chateau and at the *Mairie*. He made me sick. I was there when he swung from the tree and watched from the crowd while they chopped off his wife's hair. I made sure they were punished. I avenged Antoinette the only way I could, and I will never, ever regret it.'

Fabienne pressed her hand to her chest. 'So, it wasn't my great-grandfather who had Saber hung in retribution for his part in the pillaging of Chevalier? That is what my family have believed for all these years.'

Eglantine shook her head, weary from telling the tale and the memory of losing her friend. 'No, it was me. Your great-grandfather was a good friend to *La Resistance,* funding us where he could, passing on whatever information he gleaned from his home in Paris and arranging safe haven for anyone who needed it. He had many friends, le Duc, decent people who wanted to help, artists and writers, good folk derided by Hitler. Your great-grandfather gave shelter to our comrades and *La Resistance* returned a favour or two, providing him with bronze for one of his friend's sculptures. Monsieur Picasso, I believe.

The Nazis said he and many other creatives were degenerate, but it was they who were so.'

At this revelation skinny-man raised his eyebrows, looking to pixie-girl who had more to add. 'It's true what you say, Eglantine, and well documented that Picasso and other artists who remained in Paris during the occupation did what they could to help. And I know that my great-grandfather and Picasso were good friends. One of the treasures that the Nazis stole was a painting given by him to my great-grandmother, a personal gift she adored. It is written in the journals how distraught she was that it was taken.'

Hearing this Eglantine smiled but then flopped into her chair, exhausted by her recollections, closing her eyes on her guests. Feeling a warm hand take hers, she was grateful for the caress when Antoinette reached out and when she spoke, concern echoed in her voice. 'Well, I think that is enough for one day, Grandmère, but thank you for telling us so many wonderful things and especially about my namesake. I am proud to bear her name.'

Eglantine opened her eyes and patted her great-granddaughter's hand. 'It was a pleasure, *cherie,* just don't forget it all. Will you write it down for me? In case I go loopy.'

At this she noticed they all stifled a chuckle, and as always Antoinette had to have the last word. 'Well, if you'd told me all this before I would have written it down already. But I understand about you and your secrets, and it isn't an easy story to tell.'

Eglantine gave a loud tut. 'I did tell you, when you met...' She couldn't remember pixie-girl's name so pointed instead. '... that I knew someone who worked there and later, when you took the job. I told you to stay away from that terrible man Hugo and his wife who was a Saber, but you never listen, Antoinette. Nobody ever listens.'

'I was only ten, a little kid, and you told me all sorts of stories – fairy stories, scary stories, stories that, quite frankly, were a bit rude and as for recently, let's face it, you tell–'

Before Antoinette could finish pixie-girl intervened. 'Ding, ding. Okay you two, it doesn't matter now because we have sorted it all out, no harm done. Once again, Eglantine, thank you. It's all been fascinating.'

Skinny-man stood and shook Eglantine's hand. 'Thank you, Eglantine. You made my great-aunt come to life and maybe I could come back soon, and you can tell me what you remember about my grandparents, when they were young. That's if you feel up to it.'

Eglantine smiled and said she would, just before one of the care assistants came over and interrupted, telling her that the chiropodist had arrived for her appointment. He had smooth hands too which she found a bit creepy and hoped her new friend wasn't a foot-fiddler, but she was too tired to ask so let it go.

They all said one more goodbye then as they turned to go and the assistant attempted to guide her away, Eglantine stopped when one of the voices in her head reminded her of something. 'Will you come and show me when you find the treasure? Antoinette told me about it. She said it's there, waiting, and all you have to do is look.'

Once pixie-girl promised that they would, Eglantine resigned herself to her fate, and allowed herself to be shuffled from the room. An hour with the creepy foot-fiddler then her husband would be there, and she was looking forward to that. She missed him, a lot.

23

MAC

They were on their way to La Fleurie so Mac could pick up a change of clothes. Antoinette had also reminded them twice that they had missed lunch and she was about to faint from hunger. They'd had to stop to buy baguettes that she'd proceeded to eat and scatter crumbs everywhere.

While Mac concentrated on the road, he listened to Fabienne and Antoinette going over what Eglantine had told them, the latter still racked with guilt for not taking her great-grandma seriously.

Mac joined in, saying he'd been mesmerised by Eglantine's story, about what happened during the war. And even though it was shocking, seeking revenge and watching a man being hung, you had to take into consideration what Eglantine and her comrades and countrymen had endured during the occupation.

'I pictured it all, grandpère losing a sister when he was little, my great-grandparents seeking justice for their daughter and their pleas landing on the deaf ears of Maire Saber who, no doubt, controlled the police. Everyone would have been living in fear while he collaborated, dining with the Germans, siding with them. He sounds like a horrible man and from what you two have told me about Veronique, it sounds like the Saber family haven't changed for the better after all these years.'

Fabienne agreed. 'You are correct. She is a terrible person and so is her brother, René Saber. Our current *Maire* is like a snake. I've only met him a few times but didn't take to him. Even at the wedding, when Papa married Veronique, Antoinette and I thought he was a creep.'

Through the rear-view mirror Mac saw Antoinette nodding, her mouth full of bread as they listened to Fabienne slate René. 'Apparently, he and Papa have been acquainted for many years, through their business dealings, he said. He and Veronique are from Cholet, a pig farm, and I remember he made a cruel comment during their wedding dinner, saying that Papa had married down. I thought it was a dreadful thing to say about his sister. He also said she'd moved away while he built his fortune in property. He loves to tell you all about it so I wish I'd known about his horrible history because then I could have put him right in his place.'

'Well, I hope I never meet him, he sounds vile. But on an up note, I have to say that Eglantine is totally amazing. I know her mind wanders a bit but once she's focused, she really can tell a tale especially about the evil Saber family.'

Fabienne agreed. 'I know, she's a mine of information and I've been thinking that we should make a little film of her telling us about the occupation and her memories of Cholet. If I ever do open a museum at Chevalier, I'd like to have a section devoted to *La Resistance* and feature Eglantine and Antoinette. What do you think?'

'That's a great idea, but we'd need more visual aids, photographs of them and the village. My mémère will have lots of Eglantine and maybe my mum too. Are there any old photographs in the cottage, Mac? We might be able to use them.' Antoinette was looking at the photo of the chateau as she spoke.

'Yes, all over the place. Mostly of yours truly, but hey, I'm gorgeous so who could blame them?' He ignored the jeers and tried to picture the photographs scattered around the cottage. 'There are some black-and-white ones though. We can look when we get there.'

Fabienne clapped her hands in excitement. 'Ooh, I love this. I feel like we are history detectives on a case. I can't wait to see if we find another one of old Antoinette, but we have to be realistic because back then money was spent on more important things so having your photograph taken was quite rare.'

'Well, we're here, so let's go find out.' Mac pulled up in front of the cottage that was lit by the afternoon sun, bearing down on the whole front of the house and lighting up the walls like a beacon, as if it was showing them the way.

The first thing they did once they were inside was scrutinise the photos in the *salon* while Mac prepared a late lunch with what was left of the baguettes. There were plenty of him and his mum growing up and a few of his grandparents on their wedding day and important family events, like Mac in his cap and gown after he'd received his degree. There were none of the older Dorés so, disappointed and hungry, they decided to carry on after lunch and check upstairs, otherwise young Antoinette (as Mac kept calling her) would faint from starvation.

They were making their way up the wooden stairs, checking the paintings on the walls as they ascended, then those on the landing but nothing grabbed their attention, so Mac suggested they check his grandparents' room and then maybe the loft. That's where the chest of bits and bobs was stored.

'Are you sure you don't mind us snooping around your house? I feel like an intruder.' Fabienne hovered outside the first bedroom.

'No, not at all. I know there's a couple in Grandpère's room and then I'll open the loft.' He pointed to the hatch in the ceiling and followed Fabienne and Antoinette inside.

Mac watched as they admired the photos on his grandmother's dressing table, a recent one of her and his granddad, and then a bouncing baby photo of his mum and then Fabienne moved to the one hung on the wall where she stopped and pushed her face closer. 'Hey, look at this one... come here and see this.'

He and Antoinette obeyed and sure enough, there, in an ornate frame, was a sepia-toned family photo. A mother, seated with a baby in christening robes, the gown making it impossible to guess the sex. To her right was a tall, suited man who definitely had the look of his granddad although his attire suggested it was his great-grandfather. And there, on the left of her mother was a young woman, dressed in her Sunday best. Antoinette, he knew it.

'It is her, isn't it? The hairs on my neck are standing up. That is our Antoinette. We have found her.' The other Antoinette rested her hands on Mac's arm and Fabienne's shoulder while they stared.

'Antoinette is so much older than Grandpère though. Don't you think that's odd?'

Fabienne answered. 'No, not really. I suspect your granddad may have been what is often referred to as a "time of life" baby. Many women who think that they are no longer of childbearing age suddenly find themselves pregnant late in life. Also, infant mortality rates were higher back then so she may have lost more babies after Antoinette, before her surprise one came along. It was unusual for the working classes to have just one child so that suggests her others may have died, or she miscarried.'

'That makes sense. Why don't you take it off the wall and we'll go downstairs, then we can have a proper look.' Fabienne nodded and Mac watched as she carefully lifted the frame that exposed a non-faded section of yellow wallpaper, big bright yellow blooms as fresh as the day the room was decorated.

Downstairs, after placing the frame on the table, Fabienne ran her fingers over it. A quizzical expression crossed her face and she gently turned the frame over. When Mac saw her take a closer look at the stamps and squiggly writing on the reverse he had to ask. 'Is something wrong?'

'No, it's just this frame...'

Mac stood closer and looked. 'What about it?'

'It's just that I have seen ones like this before, many times at work. It's a Parisian-style Montparnasse frame, very popular with Impressionist artists and if I'm correct, a collector's piece. Remember I said that recently? Vintage frames have become sought after. Well, this is a great example of one. It was the carving that caught my attention, the wavy surrounds and the filigree design with gilt overlay. Sometimes they are more simple, geometric designs on varnished wood.' She ran her fingers over the front and pointed to the detail then turned it over. 'And see this label. I recognise the name, Ateliers Emile Bouche. They are renowned Parisian frame makers and here, there is a date, handwritten, it would be when it was made, in 1931.'

Antoinette reached out and took the frame from Fabienne and admired it while Mac had a question. 'Fancy my great-grandparents owning something as valuable as that. Maybe they went to Paris on a day trip or something.'

Fabienne's next words took him by surprise. 'Yes, that is what I am thinking because look around you. All the other photo frames are the type you would buy from a normal shop. Some are quite modern and a few appear to be home-made so I am wondering, given your great-grandparents' circumstances, why they would pay so much for a frame like this. And there's something else.' Fabienne held out her hands for Antoinette to pass it back. 'Look here, the seal has been broken which tells me that after the original was mounted, that someone opened the back. Traditionally you seal a frame with tape to prevent dust mites or damp getting inside and you can see where this has been cut.' Again, she pointed towards a seared line that ran around the tape.

'Do you think there might be another photo inside? My mum used to do that, keep all my school photos in one frame, adding the most recent to the top.' Mac hoped it might be another one of Antoinette, maybe a portrait so they could see her clearly.

Fabienne didn't answer Mac's question and instead, asked one of her own. He noticed she looked tense, and her cheeks were flushed too. 'Mac, would you mind if we looked inside. I will be very careful?'

'Yeah, go for it.' Mac sensed that something was wrong and glanced at Antoinette who gave him a quizzical look, then they watched as Fabienne began to remove the back of the frame, all of them completely silent.

As she peeled away the back cover, the first thing they saw was an envelope and a folded piece of paper and underneath what appeared to be a canvas. Nobody said a word as Fabienne gently removed the notes and placed them on the table then carefully prised the canvas out of the frame. Mac hadn't a clue what it was but held his breath as she turned it over and heard her cry when her eyes fell on what was clearly a painting.

'*Oh, mon Dieu...*' Fabienne's hands had begun to shake and when Mac looked at her shocked face, he could see tears welling in her eyes.

Antoinette also looked astounded; her voice hushed. 'Fabienne, is that what I think it is?'

Mac was really confused because now, Fabienne was sobbing. 'What? What is it? Fabienne, are you okay?'

When she answered, her voice was a mixture of happiness and incredulity. 'Yes, Mac, I am fine because we have found the Chevalier treasure and it's been here all along… on your grandparents' wall. This is the Picasso that we thought the Nazis took from the chateau, a gift to my great-grandmother before the war. We thought it lost forever and I think that our dear Antoinette managed to save it. The clever, loyal, wonderful girl.'

Antoinette took the painting of a woman reclining on a chair, her head tilted to one side, beads around her neck, one breast exposed and stared at it in complete awe while Mac took Fabienne in his arms and let her cry. He knew how much objects, paintings, memories and her heritage meant to her and finding the Picasso was a dream come true, worth more to her than money because she had been able to touch something that was a link to the past, her birthright.

'It is truly beautiful. I can't believe I am holding something in my hands that was painted by a master. I will never forget this moment ever, not in my whole life.' Antoinette was also overcome and wiped away tears. 'We must read the notes, see if there are clues. Fabienne, shall I do it or do you want to?'

Mac decided for her. 'You do it, let's sit. I think Fabienne needs to get over the shock.' He kissed the top of her hair, and then pulled out a chair and once they were all seated, Antoinette rested the painting on the frame and carefully unfolded one of the letters, a torn page, ripped at the edges. 'It is from our Antoinette… dated November 15th, 1940.' Again, a hush fell on the room as young Antoinette read the words of her namesake, Antoinette Doré.

Tonight, the Nazis came to Chevalier. Never in my whole life have I felt such terror and I am still shaking now. My heart stopped when I saw their cars and wagons come speeding up the driveway and then the soldiers piling out of the back, like grey angry insects swarming over the grounds, waving their guns at our poor majordome who looked terrified. He raised his hands in surrender and the driver of the truck that bore the paintings was dragged away. For a second, my body froze, but my legs shook so badly I thought I might collapse.

I had been busy packing a valise that contained the personal belongings of my Duchesse. I had gathered everything she asked for – the Fabergé egg, her jewellery, the Bassano vase she brought back from her Grand Tour, the dresses given to her by Mademoiselle Chanel, the books signed by Monsieur Hemmingway and Madame Stein, so many other things that took an age to collect and wrap properly so they would be safe during their journey.

I was in such a flap because the painting from Monsieur Picasso would not fit inside so when I spotted the Nazis from the bedroom window I panicked. They were running everywhere, and I knew that I would never get away. Then an idea came to me, so I picked up the valise and ran so fast, from the bedroom to the section of panelled wall that la Duchesse had shown me. It was our secret, she said, and it was where she kept her love letters. From whom, I have no clue because I would not pry but she asked me to hide them there, if any arrived while she was away in Paris. I opened the panel, you have to do it just so, then I shoved the valise inside the space on top of her letters.

It only just fit but to my horror there was no room for the painting, and I could hear the soldiers' boots as they came up the stairs, so I pushed it inside the deep pocket of my pinafore then ran back to the bedroom and began pulling at the sheets, rolling them into a bundle that I held in front of me. When the soldiers entered the room, they saw a silly servant girl doing her job and began shouting at me. I thought I would die of fright because one was waving his gun and pointing to the door while the others began ransacking the room.

Doing as I was told, I ran, passing soldiers on the way down, seeing others scouring the lower rooms as I went. Cook was in the kitchen when I arrived. She was crying and looked so scared and told me we had to go, immediately. I dropped the sheets where I stood. Cook passed me my coat that I threw on and buttoned up as we left. Both of us held on tightly to the other as we ran to the town where there were even more soldiers. Cook went to her sister's, and I came back here, to where I felt safe with Mama and Papa and dear baby Claude.

It breaks my heart to know that I have left my things at Chevalier, the love letters from my Gregoire, but my greatest fear is that they will find the valise so I pray it remains hidden and that one day la Duchesse will come home and I can return it to her. For now, I must hide the painting by Monsieur Picasso because she told me it was her greatest joy after her children, and I have found a way to do so.

I have taken the photo from my parents' bedroom wall, the one of us all at Claude's baptism and put it inside the pretty frame, covering the painting. I will present it to Mama as a gift. I will have to tell a lie and say that it was one that la Duchesse no longer required and gave to me. I promise to go to confession and pay penance for my sin, but I shall be vague and not admit it all to le curé. It will be worth it because Mama will be thrilled, and the painting will be safe here on her bedroom wall.

I will not say a word of this to anyone, not even Eglantine because it is too dangerous and if it slips out, I fear the Nazis coming to La Fleurie and taking Papa and the painting. I have done my best for la Duchesse so all I can do now is wait and pray for so many things. For my darling Gregoire, for my precious Chevalier and for my beautiful France.

When Antoinette finished reading, Mac saw her lips wobble and wondered if she was thinking the same as he.

It was Fabienne who spoke first, wiping her eyes as she did so. 'Oh, the poor girl. She had been so brave and clever but didn't know when she wrote that, what was going to happen to her. It is so, so sad.'

Antoinette then filled in the blanks. 'I think that she wanted to write it all down and get it out of her system, and then realised that even an entry in her diary would have been dangerous so tore it out and put it with the painting. And now we know why she went back to Chevalier so often. She was worried about the valise and maybe she did hope to get inside and get it back, but it was impossible. Then they caught her and... you know.'

They were all silent for a moment. Mac didn't want to think what terror his great-aunt went through, so focused his attention elsewhere. 'And now we know that somewhere at Chevalier is a case full of the Duchesse's personal effects. Have you any idea where this secret panel is?'

The two friends shook their heads, Fabienne answering for both of them. 'We know there are secret passages all around the chateau, marked on the original plans for the house, which are kept at the apartment. But I have never seen anything that refers to a panel and I honestly wouldn't know where to begin because apart from the attics and kitchen, most of the walls are lined with oak or mahogany.'

Antoinette had an idea. 'It must be on the first floor though, near *les grandes chambres* where we know la Duchesse had her private rooms so we should start there. Or maybe it's in the gallery, because Antoinette said she had to run fast.'

'I think we could re-enact the scene, that might give us something to go on.' Mac had a feeling it would be a challenge, finding the mystery location of the valise and then pointed to yet another, the letter they hadn't read yet. 'Shall we see what's in the envelope? It's addressed to the Duchesse at the chateau and the writing looks old.'

Fabienne reached over and picked it up, smiling as she read the front and then pulled out the paper inside, slowly unfolding the letter and no sooner had she read the first few words, then scanned down to the bottom when her hand flew to her mouth. 'It's from him... Picasso. Do you realise what this means?' She looked up at Mac and Antoinette who both shook their heads. 'Provenance. Not only do we have an original painting signed by one of the world's greatest artists, we also have a letter written by his own hand, gifting it to my great-grandmother. Irrefutable proof that it belongs to my family.'

Antoinette disagreed immediately. 'No, Fabienne it does not. As the will states, the Picasso is a chattel passed down from female to female and that means it belongs to you. And do you see what this means? We are like musketeers and together with the help of our dear Antoinette and her crazy friend Eglantine, we have done it, we have saved Chevalier. It's all going to be okay.'

Mac spent the next few minutes consoling Fabienne who could not stop crying, while Antoinette headed to the kitchen to fetch glasses and wine, saying her nerves were shot and she needed a drink. And while Fabienne sobbed, and Antoinette searched for crisps, Mac looked around the *salon* at his grandparents' things. Before, he would have regarded them as clutter but now, even though they weren't worth a small fortune, they were just as priceless. They were his heritage, his treasure and even if eventually he stored them in a box, he would keep them close and cherish them and the memories of two people he would love and remember, forever.

It was early evening and the three musketeers had talked and talked of nothing else, other than their discovery, in between rereading the letters and gazing at a masterpiece. No matter how euphoric they were, serious plans and decisions eventually had to be made.

'So, what do you have to do now, with the painting?' Mac had no idea how these things worked.

Fabienne rubbed her eyes that were still pink from crying happy tears. 'We need to get it authenticated and keep it safe. That's the priority right now. I'm so sure of its provenance that I can inform our accountants and lawyer straight away and ask them to hold the bank off for a bit longer. Once they hear about the Picasso I doubt it will be a problem especially when the news breaks because it is going to be a massive story. You both know that don't you?'

There followed a squeal and flurry of excited questions and fanciful scenarios from Antoinette who was already imagining being interviewed on television and radio, because, after all, she was Fabienne's newly appointed agent, manager, PR woman, not to mention oldest and most loyal friend and resident archivist at Chevalier... the list went on. Mac brought a semblance of calm when he asked Fabienne what she was going to do first.

'I have a friend who works at the Picasso Museum in Paris, quite close to the apartment and I want him and his colleagues to see it first because I know how thrilled they will be. I need to take it there tonight. I can put the painting in the safe at the apartment and go to the museum first thing in the morning. It's about a four-hour drive so if we set off now, we will be there around ten. And if Papa is awake, I can explain.' Fabienne looked up at the startled faces of Mac and Antoinette.

'What, you want us to come too?' Mac was secretly over the moon that she wanted him along whereas Antoinette declined.

'I can't come. I just realised I'm taking Grandmère to a hospital appointment tomorrow, and she won't be happy if I don't show up. But it doesn't matter; I can tell her about our discovery, which she will be so excited about. You two lovebirds will have to go without me.'

Fabienne looked disappointed but said she understood then turned to Mac. 'Looks like it's you and me, partner, so get a move on. We are going to Paris, tonight, now!'

Within seconds they had sprung into action, taking glasses and bowls into the kitchen while Mac raced upstairs to find something half decent to wear for his unexpected trip and as he grabbed underwear and socks and threw them onto the bed, something else occurred to him: that he wasn't the only one having a surprising day because unbeknown to good old Hugo, in a few hours he was going to get a knock on the door and a bit of a shock himself, in more ways than one.

24

VERONIQUE

The waves of nausea were getting stronger with every passing hour. Each time she tried to get hold of René the automated voice told her his phone was switched off and the bile rose in her throat, the acid sting a by-product of an empty stomach. Veronique was weak from nerves and hunger; this and running out of her pills only exacerbated the tremors in her hands that just would not be still. There was no way to prevent René from carrying out his plan that she had memorised word for word, and this only added to her anxiety because she could picture it all. Where he would be, the lone gunman, a black panther stealthily approaching the apartment?

When dusk fell at 9pm and the street lights flickered on outside the apartment Veronique had tried one more time to ring René only to receive the same reply. He had switched off his phone for this very reason, because he knew she would want to back out. *You fool. You ridiculous, stupid fool. When will you ever learn?*

One hour later and realising that her incessant pacing was a giveaway to her heightened state of unease, she sat, hands clasped, the nail of her thumb digging into her palm as she looked over to Hugo. He was smoking a cigar. Only the best for him because of course, he still believed that Quai d'Orsay was emblematic of French taste and a luxury lifestyle, and while he polluted the apartment, inconsiderate of her dislike for the habit, Veronique's eyes flicked over her withered husband.

His hair was styled as always, parted on the left, silver-grey but barely thinning, his skin smooth because vanity still afforded a visit to the barbers for a wet shave while the utility bills piled high. He was wearing his habitual shirt and tie, all buttoned up and proper, cuffs fastened with links, his father's Cartier at his wrist. Next her eyes moved downwards to the awful moss-green slacks he favoured, her gaze resting finally on his socks, fastened with hideous garters and on his feet, his old man slippers. Gone was the rakish chap she'd once lusted after and in his place sat a man who resembled the faded portrait of his father, the last good Duc of Chevalier.

The volume on the television was at full blast and each commercial jingle jangled her nerves, pinging each one like a taut elastic band. Hugo was watching his favourite programme, *Des Racines et Des Ailes,* a documentary series devoted to heritage, history and knowledge.

How ironic, that the man who had zero respect for most things had somehow convinced himself he was still part of the landed French hierarchy, revelling in glory days of old, and it made her sick. When the old Duc died suddenly in the sixties, his loyal heir, Hugo's father, picked up the baton and at least tried to keep the Chevalier faith. Guiding the Bombelles through a worldwide oil crisis and then a recession that wiped millions off their shares. Then sadly, it was the turn of the old fool seated opposite and it was he who had finally brought them to their knees.

Glancing at the clock, Veronique attempted calm by sucking in the air then immediately regretted it when her lungs filled with poison more putrid than the thoughts that filled her brain. It was 10.05pm – almost time – and she thought she might die of fear as she went over what her brother had drummed into her.

The man René had hired would wait until it was dark then, keeping his face well-hidden, the black-clad gunman would wind his way through the backstreets of Paris and approach the apartment block from the rear.

The robbery was scheduled for a Wednesday when the concierge always left the back gates to the yard open for the binmen to enter the following morning at 5am. Unlike the front of the building, there were no security cameras in the utility area. The door to the ground-floor yard was always locked, however, on refuse day it was often left on the catch and used frequently by residents and, if you were lucky enough to still have one, your cleaner. Therefore, it would be easy to hide in the shadows and while someone disposed of their rubbish, sneak inside. But just in case it was locked, the gunman had been provided with a spare key, courtesy of Veronique.

Once inside, the gunman would make his way up the stairs, preferably unseen by any other residents who, if they did pass by, would think nothing of someone receiving a visitor, presuming they had been buzzed in via the intercom on the front of the building.

Once at the door of the apartment, the gunman would ring the bell and wait until he heard the clip-clop of heels approaching from the other side and Veronique call out, *'un instant'* and only then, would he pull on his ski-mask and take out the gun – a fake, although Veronique wasn't to let on, but to act terrified when she opened the door. He would then force her into the *salon* at gunpoint.

All being well, Hugo would capitulate immediately, seeing his wife with the barrel of the silencer pressed against her temple and if not, the gunman would turn his attention on Hugo and then his adoring wife would step up, open the safe and save his life.

The gunman would then tape them both to chairs before making his getaway. And, because he was a helpful kind of criminal whose mother brought him up well, he would take Veronique's bag of rubbish with him and after popping it in the bin, he would leave the same way he came in.

Veronique knew it all by heart and going over it again had left her quaking, her mouth bone dry and she was about to stand, thinking she might keep down a sip of water when the sound she had been dreading pealed through the apartment. The shrill ring of a bell reverberated down the long corridor to the *salon* at the far end.

When Hugo looked across his surprise preceded the note of irritation in his voice at his programme being rudely interrupted. 'Are you expecting someone? If it's that annoying woman from next door inviting us for drinks again make sure you say no. She's an unbearable bore.'

Veronique stood as he resumed his viewing and then on shaking legs, she made her way to the door, reciting the assurance René had given over the phone. *'Keep calm. Remember that the gun is fake. No bullets. He won't harm you. Do not be scared of the mask. Just play along and do as he says. Be brave and then you will be free to start a new life. Focus on that. I have done my part. Don't let me down'.*

The bell rang again and, just as she had been told, she made sure her heels clicked hard on the tiled floor and said the words 'One moment.' She could see her hands shaking as she turned the catch and with the other pulled open the door and there, just as expected, stood a black-clad figure, the hood of his jacket pulled up and underneath he was wearing a ski-mask, only his eyes visible, one hand tucked inside his jacket as he stepped into the apartment. After closing the door, holding her breath she turned to face the gunman and waited for the scene to play out, resigned to making this look real. No going back.

The sound of the commercial break and then Hugo calling her made Veronique start. 'Who was it? I'm having a drink. Shall I fix you one?'

When she saw the gunman raise his leather gloved finger to his lips she obeyed and prepared for the scene to commence but when he began to tug at the ski-mask her blood turned to ice. As the face beneath was revealed and her lips became numbed by horror, Veronique managed to mouth the word, *'René.'*

Taking two steps backwards her body slammed against the front door, and she almost lost control of her bladder and bowels as he pointed the gun in her direction and sneered, 'Hello, sister dear. Surprise.'

Her whole body shook as she whispered, 'What are you doing? Why are you here? Why this pretence? I do not understand.'

Tutting and shaking his head, René stepped forward and laughed quietly in her face. 'Did you really think I would risk involving a third party when I could enjoy another one of our little charades, you know, like the old days?'

'But the plan, the mask...'

'Oh, do keep up, Veronique. I couldn't just roll up at the front like a regular visitor and have everyone see me; that would be foolish. I had to make sure some low life was picked up on cameras here and there along the route, and that the man I passed in the foyer will remember the ignorant hooded guy who couldn't be bothered to say hello. And once the *gendarmes* have put it all together everyone will believe what is going to happen tonight was just an armed robbery that went horribly wrong.'

'Oh God, what are you going to do?' Veronique could barely

speak or focus, tears clouding her vision while invisible hands squeezed her throat and lungs.

'Well, let's go inside and see, shall we? Come along, sister. I've been waiting for this for years, oh, and in case I forget later, thank you for giving me the perfect excuse to finish some family business. You really came good when you married Hugo. I'm almost proud of you.' The sarcasm in his voice was replaced by a harder edge that was enforced by the butt of the silencer being flicked in the direction of the *salon*. 'Now move.'

Doing as she was told, staring down the barrel of a gun that she now knew was loaded, Veronique sidled past her brother and holding in a sob, made her way towards her husband. Somehow putting one foot in front of the other, the most bizarre thought suddenly came to Veronique. She hoped that Hugo had drank his cognac, slugging back a nice big measure of his finest cru because as she felt the prod of steel between her shoulder blades, she feared it would be her husband's last.

Hugo had his back to them when they entered the room. He replaced the cap on the decanter, picked up two glasses and then turned as he spoke. 'Ah, finally got rid of the nosey old crone. Here, I poured you–' When he saw Veronique with René he faltered, caught off guard before rallying. 'Oh, René. I didn't know we were expecting you. I'll pour another.'

Veronique wanted to scream that there was no need to be cordial anymore, or to pretend one didn't despise the other, albeit for completely different reasons. Instead, she screamed silently, *He's going to kill you, Hugo. He wants revenge, not a glass of cognac.*

It was when René stepped sideways and pointed the gun at her husband, she saw the light dawn in Hugo's eyes as she listened to her brother's instruction's. 'Veronique. Close the curtains quickly and then turn off that crap on the television. Hugo, sit on the chair, that one, now.'

Obeying, she rushed over to the first of the two windows that were covered in voile, partially obscuring their *salon* from the apartments across the way, praying as she unhooked the ties and dragged the heavy drapes across that a nosey neighbour might just be able to glimpse what was going on. After she'd closed the second set, Veronique faced the room as Hugo found his voice.

'What the hell do you think you are doing? Barging in here waving that thing about and threatening my wife.'

René harrumphed and ignored Hugo completely and instead put his hands in his pockets and pulled out a roll of silver tape which he threw on the chaise. 'So, who is going to do the honours and open the safe? Hugo, perhaps you would be so kind and then I won't have to shoot your dear wife who you suddenly care so much about. Or perhaps I should just save time and blow your brains out then she can get on with it. She's good at doing things for me, aren't you, Veronique?'

Never had she hated anyone like she hated René in that moment, because of all the things she'd suffered, her years at the farm, her father, all of it. The worst thing of all was how René never let her forget. Each time he referred to it, another part of her died.

Hugo was furious, spittle flicking from his lips as he pointed at René. 'You won't get away with this, and I won't open the safe. And neither will Veronique. She doesn't even know the code so you're wasting your time.'

When René threw his head back and roared with laughter, Veronique could have bet her life on what he was about to say.

'Of course she knows the code, you idiot. Who do you think came up with all this?' René waved his hand and raised his eyebrow as he smirked. 'It was my clever little sister's idea to stage a robbery, and shall we say, liberate you from whatever is in the safe. But what she didn't know was I'm going to liberate you, Hugo. That little pleasure is going to be mine.'

When Hugo crumpled at the knee and staggered towards his chair, Veronique experienced a moment of compassion for a man she had come to despise because she knew exactly how it felt, the kick in the gut after being betrayed. When Hugo looked at her, she expected sorrow or disappointment and experienced another shock wave, ripping through her core when instead she saw hate, pure unadulterated hate.

'I should have known you'd be in on it, you bitch, and after I took pity on you when you turned up here penniless. God, you two are as bad as each other so go on, tell me, was it all a con from the start, you being in Paris? Nothing would surprise me anymore, not where Sabers are concerned and to think, I was prepared to let bygones be bygones.'

Veronique tried to speak but Hugo was so angry he didn't give her time.

'I was so glad to see you again despite everything that happened all those years ago. Even though he used me, I believed you were different.' Hugo gave a jerk of his head in René's direction but didn't look him in the face, as though doing so really would make him sick.

Veronique watched as Hugo slumped in the chair and shook his head. He looked weary, as though the fight had left him, and he was resigned to his fate. This thought completely rocked her. These could be the last few minutes of his life, both their lives, and it made her determined to set the record straight. Even if she didn't love him in the way she should, she bore him no real malice, not enough to want him dead. So, if they were both going to die in that room, she wanted him to know who she really was, or who she wished she could be. But before she could speak it seemed René had other ideas, striding over and dragging her roughly across the room towards Hugo.

'Tape his arms to the chair and then we can get on with it. I haven't got the time or patience for a stroll down memory lane. Move it, now.'

Still terrified that René might be planning to shoot her, too, Veronique picked up the tape from the chaise and knelt before Hugo and as she did, heard the sneer in her brother's voice. 'That's right, sister, on your knees where you belong.'

Without thinking Veronique's head spun around and she looked him in the eye. 'Just fuck off, René, you piece of scum. Just fuck off.' When the back of his hand made contact with the side of her face, the ring on his middle finger caught her cheekbone, chafing her skin and drawing blood. It took her straight back to the farm and the sting of her father's temper. But she wasn't a little girl anymore and she would not be cowed, not by the hand of a man or a bullet from a gun so refusing to cry, she grabbed Hugo's arms and shook him.

'Hugo, Hugo, look at me. Please.' Slowly he lifted his head, another cold hard stare met hers, clearly unmoved by the sight of her bloodied face, or maybe he was in shock. Whichever, she tried to make him understand. 'Hugo, I swear that our meeting at the café was purely by chance, and *he* had nothing to do with it, God's honour. Yes, when you came into my life, I was destitute and I was grateful because you saved me from having to turn to him, so no matter what you think of me right now, I thank you for that and I want you to know from the bottom of my heart that I am so sorry for this.' Again, he simply stared as René slapped her hard around the back of her head, making her brain rattle and for a second or two everything went fuzzy, and she thought she might black out. Only her brother's angry voice brought her back from the edge and sharpened her wits.

'Get on with it.'

As she taped Hugo's arms to the chair, she let the tears fall as her husband found his voice.

'Why, why did you do this? I don't understand. I know we are not the perfect couple, but we rubbed along, we understood each other, two of a kind.'

Looking into his eyes she saw they had softened slightly, and this made her cry. 'Because I've had enough, Hugo. I just wanted to go, by myself, away from the arguments about money, and the worry of it all. I could see that if anything happened to you then I'd get nothing because you have nothing. I would never get my villa by the sea, so I settled for escaping, from him more than anyone.' Veronique gave a flick of her head towards René who stood right behind her. 'I thought I could rent a room, put some money aside, get a job and live a quiet life. But I never wanted this, so please, if you believe nothing else, please believe that.'

He looked deep into her eyes, as though thinking it through and when he gave a gentle nod, Veronique broke down, curling into a crumpled heap on the floor, incapable of anything while she listened to Hugo's angry voice.

'Before you kill me, René, because I know I'm not getting out of this room alive, I want you to know one thing. That I am proud to be a Bombelle, a good and honourable family and even though I have made many, many mistakes of which I am ashamed, I thank God that I am not a Saber, and I don't come from perverted, tainted stock that is riddled to the core by hate and ignorance that eat at you like maggots.'

René stepped forward and pointed the gun as Veronique raised her throbbing head and willed Hugo to be quiet. Her brother's eyes were wild. 'You had better shut the fuck up, old man, or I will finish you right now.'

Still Hugo taunted him. 'And remember this, René, that even if you do get away with killing me, the Bombelle legacy will not die. Fabienne is worth a thousand Sabers and you are not fit to lick her boots. So do your worst because I will die happy knowing my daughter lives on, and so will our name.'

When René began laughing, manically, like some deranged cinematic madman, Veronique looked to Hugo and saw the fear return to his eyes while she experienced a deep sense of foreboding.

Her brother pushed his face closer to Hugo's, his voice pure malice. 'Not if I have anything to do with it, old friend. Because while I'm putting a bullet in your head, I have arranged for another tragic event to take place. Just imagine the headlines, they will be magnificent.' René straightened then raising his hand in a dramatic gesture, pictured the news. *Bankrupt Hugo Bombelle stages insurance fraud that went horribly wrong.*'

Veronique screamed at René, no longer fearing her own mortality. 'What have you done? René, for God's sake what have you done?'

'Keep up, you cretin. Can't you see how easy you made it for me to wipe the earth clean of the Bombelles and frame this pathetic piece of shit at the same time. Even when he and his daughter are dead and buried their name will be remembered with shame.'

Hugo was like a man possessed, screaming obscenities as he pulled and shook the chair, desperately trying to get his arms free as panic ravaged his face, escaping via his voice. 'What have you done? Where is Fabienne? If you have hurt her...'

'What? What will you do, old man? Nothing, as always because,' he gave a flick of the wrist and checked his watch, 'right now, Chevalier is on fire and if they have done their job as I instructed, it will be razed to the ground and whoever is inside will perish. Poof, gone, just like that.'

It was the sarcasm, and the click of his fingers and the sheer disregard for human life that flooded Veronique with rage she'd never experienced and in one cat-like movement she summoned enough strength to pounce, punching him in the gut so hard she thought she'd broken her wrist. When the butt of the gun caught her full force, square on the jaw and her head connected with the side of the coffee table, pain seared through her skull then a second later, the room went black.

25

FABIENNE

They climbed the stairs to the apartment and all the while, in between exclaiming how grand and beautiful the interior of the building was, Mac reminded her how desperately he needed the loo and a change of clothes. Due to an emergency stop as Fabienne negotiated the notoriously hazardous roundabout at the Arc de Triomphe, Mac had spilt a whole cup of coffee down his shirt.

'I can't meet your dad looking like this. What will he think? I look a right mess.'

Fabienne tutted. 'Well, it's your own fault for taking the lid off.'

'It was too hot! They always make drinks too hot.' Mac pulled at his soggy shirt that was sticking to his chest.

'Well, at least it had cooled down, otherwise we'd have had to stop by the hospital and get you treated for burns. Anyway, we are here. You can use the loo and change in there if it makes you happy. I will go find Papa and explain what's happened.' Fabienne knew her father and Veronique were up because when she pointed to the apartment from the road, she could see a slice of light through the curtains.

'Well, hurry up and open the door because I'm bursting here.' Mac jiggled on the spot like a child.

She took out her key to the apartment, unlocked the door and pushed it open. As they stepped into the hall she pointed to the first door, which was a guest bathroom. Giving her the thumbs up Mac rushed inside, taking his rucksack with him, while Fabienne placed her overnight bag on the floor and took the painting, wrapped in brown paper with her.

Her Converse shoes made no sound on the marble floor so as she headed towards the *salon* at the end of the corridor, she heard a raised voice. Pausing, Fabienne listened.

'Veronique, Veronique, wake up! Get up. For God's sake, what have you done?'

What the hell? Fabienne's hand flew to her neck. Were they having a row? Her father sounded angry and she was unsure what to do. And then came her stepmother's voice, groggy and weak. Maybe she was drunk? Instead of announcing herself Fabienne moved closer to the door. Over the next few short minutes as she tried to picture the scene in the *salon,* the eavesdropper would hear no good, about anyone or anything.

'It's okay, Hugo, I'm fine... all this, it is nothing, I'm used to it... some things will never change and it's true, what my dear demented brother says about me, the hints, the digs, the sarcastic looks. He is right.' There followed a pause before she continued and when they came, laboured but clear, Veronique's words took Fabienne's breath away.

'Yes, I was a whore... because from childhood my brother made his little sister do things that no child should... for a crust of bread, a bicycle. And I tried to escape him so many times... but I am weak, pathetic. The demons in my head always catch up and ruin what happiness I find... and look, even now I can't rid myself of him. Even you couldn't keep me safe or give me the one thing I truly craved.'

Fabienne covered her mouth with her hands, horrified as in between sobs, Veronique's words had been laced with sadness and then came her father's voice, mirroring that of his wife.

'And what was it, this thing you craved all these years, Veronique? Money?'

Another sob. 'No, Hugo. I wanted a home I could call my own, a place to rest my head, then lift it up and not feel shame but most of all, I would have liked someone to be kind, and love me for what is in here.'

Fabienne knew that Veronique would have touched her heart and it made her own break for the woman she'd gravely misunderstood. But it was the sound of a third voice that came as the greatest shock.

'Bravo, Veronique, bravo. That was most touching, I must say.'

René. She recognised his voice, all her assumptions about him were now brought to bear but when Fabienne heard the slow clapping, white hot rage consumed her. She was about to open the door when she stopped.

Her father's voice again, raised and angry. 'You're mad, completely mad. I always thought you were and then after the accident, that's when I knew for sure, when you started blackmailing me. I saw it in your eyes, how much you enjoyed manipulating me and everyone else who was unfortunate enough to cross your path, even your own sister. You disgust me.'

What did he mean about the accident? Fabienne listened to René's reply.

'Pah, don't feel sorry for that whore because she deserves everything she gets, especially you. The pair of you are a drain on humanity, you make me sick. I don't know who I despise the most, that thing over there for being such a pathetic, pill-guzzling mess or you, the man who killed his own wife and child, running them off the road and watching while they burned to death. And all for a bet.'

Fabienne thought she was going to collapse and had to use the wall to support herself as she listened to René mock her father, the man who she now knew was responsible for the deaths of her mother and her brother.

'And I remember that night so well. You, crying like a baby, saying you didn't want to go to jail, that it wasn't your fault. But it was your fault, Hugo. You were completely drunk and on the wrong side of the road when your wife came around the corner.'

'ENOUGH! I won't listen to another word. I've had this hanging over me for years while you bled me dry, roping me into investment opportunities that always turned sour, calling in one favour after another but I have nothing left to give so go on. Tell everyone what you know. I don't care anymore. Do you hear me, René? I DON'T CARE!'

There followed a heartbeat of silence and in it, Fabienne pushed open the door and took in the scene, confused and not believing what she saw. Her father was sitting, his arms taped to a chair, eyes bulging from his ashen face, while Veronique crouched on the floor by his side, her face smeared with blood. Opposite stood René, his back to Fabienne, unaware of her presence.

Those facing her looked shocked when she entered the room and Fabienne was just about to say, 'But I care, Papa,' when René slowly turned and although it took a millisecond to register, Fabienne's words evaporated when she spotted the gun.

Think, think, don't panic.

As a million thoughts raced through her head, knowing that at any second Mac would emerge from the bathroom and alert René to his presence she slowly placed the painting on the bureau by her side and then raised her hands and just as she said loudly, 'Don't shoot, please don't shoot,' her voice muffled the sound of the bathroom door opening.

She caught a flicker of movement to her right, inwardly relieved when Mac stopped but she could feel his stare, knew he would be as terrified and panicked as she. She prayed he would remain silent, not give himself away while they listened to René's special brand of sarcasm.

'Well, well, well. If it isn't my dear step-niece. How kind of you to join us, Fabienne. I have to say it's something of a surprise but hey, you're here now so come and join the party.' René sneered and gave the gun a flick, indicating she should move further into the room as her father watched and whispered, 'Oh, God, no.'

She had to convey to Mac exactly what she could see so he could alert the police and as she moved forward raised her voice in anger. 'Why is my father tied up and what have you done to Veronique? Why is she bleeding? And please stop pointing that gun at me!' Once she had taken up position between her father and Veronique, Fabienne faced René and prayed that Mac didn't decide it was his day to be a hero and come barging through the door.

'Ooh, feisty. I like that but it's a pity that I don't have time to waste listening to your smart mouth so shut up and do as you are told.'

Fabienne noticed the beads of perspiration on René's forehead and suspected her arrival had rattled him. But his hand was steady and his eyes glazed, and that was not a good sign, and neither was her father's plea.

'Please, René, let her go. Kill me like you planned but spare her. She has done nothing wrong, so I beg you, don't hurt her.'

Fabienne gasped as the magnitude of her father's words hit home, full force as she watched René sneer. 'Veronique, get up.

I need you to do the same to her as her father. Then you are going to open the safe. MOVE.'

As Veronique struggled to her feet, Fabienne forced herself not to look at the door in case René noticed so instead she focused on her stepmother who was in a bad way, clearly dazed and in pain, blood seeping from the back of her head and matting her hair. It was as Fabienne attempted to help Veronique to her feet that they heard a strange noise, and when she turned saw that her father was in distress, his face contorted with pain as he gasped for air. She didn't even have time to call his name before his body slumped forward, his head flopping to his chest, then silence.

'Papa, PAPA!' Fabienne dropped to the floor and began to shake him, then began feeling for a pulse, begging him to wake up.

Veronique crawled towards them, repeating the word *no*, over and over before screeching at her brother. 'Look what you have done... Are you happy now? You got what you wanted; he is dead. You killed him, so bravo, René, bravo, you animal.' The yelp when he kicked Veronique in the ribs made Fabienne wince, and seeing he was going to do it again, she threw her body in the way and screamed 'no!' The toe of his boot connecting with her biceps made her cry out.

'Shut up, bitch. Now both of you get up or I will shoot him in the head just to make sure he's dead. UP. NOW!'

René had the gun pressed against the top of her father's bowed head giving Fabienne no other choice than to do as he said. She turned to Veronique. 'Please, try to stand. I will help you, come on. It's going to be okay. We can do this.'

It was a struggle, made worse by the fact that if her father wasn't dead already, he soon would be. He needed urgent medical assistance so she prayed that Mac had called for help. But it was as Veronique got to her feet, unsteady and dazed, that a figure appeared in the doorway edging closer to René, a fire extinguisher raised and ready to strike.

While Fabienne was in control of her senses, Veronique was not and as she raised her head the sight of Mac startled her, causing her to cry out. It all happened in a split second, René realising what was happening then spinning around, pointing the gun, a muted shot, the strange popping sound of death in a bullet as it powered through cloth and skin, then Mac hitting the ground.

René took three steps backwards and not caring if he shot her too, Fabienne leapt forward and crawled the last few centimetres on hands and knees to Mac's bloodied body. 'NO! No, no, no...' She patted his face as blood oozed from a shoulder wound and when he stirred relief flooded her body. 'It's okay, Mac, you're going to be okay. Try to stay awake, that's good, keep your eyes open.' She had no idea whether that was the right thing to say and was repeating stuff she'd seen in films, which reminded her to stem the flow of blood, so she looked around and seeing nothing useful, resorted to her own T-shirt that she dragged over her head and scrunched into a ball.

Mac was staring at the ceiling, muttering. 'I'm sorry, I messed up, don't hurt her, please don't hurt her, the police are coming... any minute...'

Inside she rejoiced, he had made the call, so staying focused until they arrived and keeping her tone as light as she could, Fabienne ripped open the front of Mac's shirt, gagging when she saw his punctured skin and the flow of red. 'Hey, looks like you've ruined another good shirt. Don't worry, we'll get you a new one.' And with that she pressed her T-shirt onto the site and pushed hard as she watched his eyelids flutter; she continued talking, but this time to René.

'You are going to hell and prison for this, and I will make sure you rot before the devil drags you down to where you belong. Mac heard everything and called the police so you might as well just give yourself up. Or you could make a run for it before they get here, which will be any second.' And when she dragged her eyes away from Mac's face and raised them to René's, she saw it. Fear.

Veronique spoke next, the tremor in her voice relaying her fragile state. 'Listen to her, René, go, now before they arrive.' Her tone wasn't one of concern, like she had the best interests of her brother at heart. More that she wanted him gone, as far away from her as possible.

Fabienne watched a nerve above his eye twitch and saw beads of perspiration running down his forehead and prayed he would take their advice and flee. She needed to get ambulances for her father and Mac. Fabienne watched René like a hawk, could see he was considering his predicament, pacing, rushing over to the window, peeping though the crack in the curtains.

Then, in the distance, the wail of sirens and she almost wept with relief and urged René to flee. 'They are coming. You should go right now.' But when the sound grew louder and she saw the reflection of blue lights in the mirror on the wall opposite, breaking through the crack in the curtains Fabienne's stomach flipped, especially when René began tapping his forehead with the butt of the gun, cursing under his breath.

They could hear the slam of car doors outside and more sirens and then the unmistakable whir of helicopter blades overhead. And then René reacted. 'Veronique, you are coming with me. Move, now.'

Her voice barely audible, Veronique begged, 'Please, René, leave me be.'

'NO! Do as you are told. You will be my hostage. They will have to let me go.'

Fabienne almost laughed. 'Don't be stupid, René. Give yourself up. You will never get away. Where would you go? Be sensible. The place will be surrounded; you have no other option.' But as she said the words, she saw his eyes drift to Veronique, sheer hate written across his face. Fabienne's heart missed a beat, and she knew what was going through his mind.

Maybe his sister guessed too. From what Fabienne had overheard René had some weird hold over Veronique and wouldn't let her go, especially when his back was against the wall. And in a moment of utter despair, two minds, two women who had once been poles apart suddenly connected.

When Veronique spoke, it was with deep sadness in her eyes. 'Fabienne, please know I am sorry for how I behaved towards you, and I wish things could have been different, that we could have been friends.'

All Fabienne could do was nod and say goodbye, because that's what it was, her lips quivering as she sucked in a sob. 'And I, too, am sorry, and I wish the same, Veronique.'

Then came the most terrible news, when Veronique's eyes widened like she had remembered something, a panicked message delivered in a rush, as though she was scared that René would turn the gun on her at any second. 'Fabienne, do as I say. When I am gone you must ring the *pompiers* immediately because he set Chevalier alight... He means to burn it to the ground. He thought you were there. He wanted you dead too.'

Fabienne froze. The image of her beloved home on fire stunned her into silence and then as the flames in her imagination lit her heart, rage ignited her soul. Balling the bloodied T-shirt into her fist she screeched and threw it in René's face. And in the seconds his eyes moved from his sister to bat it away, Veronique ran from the room, punching open the door to the next.

René didn't miss a beat and flung the T-shirt to the floor then followed and the second he disappeared from view, Fabienne began searching Mac's body for his phone begging some unknown and unseeable force for help. 'Please, please don't let her die, please God don't take her from me. Antoinette, please hold on, don't leave me, Antoinette...'

Fabienne winced when Mac groaned as she moved him, finally locating the phone in his back pocket and with hands that could barely stay still long enough, she prodded the screen and called for help. Time was running out for Antoinette, for Mac, for her father. And for Veronique.

26

VERONIQUE

Staggering, her stupid heels slowing her down while concussion blurred her vision, Veronique made her way through the dining room and towards the balcony. She could hear the devil only metres behind and any second expected a bullet to hit her in the back yet still she ran, one hand dragging along the wall, the other arm outstretched as her fingertips swept aside the voile that blew in the evening air.

Veronique knew she would be trapped, but it was the only place to go, and her only escape was to jump over the edge. She listened to the desperate voice in her head that screamed at her to run, and she didn't care if it hurt when she hit the ground as long as she was away from him. As she burst onto the balcony and felt the warm summer night brush her skin, Veronique had no fear, she was elated and gloried in being moments away from freedom as she prepared to leap to her death.

But when rough hands grabbed her hair and dragged her down, she screamed in terror as her knees connected with the floor tiles and René's fingers pulled hard at her roots causing her to squeal like one of her father's pigs. Veronique raised her hands and grabbed his, attempting to prise them away as a tinny voice echoed in her ears and the barrel of a gun pressed against the side of her head.

'This is the police. Do not shoot.'

She opened her eyes and saw that the walls of the apartment opposite were lit with blue flashes from the police vehicles down below. Through the rails she saw the street was packed with them. Above, a bright white beam of light shone onto her and René, actors on a stage, caught in the spotlight. Again, the voice from the loudhailer.

'René Saber, drop the gun and raise your hands. You are surrounded. Give yourself up.'

Veronique felt his grip tighten as he twisted her head, forcing her to face him, his back to the apartment wall, hers to the street. Taking up position in front of her, René yanked her head back and slid the barrel along her skull until it rested on her forehead.

Looking up, she stared into the eyes of evil. 'René, stop this. Give yourself up. It does not have to end like this.' But Veronique heard how weary she sounded and, in that moment, knew she did not care anymore. Not about herself. Every part of her ached; her knees, her face but most of all her heart yet amongst all that she was calm, not afraid, almost serene. She had been prepared to die when she ran outside but right there and then it occurred to Veronique that this way might be better. Quicker perhaps, a bullet in the brain, and not a sin which meant she might even get to heaven and see Mama again.

Over the balcony René called out to the police. 'I will kill her unless you back off. I mean it. Drop your weapons or she dies.'

'It's useless. They will not let you go.'

'Fuck you, bitch. This is all your fault.'

And then it came, a flashback to a young boy falling from a tree, fear in his eyes and all those years later Veronique saw it again but this time, she wouldn't hold out her hand and, if she got the chance, would let him fall. Things had changed.

'Are you scared, René?'

'Shut your mouth.'

Veronique smiled, yes, he was terrified, so she persisted because time was running out. 'Was Alain scared? When you took him from me?'

Such immense joy spread across René's face that Veronique shuddered and as she stared into the gleeful eyes of the devil incarnate, he gave Veronique the answer. 'Ah, finally she dares to ask so yes, he was scared and begged for his life just after I told him all about you, the woman he wanted to marry.'

'What do you mean.'

René's eyes were wild now. 'Ha, the old-fashioned fool came to me and asked for your hand, even showed me the ring. It's a good one too, so you can rest knowing that he wasn't a cheapskate.'

While a part of her died before her real and imminent death occurred, another part of Veronique screamed that she shouldn't ask, but she did; she had to know. 'What did you do to him?'

'Well, put it this way, the crops in Monsieur Juet's cornfield were treated to some extra special fertiliser and his pigs really enjoyed their lunch. Does that answer your question, sister, dear?'

From deep within, the swell of nausea began to rise while her body sagged and now all that held her up was the clutch of René's hand, her head flopping backwards, no fight left. It was then that she saw movement to her left, a shadow man on the next balcony, and noticed the red dot that shone on René's forehead like the one flickering on his neck and she knew the end was close.

Her voice weak, the fight almost gone, Veronique willed it to be over soon. It was time to say goodbye to her brother, at the same time as goading him into pulling the trigger. 'Know this, René, that even though you took Alain from me, I never stopped loving him, and you can never take away the joy he gave me, something so wonderful and precious, a love you will never know, are incapable of. You're going to die, any second and then I hope you rot in hell because that's what scum like you deserve.'

'BITCH!'

She felt his body tense, fingers ripping away the roots of her hair, nails digging into her scalp. Blue lights flashed, the police on the ground monitored the scene above, sights trained on the target, whirring blades of the helicopter hovered in the night sky. And then amidst the stillness of a siege, somewhere below a door slammed, startling a lone turtle dove that broke cover, panicked, swooping, flapping its wings above René's head. In that split second, a trigger was pulled, and a shot rang out.

The end was swift. And as sirens wailed and ambulances sped to the scene, the turtle dove soared into the Parisian sky, fleeing the drama below. Free, just like Veronique.

27

ANTOINETTE

They were on the terrace, her and Joel, Fabienne and Mac and someone was cooking a barbeque. She could smell the smoke; it was strong and burning her nose, but she'd had far too much to drink and didn't care. Sleepy, so sleepy. She curled into a ball and told the others to save her some food. 'I'll eat later, too tired.'

And then a fly, something buzzing in her ear, so she batted it away, but it wouldn't stop, no matter how much she swiped. Then the buzz became a screech, then crackling, like a radio signal being tuned in, someone turning the dial, so that the sound flattened out and when the line was straight, she heard a voice. Faraway at first but even through the grog of wine Antoinette managed to focus, hear the words.

'Antoinette, wake up. Please, you must get up.'

She stirred.

The voice was louder now. 'Wake up, hurry. Antoinette, please listen to me. You have to go.'

So annoying. 'Fabienne, let me sleep. I drank too much. I'll see you in the morning.'

'No, please get up. You have to leave. There is a fire; there is a fire.'

A fire? No, it's just the barbeque... but the smoke was hurting her nose... and her throat. She needed water so tried to open her eyes, but they were too heavy and then, even though glue was sticking her eyelids together Antoinette saw a glint of light, the moon at the window. Where was she? Where was Fabienne?

And then she realised. *Paris.* Then who was calling her name?

'That's it, wake up, open your eyes.'

Doing as she was told Antoinette forced her eyelids open and in that second, when realisation collided with terror, the word she'd heard made sense and panic took hold. The room was thick with smoke, swirling in the beams cast by the moon. The chateau was on fire, yellow flames coming under the door that led to the library. She was in the *salon,* had fallen asleep on the chaise. She had to get out.

She couldn't breathe. Clasping her hands over her mouth, Antoinette stood and kicked over one of the empty wine bottles, hearing it roll across the floor. She had to get to the door but couldn't see properly because her eyes stung, and her chest was so tight she couldn't breathe. And then above the terrible crackle of flames and splitting wood, she heard the voice again. Soft, calm, telling her what to do.

'Follow me, Antoinette. Listen to the sound of my voice and follow me. That's it, move towards the moon.'

Doing as she was told, confusion and panic mingling with fear like she'd never known, Antoinette tried to work it out. The window was to the right. Follow the moon, open the window, breathe the air. With one hand over her mouth, the other outstretched, she staggered forward while to her left the flames grew higher, the door completely alight.

The desire to breathe fresh air was the only thing that kept her going, each movement torture, her limbs barely able to move but when she fell against the glass, Antoinette knew she hadn't the strength to lift the sash, so feeling to her right her fingers grasped the first thing they touched, a brass lampstand. Swaying, mouth clamped shut, she lifted it high and not caring if she was cut to pieces, with both hands, smashed the base against the glass, almost screaming with relief when she heard it shatter and felt the fresh summer air flow into the room, brushing against her face, filling her lungs as she hung her head from the window.

And then a sound, wailing, a blue banshee coming up the drive, lots of them racing towards her as she bashed away more glass so she could climb outside and escape the unbearable heat and the flames. She was climbing out of the window when strong hands took hold and pulled her out, and when they asked her if anyone else was in there she said no, she was alone.

And while others rushed in to put out the fire that was raging through the library, the windows a blaze of orange, Antoinette was carried away in the arms of a *pompier*. From over his shoulder, she sobbed when she saw her precious Chevalier alight and unable to bear it, she was about to turn away when through the smoke she saw a figure standing on the lawn. Someone she recognised. A maid, dressed in black, wearing a white pinafore and just before she was lost in the grey swirling mass, she slowly raised her hand.

Knowing exactly who it was, she did the same and not caring if the *pompier* heard, called out into the smoky night. 'Thank you, my brave friend. Thank you, Antoinette.'

28

FABIENNE

She held Mac's hand as they walked silently from the cemetery, a moment of reflection after paying their respects to those they missed and would never see again, all made easier by having him by her side, someone who understood. The sense of bewilderment, loss and not being able to say goodbye, sorry; all those things we think of after the event, the moments we are robbed of.

It was the first of November and a national holiday. *La Fete de la Toussaint,* All Saints Day, and along with most of France, Mac and Fabienne had been visiting the gravesites of their family. The chilly day was brightened by a determined winter sun making the sky shine white. Above, a bird, indistinguishable, silhouetted against the clouds flapped and swooped before taking refuge in a tree, catching Fabienne's attention as she shielded her eyes from the glare.

Dodging an elderly couple who, like everyone else carried a pot of chrysanthemums, the traditional flower of mourning, Fabienne hoped that their pilgrimage would bring them comfort whereas for her, grief was raw, reignited by the events at the apartment and a large serving of truth.

Three months, yet it seemed like yesterday when she'd been caught up in a scene that continued to haunt her dreams. It had passed in a whirl, since the euphoria of discovering the painting and then hours later walking straight into a siege. But slowly, they were trying to come to terms with everything that had happened that night and the furore and media frenzy afterwards.

In the strangest and most cruel of circumstances, in the glare of publicity – zoom lenses shoved in their faces, the phone that never stopped ringing – they'd pieced together the past. Even amidst the sadness and tragedy tinged by such bitter disappointment had come knowledge and with it, a certain sense of liberty. Despite the horror surrounding the deaths of her mother and her brother, the knowledge had solved a mystery. The last of the dots had been joined.

And then came facing up to what her father had done. Then the shame, women crawling out of the woodwork, claiming their five minutes of fame by exposing Hugo the cad who had loved and left them, before, during and after his marriage.

Yes, she had been aware of his infidelity but never in a million years could she have guessed that he was responsible for the crash. The shock revelation was one thing, but what had truly rocked her world was that, once it sunk in, she wasn't that surprised by her father's behaviour. Driving when drunk to win a bet and then for over twenty years, keeping what happened in the last few moments of his wife and child's life a secret. How low could a man stoop?

Not only that, once they were in the ground, swept aside, divorce courts swerved, he had got on with it, soaking up the sympathy, playing the grief-stricken husband in public while in private he was womanising, gambling, drinking, being a terrible father. He hadn't even tried to atone, put his all into doing his best for his daughter and no, shuffling her off to a fancy school did not cut it.

In his role as devil's advocate, Mac had suggested that her father must have been riddled by tremendous guilt and in a way, had been punished for his crime. Living a lie, being blackmailed for years to keep his secret safe, not having a proper relationship with his daughter and going from one failed relationship to another. He must have been a very troubled and lonely man and perhaps, being from an era where men didn't discuss their emotions, he simply didn't know how to deal with what he'd done.

Fabienne knew Mac was trying to be kind and make it easier for her to come to terms with it all, but nothing he said would water down how she felt about her father. He was weak. A man without honour or moral fibre who even before he made his greatest mistake had already failed his family in so many ways and for these reasons, that night in the apartment when she'd heard the paramedic pronounce her father dead, she'd felt nothing.

In hospital, while Mac had recovered from his gunshot wound, they'd talked it over and over, and he'd put her numbness down to shock when she confessed to feeling little sorrow for her father but really, how could she? She couldn't mourn a relationship they never had or pretend she didn't despise the man he'd always been.

And him dying had saved them both the indignity of faking it, her sitting by his hospital bed, waiting for him to recover so she could forgive and forget. That was never going to happen. And she wouldn't have been able to bear more lies and excuses or worse, witness his arrogant reluctance to face up to what he'd done or say he was sorry. With him, it could have gone either way so seeing his body wheeled from the apartment in a black bag was for the best. He was gone, and she would deal with it.

They had reached the gates of the walled cemetery, nodding politely to a couple on their way in and it seemed that once outside the spell was broken and the dead let go, their grip on her heart slowly easing with each step along the pavement. It even allowed Mac to lighten the sombre mood that chatting to headstones and memorial plaques had cast over them.

'I think I've found the answer to my financial situation... I'm going to open a chrysanthemum shop. Have you seen how many there are in there?'

Fabienne smiled. It had been the same scene back at Chevalier where they'd visited the family plot, placing tributes where her mother and petit-Baptiste lay, and only out of propriety, one for her father. In the cemetery, they left some with Mac's grandparents, finally stopping to speak to Antoinette. The old one, not the current one who was back at Chevalier doing a Zoom interview with an online magazine about her namesake who had saved the chateau from ruin.

Fabienne was so weary of being interviewed and had happily passed over the baton to her PR woman and full-time resident archivist who almost burnt to death in an arson attack. Antoinette revelled in the drama of it all.

'And what would you sell for the rest of the year? I think the chrysanthemum ship sailed a while back so you might need to think again.' Fabienne knew that Mac's levity was all a front and deep down he was becoming more and more concerned about the future and how he could sustain himself in France.

And if he'd told her once, he'd told her a thousand times that he was not going to be a kept man, like some sex slave to the millionairess who lived in the chateau. Fabienne smiled at this and hoped that soon, she would have the solution and one that didn't entail locking him in the dungeon.

Mac gave her a nudge. 'Hey, do you reckon Antoinette's telling them all about how she was woken from her sleep by a ghost who whispered in her ear, and a misty figure led her to safety? She's adamant that it happened, and I swear we will never hear the last of it, or that it was her idea to take all the books out of the library and that's what saved them from going up in smoke. I can repeat it word for word now. She'll be saying she drove the fire truck next!'

Fabienne was laughing. 'Bless her, but I think after what she went through, seeing the library on fire and how scared she must have been alone at Chevalier, we can indulge her for the next God knows how many years. Which reminds me, I need to ring the insurance company tomorrow. They are so slow, but at least they are going to pay up and we can start repairing the damage. But first, I have a big surprise for you.' Taking out her phone she was prepared for twenty questions from Mac but before he could begin, she raised a finger to silence him while she read her messages.

'Okay, we are all set. Come on, we have to meet Antoinette at La Fleurie. She's all done being famous.' As they headed for Mac's car, she ignored his demands for clues and even his sad face and puppy-dog eyes routine, and as he rummaged for his keys, she started to lose patience. 'Will you hurry up and get in. We're going to be late.' Finally, he found them and within seconds they were heading out of Cholet, direction, La Fleurie.

Mac never knew when to give in and had exhausted every conceivable scenario known to man, or him anyway. They varied from his least favourite option, another surprise visit from his mum. She had flown out the minute Fabienne had told her about the shooting and refused to leave until his wound was starting to heal. Mac said it was the longest two weeks, four days, nine hours and twenty-seven minutes of his life.

His next guess was ludicrous, about going to space and the one after that was just plain rude so he went back to his astronaut ambitions. 'I mean, let's face it, only millionaires get to go on a space flight and Monsieur Picasso more or less bought me a ticket *and,* I did throw myself in front of a bullet to save your life...'

'Mac! You are worse than Antoinette for gilding the lily and you did not throw yourself in front of a bullet, you got shot because you were trying to whack someone on the head with a giant fire extinguisher when, I might add, you walked past two bronze statues and my grandfather's auction gavel that would have done quite nicely. So, it was your own fault!'

'Ungrateful, that's what you are, mademoiselle, so in that case I'll settle for my last guess; that'll do nicely.' Mac glanced across and gave Fabienne a cheeky wink.

'No chance, monsieur.'

They traversed the country road for another mile or so in companionable silence, apart from the radio and Mac's tone-deaf humming, giving Fabienne's mind time to wander and as was often the case, it took her over the events of the past few months. After she'd skilfully circumvented the horrors of what happened at the apartment, she focused on the reaction to the painting and how, as she'd suspected, it had changed her life.

The Chevalier Picasso as it was now known, ended up on the front pages of almost every newspaper all over the world because it was, beyond a shadow of a doubt, an original. Fabienne had been immensely relieved when her friend Marc and his colleagues, after they had almost died of excitement, secured it in the vault at the museum.

She'd already estimated its worth on the drive up to Paris, knowing that the most recent Picasso to be sold was in 2020 when *Marie-Thérèse* went for $103 million. It was painted in 1932, a year after Ophélie's gift was delivered to Chevalier.

No decisions had been made as to whether she would sell the painting and, in her heart, after it had been hidden for so long behind a family photograph, Fabienne hoped it would see the light. Her favoured option would be to have it displayed in the Picasso Museum and then loaned to galleries around the world, so that others may see its beauty and hear the story of how it was saved from the Nazis by a brave young woman named Antoinette.

In the meantime, Fabienne would be able to borrow against the estimated worth of the painting, as art loans were commonplace. Then she could begin restoring Chevalier to its former glory, room by room, piece by piece. She could do it properly, employ experts and finish what her great-grandfather had begun after the war.

The apartment in Paris would also be renovated and then let to someone with more money than sense. It had been the suggestion of her beleaguered accountant old Monsieur Landry that the estimated income from an apartment in a much sought-after arrondissement would easily pay the interest on the loan. She had no desire to visit there, let alone stay but just like Chevalier, it was part of her heritage, and she wasn't ready to let it go. Maybe that decision could be left to the next generation of Bombelles or even the ones after.

And she had another task, a mystery to solve and that was trying to find the valise that was hidden somewhere in the chateau and if she found it, Fabienne already knew that she would never ever let the contents go. The precious and personal treasures and letters that belonged to la Duchesse Ophélie would remain in the Bombelle family forever and she could not wait to hold them in her hands, touch a piece of history and make a connection through time.

Fabienne had a job to do. And thanks to Antoinette Doré, the chateau would survive for future generations. And for others. For visitors who would wander through the rooms to admire the treasures; for artists to display their work on the walls; for guests who stayed the night and diners soaking up the atmosphere; for couples getting married, or for those who just came to sit on the lawns where chevaliers once practised their skills, ready and waiting to protect king and country.

Chateau de Chevalier would be her legacy, a homage to all those who had gone before, lived, died and served there, and when her time came, she would have done her best, for her family, for the future, for everyone.

29

MAC

Fabienne had that look on her face when someone thinks they have bought you the best present in the world and can't wait for you to open it, but the flaw in his theory was the distinct lack of anything that looked like a gift.

Playing along, he had followed her around the side of La Fleurie to the fence and the little gate that led to the woods and here he waited until she had delved into the huge floppy bag slung across her chest. When she pulled out his granddad's notebook, Mac became really curious.

'Okay, what are you up to?'

Fabienne smiled. 'Come on, I'll explain as we walk. I gave Antoinette a copy of the map and she's going to meet us there with a picnic. She insisted we made a special occasion out of it. You know she doesn't go anywhere without food.'

'Occasion out of what? And Antoinette's in on the surprise... that's a miracle, that she managed to keep quiet. And what do you mean, the map?' Mac was putting two and two together and had decided that this was something to do with his family, or maybe all their families and they were going to have a wake in the woods, after all it was *La Toussaint*.

Happy to participate, even though it was a bit chilly, Mac hoped Antoinette had made a fire and brought blankets like they used to when they were kids. He followed Fabienne along the track, watching as she opened the notebook and flicked through the pages, stopping at a certain one. Looking around he saw her squint at an elm and then grin, before facing him, eyes wide with excitement.

'Okay, we need to follow this map. You can do the honours seeing as you've been here before. Your granddad left it, just in case you'd forgotten and got lost.' She passed him the book and pointed at the pencil-drawn instructions, written in Claude Doré's elaborate hand.

At the top of the page, underlined were the words *Le Verger*. 'The orchard. I can't remember there being an orchard in the woods. All Grandpère's apple trees are around the cottage, some pear and plum trees too.'

'Oh, I assure you there is, it says so in there. I came to it a few nights ago while you were snoring away. Now pay attention because your grandpère marked the trees along the way. It says you must remember how he taught you the different varieties. You point the way while I explain what it says. Come on, this way, I found the first one for you.' Fabienne set off, taking a route to the left where he looked downwards, and could see the imprint of boots on flattened grass.

As they made their way further into the woods, in silence at first, the only sounds were those of the birds and the rustle of leaves and the wheels of a cart as they wobbled and bumped along a worn track, and when the hairs on his neck stood on end, Mac knew for sure that his granddad was right by his side.

Fabienne agreed that it would have been difficult for Mac to translate all of his grandfather's words because he wrote in the old style, the handwriting elaborate and hard to decipher in places but the entry *Le Verger* was clearer, more recent, written one year earlier and just four months before Monsieur Doré passed away.

He had continued to tend the little oak trees year in, year out, adding more saplings, moving the fences wider, even when Mac failed to visit. At the ten-year point, when they should have started to bear fruit, Claude Doré was hopeful that the truffle spores would have worked their magic underground. He had been disappointed but remained vigilant and kept the faith. When Mac's grandma died, his granddad lost interest in everything, and it had been a struggle to muster the strength to tend his garden and vegetable patch let alone trek through the woods to the orchard of little trees.

However, when he woke early one morning in September, feeling unusually refreshed and positive, before the feeling wore off and it became too hot, Claude sailed on his second wind and headed into the forest. It had taken an age and he was thoroughly exhausted once he'd arrived but, to his utter delight, when he checked the base of the trees he saw what he'd been waiting for. Tiny fruit flies. It was a good sign that below the ground, magic was occurring.

Knowing it wasn't the time to dig and he should wait until the winter when the truffle season began in November, after sitting a while and remembering things that old fools do, he set off for La Fleurie and there, before he nodded off, Claude wrote it all down in his notebook; what to do, when to dig, and a map of how to find the treasure. Sadly, a few days later he was taken ill and spent the last of his days in hospital and never got to go back to the woods to dig for diamonds, but he was sure they were there, and all Mac had to do was find them.

They emerged from the trees into the clearing exactly as it was marked on the map and there waiting for them was Antoinette with a man he didn't recognise and a very giddy dog. Mac was still recovering from what Fabienne had told him and attempted to pull himself together before greeting the others. It had hit him hard, hearing the words and voice of his granddad and his heart broke again when she got to the part where he'd made the trek alone and fallen ill shortly after. That was a period Mac wanted to forget, his inglorious history where he got it all so very wrong.

After the telling, they had walked hand in hand in silence. Fabienne, as always being a sensitive soul, had left him to process his thoughts and point the way. And now they were here, the scents of the forest; pine, wild garlic and the last of the hardy mint was swirling in the air with the woodsmoke from the fire. Antoinette, a blanket around her shoulder, had read his mind and was waving from one of the two logs that he and his granddad had rolled into place all those years ago, and then they'd eaten their lunch and he'd learned all about the magic.

While Fabienne strode over and said hello, shaking hands with the man and ruffling the head of Giddy Dog, Mac took it all in, his mind rushing back to a day long ago when he'd stood in the very same spot and saw the fences and by his side, his granddad explained all about the little orchard they were going to plant.

Fabienne called him over. 'Mac, come and meet Olivier, a friend of Antoinette's father's cousin and this little chap is Albert.' She crouched to stroke the dog who was pulling on his lead and explained further. 'Olivier leads the truffle hunt down in Saumur and I asked him to come here today with his special dog to see if your grandpère was right and there are some black diamonds here, after all.'

At this point Olivier stepped forward and shook Mac's hand. 'Fabienne has explained everything, and I must say Monsieur Doré has done a fine job protecting his orchard but please do not get your hopes up. We may not find any and the flies could have been a coincidence. Then again, there may be one or two truffles hiding in there somewhere.'

It was Antoinette who, impatient as ever hurried them along. 'Well, what are we waiting for? Come on, let's go in and solve another mystery and then we can have our picnic. I'm starving.'

Fabienne rolled her eyes at Mac, who was also eager to see what would come of that hot summer day from so long ago. Leading the way, just as he had seen his granddad do, he wiggled the middle fence panel and, when it was loose, pulled it from the soil, and they all stepped inside the orchard. Olivier let Albert off the lead and within seconds, he was racing up and down the rows of trees, getting the scent, moving in a random pattern until he stopped by one particular tree and then to Mac's astonishment, began frantically digging.

Olivier was there in an instant followed by the others and after he'd moved Albert to one side and gave him a treat, he took a trowel from his jacket pocket and resumed digging. Mac crouched and watched, his heart beating wildly. Seconds, that was all it took. Olivier stopped, then reached into the earth and pulled out what at first looked like a black rock, or a bumpy piece of coal the size of an egg, which he gently placed in Mac's palm.

'*Voilà*, a black truffle and it is a good size too. I'd say about sixty grams. A thing of great beauty. Smell it, take in the scent of something that has been growing in the earth for many years, waiting to be found.' Olivier looked immensely pleased, so doing as he was told, Mac inhaled the scent of the forest, a musky earthiness, oakwood and nuts.

Turning the truffle in his hand, running his fingers over the dusky surface, Mac wished more than anything that his granddad had been there to see this, and then a voice in his ear whispered that he was. *Of course I am here, always by your side, to hold your hand and guide you when you need me.*

Looking up, unable to speak, he passed the truffle to Fabienne who looked as moved as he felt and as she took it from him, Antoinette tapped Olivier on the shoulder. 'I think Albert has found another one, look.'

They all turned and sure enough, the springer spaniel was digging furiously at the soil and flicking it everywhere in his eagerness to find the prize. Rushing over, Olivier repeated the process and again produced a truffle but this time even larger than the first then no sooner had he handed it over, Albert was once again on the trail.

Mac sensed the excitement of the others as they ran to where Olivier had begun to dig then seeing Albert shoot off once more, he stood, pulled another trowel from his pocket and handed it to Mac. 'You finish here, I will follow my crazy dog. Look, he has not had so much fun in ages.'

Doing as he was told, Mac got on his knees and as Olivier had done, scraped back the soil and when he saw something appear, a blob of black, he couldn't hide his delight. 'I found one, look... and there's another.' Turning, he called over to Olivier, 'How many will there be around each tree?'

'Sometimes a kilo per tree, maybe less, just keep looking because I think we have struck gold. Antoinette, bring the bags from my rucksack and put the truffles inside as you find them. I have a feeling we will be here a while.' Olivier was trying to dig and keep an eye on Albert who was zigzagging across the orchard.

Antoinette was fetching the bags while Fabienne knelt by Mac and placed her hand over his, halting his digging for a second. 'I am so happy for you, and for your dear grandpère. This is a very special day and I am honoured to be part of it.'

Mac let go of the trowel and leant over, cupping her face in his hands before kissing her gently. 'And I am happy, too, and I know lately, things have been totally crap, but I wouldn't change any of it, not one thing because in the end it brought me back here, to you.'

Fabienne smiled, her face covered in mud that Mac decided not to tell her about and instead he got back to the task in hand, digging for treasure in a field of black diamonds, his granddad by his side.

Later, at Antoinette's insistence, they were seated around the fire eating and making plans. According to Olivier, Mac's orchard was a veritable goldmine and they had already agreed to go back the following day and harvest the rest of the truffles, once he'd rang his restaurateur contacts and got them to place orders.

First though, Olivier had more practical suggestions. 'Did you notice that some time recently your grandpère planted more saplings? It means that another section of your orchard could already be producing and if I were you, I would extend the plot and create a sustainable crop that will yield truffles year after year.'

Mac couldn't hide his surprise. 'What, you mean I could start a business, have a proper truffle farm?'

Olivier was animated. 'Yes, of course. Your grandpère has laid the foundations and all you need to do is learn about trufficulture, tend the soil and saplings and of course your established trees and *voilà,* nature will do the rest. I will help you all I can, in return for a truffle or two.' Olivier winked at Mac.

'Of course, and thank you. But how much could I expect to earn? Would it be enough to live off so I can stay in France?' Mac didn't miss the look on Fabienne's face, and he suspected she wanted Olivier's answer to be 'yes' just as much as he. So when the old truffle hunter began chuckling into his wine glass, Mac wasn't sure which way it would go.

'Monsieur Mac, the first truffle we found today is probably worth around ninety euros, and one kilo can sell for as much as eight hundred.'

For a second, Mac thought he'd misheard. 'For one kilo?'

'Yes, and I estimate that once we harvest all fifty of the mature trees, at approximately a kilo per tree, well, I will let you do the maths.' Olivier raised his glass and smiled, then busied himself with a chunk of Comté while Fabienne whipped out her phone and began tapping in the numbers.

'*Ooh la la.* Mac, look.' She turned the screen to Mac who, clearly having a better grasp of mathematics than Fabienne, had already worked it out. He'd also realised that now he could stay and make La Fleurie his home, just as his grandparents had always wanted.

Once the shock wore off, it was replaced by excitement and Antoinette suggested that alongside selling the truffles, Mac could produce a range of products like infused oil and jars of preserved truffles, and when it was up and running, Hôtel Chateau de Chevalier could use and sell products from La Truffière La Fleurie and maybe even send guests there for a tour of a truffle farm.

When the fuss died down, Olivier said his goodbyes, eager to get home and make some calls but promised to return bright and early the following day to help with the harvest. Antoinette said she needed a wee and promptly disappeared into the bushes, saying they had to listen out in case she saw a wild boar, or a wolf or a grizzly bear.

After watching her go, Mac took one of the truffles from the bag and held it in his hand. Taking a moment to admire something that had been hidden in the dark for so long, it reminded him of the Picasso that had laid beneath a family photo for almost eighty years.

Closing his fingers around the truffle, feeling the soft, bumpy flesh beneath his skin, Mac held out his free hand to Fabienne, which she took. 'I get it now, I really do. Your affection and affinity to things, objects, stuff that might not have a heartbeat but somehow, they touch your soul. It's true the past sticks to them, and then when you hold it in your hand a bit of their life and essence sticks to you.'

'Inanimate objects, do you have a soul which sticks to our soul and forces it to love?' Fabienne answered Mac's puzzled look. 'It's my favourite poem by Lamartine. I recited it that day in the gallery and it totally sums up how I feel about Chevalier, and La Fleurie and that truffle you are holding in your hand. It's also how I feel about you because you have stuck to my soul and if there was ever a time to say it, that I love you, well, it's right now.'

Mac shuffled closer. 'And, mademoiselle, you have stuck to mine and I love you too.'

Always knowing when to ruin the moment, Antoinette reappeared from the bushes, oblivious to her gooseberry status. 'That feels better but this is not the weather for taking a wee outdoors. My lady bits are completely frozen.'

Sighing, Fabienne then told her to be quiet and take a seat because she had something else to show Mac and she took the notebook from her bag. 'Your grandpère has left you a message, it's the last entry and I think he wrote it the day he came here, once he'd discovered the truffles had worked. Would you like to read it, or shall I?'

When his throat constricted and his eyes began to water Mac knew he would be incapable so simply shook his head, and then watched as Fabienne nodded and turned to the page. When she began to read, it was as though the whole of the woodland was listening, drawing closer, gathering round to hear the last words of a grandfather, to the grandson he adored.

To my beloved grandson, Mackenzie Donald.

The apple of my eye, the son I longed for, our summer boy who came back to us each year bringing love and laughter, filling our days with memories and our hearts with so much happiness they almost burst.

But we always had to let you go, no matter how much we wanted you to stay. And at the end of each visit, while feeling sad we took joy in what you had left behind – your paintings, your dirty boots, the handprints on the walls, the bonbon wrappers your mémère would find under your pillow. They all reminded us of you, and we hoped that when you went, you took a piece of us in your heart, on your journey through life.

My grandson, I have watched grow, from a tiny twig into a tall elm, and how proud you have made me. You were a good boy, you did well at school, got your cap and gown and how your mémère was proud of that photo of you, all of them, showing your travels and achievements. We lived through you, told all our friends about how well our grandson was doing, and we understood why you could not always come back. I promise you we did.

I understood more than you know. Your mama explained. Love captures all men's hearts and turns our heads. It is the way of the world so please, do not feel bad. I would not want that. All men make mistakes.

I am very tired and I miss my wife. I know the sun is about to set on what has been a long day and a good life, so before I go, I hope I have assured you of many things, and that I can leave you knowing how much you were loved. And with a memory.

You and I, pulling a cart, side by side, our journey through the woods to a field where we buried treasure. I remember every moment of the day we made magic, and it is my hope, my last wish, that when you find the diamonds that they bring you happiness.

If you decide to stay, dig, get your hands dirty, toil, grow, dream, love, laugh, cry a little, but then eat, drink, and be merry once in a while.

If you decide to go, know it is with my blessing.
La Fleurie is your home, but your life is yours to live.
Be happy my precious boy,
Grandpère.

30

VERONIQUE

Each morning, when she pulled back the curtains, the view of the Mediterranean never ceased to fill Veronique with immense joy. It took her breath away and she would say in her head, '*Look Mama, what a beautiful day.*'

Pulling on her sweater, she unlocked the balcony doors and stepped outside, embracing the Saharan wind that swept over the sea and sand, and whipped around her legs. She had taken the small apartment for the winter months while she searched further along the coast for her forever home, one that her mama would have approved of and where she could sit on the rocks and watch for the little mermaid. There, she would be able to forget about the past and make a good life for herself, start over in a quiet place, live comfortably, never have to worry. It would be a world away from everything she had endured, all that had caused her pain and most definitely somewhere she could hide.

It had been a terrible time, her whole life, all of it. And then after the robbery, it was as though the ordeal of simply being her would never end, made worse by gossip and being hounded by the press. What vultures they were, not respecting that she and Fabienne had just lived through a nightmare with no wish to relive it over and over again, no matter how much they offered for interviews, exposés, even her biography for goodness' sake. Who on earth would want to hear about all that? She just wanted to forget it all, move on.

The police wanted to hear it, though, and Veronique hadn't minded telling them what they needed to know about her brother, the one whose skull had splattered over the balcony and her. In a fluttering of wings, a second's worth of distraction when René took his eyes and his gun off her head, the marksman had taken his shot and set her free.

Veronique had been glad to help, so grateful was she for them saving her life. She explained in great detail why her brother wanted to frame and kill her husband, and her. The answer was simple. Jealousy and revenge, obsession and greed all rolled up into one very damaged and dangerous man.

While she lay in her hospital bed, after she had recovered from severe shock and concussion, Veronique started right at the beginning. The terrible life she and her mother endured on the farm and once her father was dead another monster took his place. Fearing that at any time her own brother would take her for himself and, how over the years his unhealthy obsession with her had manifested itself in evil, resulting in murder.

To make her point, she explained about Alain and in doing so had a difficult decision to make. Should she tell them the whole truth about what had happened? His mother did not deserve to think of her son dying that way. There would be no evidence, not after all these years, unless they were going to dig up all of Monsieur Juet's cornfields, and his pigs would have been made into sausage meat long ago. Or should she let a mother wait for a son to come home, leave her with a sliver of hope amongst the confusion and despair?

Veronique found a compromise; still making the police understand what a deviant her brother was, she gave Alain a better death.

When he knew he was going to die on that balcony, in a last malicious act René had confessed to Alain's murder, knowing it would cause her pain, telling her how he shot her lover and after throwing him in the Atlantique, had disposed of his car. That would be easier for Hélène to bear than the truth.

The officers who took her statement were kind and understanding, sitting through hours of her life where her cruel father and depraved brother reigned supreme. One a drunken bully who beat wife and child, the other who preyed on a hungry little girl and sold her for a bicycle, all because he gave her a crust of bread.

Passing on what she'd learned from many years of therapy, she explained that she had fallen into the trap of the abused being unable to escape the grip of the abuser, giving them chance after chance to change their ways, make it right, be the person she wished them to be.

But René had been riddled with jealousy when she met Alain, and even when she fled, sick and tired of his games, her brother had revelled in every failed relationship she'd ever had. No matter how hard she had tried, her fragile mental health always sabotaged any hope of happiness.

There was no need to mention that she and Hugo had once been lovers, that secret had died with René and her husband, and she was glad that Fabienne hadn't overheard that part of their conversation. Instead, Veronique focused on her chance meeting with Hugo, an old acquaintance, and how they'd hit it off, and how their subsequent marriage must have been the final straw for René. A Saber and a Bombelle, his sister and the enemy, her brother's worst nightmare. Riddled with jealousy and spite he bided his time and when he saw his chance to strike, he'd taken it.

Then they asked about his obsession with the Bombelle family. In a history lesson worthy of Sister Mary Marguerite, Veronique described her father's hatred of everything, and everyone associated with Chateau de Chevalier, his desire for revenge, a quest that had been passed down through generations. And once they'd unearthed René's links to the far right, subscriptions and donations, photographs of him at violent political rallies, they were able to picture better a warped fascist whose family grudge finally got the better of him.

Veronique did take some of the blame, letting slip to her brother that she and her dear husband were on their uppers and Hugo was at his wits' end, hence René's attempt to frame a desperate man by torching his house and staging a robbery, one that would leave the Bombelles' name tainted with shame and her poor, darling husband dead.

Her statement tied in with what it seemed Fabienne had overheard which, it transpired, did not include any of the conversation that implicated Veronique in the robbery. And she had been kindness itself, the stepdaughter who she'd once regarded as the enemy. Fabienne had visited her every day in between visiting Mac who had taken a bullet, thanks to Veronique's stupid outburst.

All had been forgiven, though, and they had talked, made amends, healed, both repeating their apologies from the night of the siege. Veronique had meant every single word. Fabienne had been sincere, promising that she would take care of financial matters and give Veronique what she'd always desired. Somewhere to rest her head, a place of her own, and a family who would be kind.

Despite all this, and Fabienne insisting that Veronique was

always welcome at Chevalier, as soon as the final charade was over, she went her own way. It was for the best. She'd played her part well at the funeral, of the bereaved wife who had so many crosses to bear. Not least having to endure lover after lover stepping forward to wistfully recount Hugo's heydays. Yet none of them could say they were la Duchesse.

She had held her head high, taking her rightful place at the graveside, stoical, loyally supporting Hugo's equally strong daughter. Hiding behind their veils, both hiding the truth about the man who was being lowered into the ground, they kept their private pact. Neither gave a statement to the press, confirming or denying rumours, and instead they let his many indiscretions and financial misfortunes be buried with him.

The day she left Chevalier, the morning after the funeral, polite invitations were made, as were promises to keep in touch and after a cordial *au revoir,* Veronique drove out of the gates without once looking back. It would be many months, years maybe before the Bombelle estate was settled but this did not trouble her unduly. She was going to be okay. In her bag were the keys to René's apartment, given to her by his solicitor who assured her that as his next of kin, she was entitled to his entire estate, once probate was granted.

Still, six months was a long time to wait when you were penniless, and she had no desire to live off Fabienne's well-meant charity. So, until his properties and bank account, his latest stupid flash car and whatever else he had amassed over the years became hers, Veronique had reverted to plan B.

Letting herself into his swanky apartment, trying to ignore how being so close to René's personal belongings made her skin crawl, exhibitions of wealth that reeked of a vain and shallow man who had surrounded himself with trophies, women included. It wasn't any of that which interested her, it was something much simpler than that.

She spotted it on a shelf, the mahogany casket that to all intents and purposes contained the ashes of their dear father. She had been there when René had scattered them amongst the pigs and watched as they'd been trodden into the mud so she knew exactly what he really kept inside it. He was a creature of habit with a warped sense of humour but it was she who would have the last laugh.

Taking it from the shelf she proceeded to the kitchen and turned it upside down and after pulling a knife from the drawer, began to loosen the four screws that held the base in place. Five minutes later, after replacing the casket, Veronique left the apartment with a carrier bag which contained the rolls of tax-free euros that René had been hiding there. And on her finger, she wore a beautiful diamond ring, the inner band inscribed with the names *Veronique et Alain*.

It was as she'd lain in her hospital bed, going over what René had said in his last moments she realised that when he spoke of the ring, it was in the present and she knew that he'd kept it, a trophy.

Raising her hand, Veronique allowed the morning light to catch the diamond so that it glinted in the sun, rays of colour sent to brighten her day. She smiled and imagined it was Alain, winking at her, saying she had done well, taking back what was hers.

Veronique vowed to wear it always, and when unsuitable men, any men at all, saw her in a bar or restaurant they would think twice about trying to catch her eye or send over a drink. And she would say to herself, *I do not need you. I am not one of those girls. I am not desperate. I am not sad. I am happy. And I am free. And I will never be hungry again.*

EPILOGUE
ANTOINETTE

How proud I am of Mademoiselle Fabienne. She has saved us, just as I knew she would. It has been such a long wait, for her to find the painting and now I can enjoy watching Chevalier be restored to its glory days, even those long before my time as lady's maid to la Duchesse Ophélie.

The chateau is a buzz of excitement because it seems the film crew who once visited now want to make a series about Mademoiselle Fabienne and the painting and document the full restoration of Chevalier. And there is to be a party to celebrate everyone's good fortune. I heard my namesake talking about it only this morning. Goodness, how she can chatter but I have to say, so did I when there was anyone to listen. Still, Antoinette is a good girl, although she does not clean the range to my satisfaction and her culinary skills leave something to be desired. But I forgive her because she is as true and loyal a friend to Mademoiselle Fabienne as I was to my own dear Duchesse.

That is why I tried so hard to save her, when those dreadful men came with their cans of petrol and started the fire in the library. The smoke was terrible, and it took all of my energy to make her hear me, listen to what I said and allow me to lead her away from the flames. Poor girl, nobody believes her.

It is most frustrating, to stand beside someone and them not know you are there, like my dear Gregoire, who I hear has been invited to the party. I cannot wait to see him again. I have watched him for years and called out to him many times, ever since he returned after the war as he promised to and found that I was gone. How he cried, in private and with dignity but he did not hear me whisper his name or know that I held out my finger each time he took my engagement ring from his pocket. On the day he left to join *La Resistance* he wanted me to keep it. He swore an oath there would never be another, and I swore the same. I refused to take the ring, insisting that I would wait here, for his return when he could place it on my finger, and we would be together for all eternity. That was our parting tryst. That is why I cannot leave yet. I am waiting for my Gregoire.

I am also waiting for my dearest friend Eglantine, and I do wish she would hurry up but that one always did like to keep everyone waiting and make a song and dance out of everything so there is no way she will miss her hundredth birthday party, that is for sure.

I did not think she would remember, the things I tell her when I visit because she hovers between reality and a place where even I do not exist but, in the end, she came through, my loyal comrade. I wanted her to pass on the message to my great-nephew so badly. And now, praise our Lord who waits so patiently for me, Mac has found his treasure. My brother will be so pleased, as was I when he grated the truffle on the eggs that Antoinette had overcooked, *again*. Terrible food aside, he is going to be all right because not only has he found his destiny, he has found his true love in Mademoiselle Fabienne.

How I adore her and blushed slightly when I heard that she was going to pay tribute to me at the party and tell the guests my story, of how I saved Chevalier. I shall stand right at the front and listen although it will perplex me that I cannot fill in the blanks, the part of the tale that nobody really knows, only those who were there. And I doubt even if they were alive anyone would admit to what they did.

I rarely think of it, the moment when the patrol crept up on me in the woods and dragged me back here then threw me before the *kommandant* and his dinner guest. I had been spying for *La Resistance* but also, some crazy part of me hoped that I'd be able to sneak back in and retrieve the valise.

When I saw Maire Saber, seated at the table beside the *kommandant*, the look in his eye and the sneer as he turned to whisper in the ear of the Nazi, I knew what they were going to do. Even now I cannot bear to... No, I shall not speak of it. Afterwards, when they had finished and even the soldiers turned up their nose at the sight of me, I thought it was over and they would let me go.

They told me to run, so I did. I made it across the lawn and through the gardens and had reached the edge of the woods when I heard the dogs, the real hounds from a hell even worse than what I had just endured. I knew what would happen if they caught me and I could almost feel their breath on my legs so when I came to the railway bridge, I knew how it would end, in one piece not torn to shreds. With the last of my strength, I tried to climb on top, but my legs failed so when the shot rang out and the bullet hit its target, I did in fact escape hell and instead, found myself here.

This is where I have remained ever since, tied to this place waiting for my dear Gregoire. There never was another, not for either of us, even though I would have forgiven him. I truly wanted him to find love, not be alone but he kept his oath and therefore I kept mine.

So, until it is our time, I will keep the Chevalier faith and watch over the house and Mademoiselle Fabienne who has a huge task before her and, I sense, more challenges to face, storms on the horizon. But I will be by her side and guide her where I can and maybe, just maybe, young Antoinette will see me again, and wonder why I stand by the window each evening, at the end of the long gallery.

I am trying so hard to show them where to look, because the valise that I hid, the private treasure of la Duchesse Ophélie and my dear Fabienne's birthright, is close by. And all she has to do is find it.

THE END

ACKNOWLEDGEMENTS

Hello and thank you for reading *Birthright*. I hope you enjoyed it.

What a joy this book was to write because I was able to visit the Loire, my favourite place, and spend summer in a rambling, crumbling chateau. Sometimes I nipped over to a little cottage in the woods and then I was off on the TGV to Paris, I even took a trip into the past and met some old friends there. Of course, all this was in my mind, but you came too, my imaginary travelling companion.

The inspiration for *Birthright* was drawn from many sources so I will start with the beautiful poem by Lamartine that appears at the front of the book. The first time I heard it, as my friend recited it over dinner, I knew that one day I would include it in a story. We were talking about how attached we become to inanimate objects and as I often chat to teddy bears, thank my car for delivering us home safely from France, and apologise to cups when I break them, I believe that certain things do stick to our souls.

Another source of inspiration came via my husband who has created our very own truffle orchard. He'd spent so long preparing the ground, digging the holes, and nurturing the little saplings that as the sun set after a very long day of planting, while we walked along the rows watering each tiny shoot, I prayed that in years to come he would find just one truffle hiding in the soil, a small reward for his labours. I decided then to write a story that included them, and a bit of Loire history. The trees are currently growing strong and I hope that underground, the magic is happening.

Then there is my fascination with *La Resistance* and the Second World War: such a poignant and tragic period in time and I don't think I will ever tire of hearing tales of bravery and the struggle to free France. I also love art, visiting galleries and the Montparnasse district of Paris and after reading that Picasso and many other artists spent the duration of the occupation there, my mind began ticking. For those of you who have read *Resistance* I hope that meeting Yvette and Vincent again, even for a moment, made you smile. I had to include them because they are two of my favourite characters of all time.

Now, I need to say a few thank yous. To the wonderful team at Bloodhound Books who take my ninety thousand words, polish them up and make them shine, give me a beautiful cover, and then hold my hand while my book goes out into the big wide world. Thank you Betsy, Fred, Tara, Abbie, and Hannah for all your hard work and dedication. A special mention has to go to Betsy, who gives me the freedom to write the way I want to, no matter where my imagination takes me. Thank you for trusting and believing in me, and for giving me the chance to do my dream job.

To Clare Law, who I adore working with, who sees all things that I don't and keeps me on the straight and narrow. I have learnt so much from you, Clare, so thank you. And to Ian Skewis for his eagle-eyed skills and erudite observations. You are a dream team.

Next, a big thank you to the beta-readers, and the Bloodhound ARC group who get a first look at my story. And a mahoosive shout out to my very own band of fabulous, loyal, and supportive ARC readers who cheer me on and mean a great deal to me. You know who you are, and I honestly don't know what I would do without you.

To you, the reader, a huge *merci beaucoup* for picking my book, and if you've read any of my other thirteen stories, again, thank you.

I cannot forget Tara-Jane Lyons for winning my competition and being named the most adored and hottest girl in Year 10. Thank you for being a good sport and also, for being such a lovely lady who patiently helps me out when I get stuck. Which is quite a lot.

To Heather and Nathan, for simply being my mates, for the laughs we share and the hours that we waste talking rubbish.

And now, to a very, very special person who as always, is there from the very beginning, before I even write one word. Who listens to my rambling plot ideas, chucks some of her own into the mix and then off we go. Keri Beevis, thank you for reading every word I write, for being honest and for the odd telling off – I love it when you go all bossy and strict. I know that this book is all the better for having you by my side. And it goes without saying, thank you for being such a brilliant friend.

Finally, as always, I want to mention my magnificent family, six people who are the centre of my world. In the words of Alphonse de Lamartine, you have all stuck to my soul, and my heart, and you are my most precious treasures.

I love you x

A NOTE FROM THE PUBLISHER

Thank you for reading this book. If you enjoyed it please do consider leaving a review on Amazon to help others find it too.

We hate typos. All of our books have been rigorously edited and proofread, but sometimes mistakes do slip through. If you have spotted a typo, please do let us know and we can get it amended within hours.

info@bloodhoundbooks.com